THIS BOOK BELONGS TO

_____

D0188211

KENDRA KANDLESTAR
AND THE SEARCH FOR ARAZEEN

Enjoy searching for Arazeen

KENDRA KANDLESTAR
AND THE SEARCH FOR ARAZEEN

BOOK
5

Written and Illustrated by
Lee Edward Födi

SIMPLY READ BOOKS

Published in 2015 by Simply Read Books
www.simplyreadbooks.com
Text & Illustrations © 2015 Lee Edward Födi

All rights reserved. No part of this publication may be reproduced, stored in a retrieval system, or transmitted, in any form or by any means, electronic, mechanical, photocopying, recording or otherwise, without the written permission of the publisher. The publisher does not have any control over and does not assume any responsibility for author or third-party websites or their content.

Library and Archives Canada Cataloguing in Publication

Födi, Lee Edward, author, illustrator
    Kendra Kandlestar and the search for Arazeen / written and illustrated by Lee Edward Födi.

(The chronicles of Kendra Kandlestar)
ISBN 978-1-927018-29-3 (pbk.)

    I. Title. II. Series: Födi, Lee Edward. Chronicles of Kendra Kandlestar.

PS8611.O45K459 2015   jC813'.6   C2014-905985-X

We gratefully acknowledge for their financial support of our publishing program the Canada Council for the Arts, the BC Arts Council, and the Government of Canada through the Canada Book Fund (CBF).

Manufactured in Canada

Book design by Lee Edward Födi
Cover design by Sara Gillingham

10 9 8 7 6 5 4 3 2 1

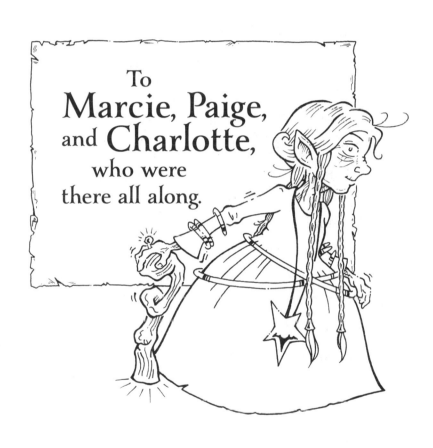

To
Marcie, Paige,
and **Charlotte,**
who were
there all along.

LIST OF CHAPTERS

CHAPTER 1
The Unseen Enemy

Being the type of reader who loves adventure, you understand all too well what it means to follow a hero on a quest. You have braved perilous seas, crossed lonely plains, and even faced dangerous foes. And, through it all, you have learned one important thing: all good adventures must come to an end. Eventually, the hero must return home and, if we are so lucky, evil has been vanquished and peace restored. But if you pay close attention (and of course you always do), then you know that no journey is complete without the hero losing something precious along the way. This might be something as simple as a token, some shiny trinket that the hero once held so very dear. It might be an enchanted weapon that helped complete the quest. Or, sometimes, it is something

1

just a bit more personal, something that forever alters the hero's path ahead.

Yes, the loss is an important part of every story—even our own. Yet, this is the strange thing about the journey, the magic thing, if you will. You see, the act of losing this precious thing is sometimes what helps us see ourselves for who we really are. The loss may seem devastating at first, but by the end it can be the greatest gift of all.

How can this be, you ask? How can losing something possibly be a gift? Ah, this is something you will come to understand. For this is a story of loss, and the incredible power it can grant us . . . if we so let it.

And now you are wondering what all of this means for Kendra Kandlestar, the twelve-year-old wizard's apprentice whom you have come to know so well. Having followed Kendra's past adventures, you know that she has already lost a shiny trinket, and an enchanted weapon, too. She has even lost her family: her mother, father, and brother Kiro. And so, you might ask, what more can she possibly lose?

We will come to that, all in good time. For now it is enough to remind you that Kendra is an Een, coming from that tiny land tucked between the cracks of Here and There. If you recall anything about Eens, it is that they wear braids and are mostly small, mostly elf-like, and mostly best at staying safe and hidden behind the magic curtain that protects their land from the outside world. Kendra, of course, is not one of those "mostly" Eens. Indeed, as we join her in this tale, we find her far away from her beloved home, standing alone in a mysterious chamber, preparing to face a powerful adversary.

Kendra couldn't see a thing in the room. She could only rely on her hearing, her sense of touch, and—most importantly—her magic. Raising her wand of Eenwood, she took a cautious step forward, tentatively reaching out with the toe of her foot to find the reassuring plane of the floor. The wooden planks creaked beneath her, but that was okay. Her rival already knew she was coming. Patient as a spider, he was waiting to make his move.

This is what it must feel like to be blind, Kendra thought as she took another step. She couldn't help thinking of the future, a future she had been lucky enough (or unlucky enough— Kendra supposed it depended on your point of view) to catch a glimpse of. In that future she was the ripe old age of one hundred and twelve, and completely blind. It bothered her to think of herself that way, but if there was one thing her adventures had taught her, it was that the future was never set in stone.

Besides, that's a hundred years from now, Kendra thought, inching forward.

Suddenly, something hot and searing hissed past her ear. Kendra's wandering mind instantly snapped to attention.

Fire bursts, Kendra realized, her heart thumping.

She fought the urge to duck, realizing that this might be exactly what he expected. This was no time to panic. She just needed to swallow her fear and focus. She tuned her mind and slowly began to feel shapes emerge from the darkness. It wasn't seeing exactly, more like a sensation of what was around her. To her left there was a chest, to the right something taller. A cask? A cabinet? She wasn't sure, except that it was inanimate, and that's all that mattered. She could always use that for cover, if necessary. She shuffled forward—only to sense something stretched in front of her. It was suspended just a hand's width above the floor.

Aha! A rope! Kendra thought as she adeptly stepped over the snare. This was no time for smugness, however—for at that exact moment she detected three more bursts of fire blazing towards her. Coolly, Kendra flicked her wand and uttered the following spell:

> *Arrows of flame, bolts of fire,*
> *Feel my magic—then expire.*

Before the flaring arrows could reach her, they simply fizzled away, falling to the floor like failed firecrackers. Kendra allowed herself a smile of satisfaction.

More fire bursts came, dozens of them. Now full of confidence, Kendra twirled her wand, deflecting every missile with ease as she moved steadily forward across the chamber. There were a few more obstacles in her path, but they caused her no grief. Her mind was working like a well-oiled machine. Just a few more steps and victory would be hers . . .

"Oomph!" Something struck her in the gut, so hard that it caused her to crash to the floor—and drop her wand in the process. Whatever had hit her (*Definitely not a fire burst,* Kendra thought) had left her completely winded. Now, as she gasped for air on the floor, she could hear her attacker stride forward. Kendra was defenseless. Desperately, she reached out into the darkness, hoping her fingers would find her wand. Instead, she felt a cold and hard foot press down on her wrist.

"Humph."

With her free hand, Kendra pulled away the cloth that had been used to blindfold her, but she didn't need to look up to know what Uncle Griffinskitch was thinking. She was an expert at deciphering his humphs, and this particular one said it all. It had that I'm-disappointed-but-sadly-not-surprised tone about it.

"Are you going to let me get up?" Kendra asked, purposely staring at the floor.

Uncle Griffinskitch lifted his foot. "You lose," he proclaimed. "Again."

Kendra collected her wand, stood up, and finally dared to look at him. He was so hunched that he was a full head shorter than her, but that didn't make him seem any less intimidating. It probably had something to do with his long, gnarled wizard's staff. Or his vivid blue eyes. Or maybe it was all that beard; there was so much of it that you just couldn't be sure what he was hiding underneath it. Indeed, the beard covered his whole body—almost, anyway; Kendra could see his two feet poking out from the bottom. That's when she realized one of the feet was suspiciously naked. The missing boot was lying nearby, its tongue lazily hanging out, as if to taunt her.

"A boot!?" Kendra cried in exasperation. "You threw a boot at me?"

A hint of mischief played in the old wizard's eyes. "You know what they say," he said as he waved his staff, causing his boot to return to its rightful place. "The most painful attack is the one we least expect."

"Seriously?" Kendra retorted. "I was fighting fire bursts. You know . . . *magical* weapons. Not an ordinary boot! How was I supposed to see that coming?"

Uncle Griffinskitch's expression turned from amusement to ire. "You are a sorceress of Een! You must not see what is ahead. You must *feel*."

Kendra glared at him, fuming. "You cheated."

"Humph," Uncle Griffinskitch growled. "Once again, you have failed to understand the lesson."

"To win at all costs?"

"No!" Uncle Griffinskitch growled, thumping his staff against the floor. "To feel the energy of things, to trust what is really there—not what you *think* is there. When it comes to the magic of Een, you must unite both heart and mind. You must become one. You must find *Arazeen*."

"Paradise?" Kendra said dubiously. "Perhaps you have forgotten, *Master*, we are not searching for some magical Een heaven written about in your ancient texts. We're searching for—"

"Arazeen is not a place," Uncle Griffinskitch interrupted. "You will not find it across the seas, floating in the skies, or hidden in some distant vale."

"Where then?"

"Here," Uncle Griffinskitch replied, raising his staff to tap

Kendra on the forehead.

Kendra pulled away with a scowl. "I thought Arazeen was an Een myth, just a place to go when you die."

"That is what Professor Bumblebean would tell you," Uncle Griffinskitch said. "But a wizard seeks Arazeen in *this* life, in the here and now. To discover Arazeen means to know one's self. To know who you are, and what you are about. To find your true power."

Kendra tugged at one of her braids. It was a habit she was trying to break, but it was difficult with seven different braids to choose from, each sticking out from her head like a long and tempting tree branch. Besides, tugging helped her think—and right now she was thinking, *I'm really not in the mood for a lecture. None of this changes the fact that he cheated.*

Uncle Griffinskitch's brow furled, as if he was reading her thoughts. "Come," he commanded. "There is something I would show you."

CHAPTER 2

Seeking the City on the Storm

Everyone

knows better than to disobey an elder—especially if that elder happens to be a wizard, and an ornery one at that. So Kendra did her best to bury her irritation, and followed after the old Een. She had to hurry, too, for Uncle Griffinskitch could truly move when he felt like it. Down the corridor they went, up the stairs, and onto the uppermost deck of the *Big Bang*, the magical airship that had served as their home for the past several months.

Uncle Griffinskitch led Kendra to the bow of the ship and together they stood at the railing. The skies were just beginning to ignite with the colors of sunset. Vibrant oranges and pinks made the clouds look as if they were on fire. With a bite, the wind whipped across the deck.

9

"You have to admit," Kendra said, raising the hood on her cloak, "I was doing great until the boot."

"Humph," Uncle Griffinskitch grunted. "Tell me, Kendra. What lies before us?"

Kendra fiddled with a braid and stared out at the skyscape. "Clouds?"

"Not what you see. What you feel."

Kendra sighed. Her head was beginning to hurt.

"Do it."

So Kendra closed her eyes and, with wand in hand, cast her mind across the sky, fishing for feelings.

She certainly knew what she was hoping to feel out there amidst the clouds—and it wasn't Arazeen, that's for sure. It was her brother. She had come so far, been through so much, to find him.

Kiro had been long ago transformed into the monstrous form of Trooogul the Unger. He had become obsessed with a quest of his own, and that was to rebuild the ancient cauldron once used by the Wizard Greeve. It was a source of dark magic, and many believed that rebuilding it would resurrect a curse that would transform the entire Een race into monsters.

Kendra shuddered at the very idea. She didn't want to share the fate of her brother. And she didn't understand why his heart had darkened, why he had decided to turn against her and repair the cauldron. She had no idea about his true motives; all she knew was that he had told her to find the City on the Storm, that she could be reunited with him there.

The problem was that no one seemed to know where this city was. Kendra and the crew of the *Big Bang* had sailed the skies all through the winter and into the spring, seeking the fabled city. They had journeyed over lands strange and unfa-

miliar, chased rumors and
clues, met both friend and
foe—but so far their search
had been in vain. Most
strangers they met
said that the city was
so well hidden that it
was impossible to find;
others claimed that it
didn't exist at all.

Kendra couldn't believe
that. The City on the Storm
had to exist. Still, as she used her
mind to probe the skies ahead, she could find no hint or clue
that suggested any scrap of civilization was nearby. She let her
mind soar further across the clouds, sending out her magic as
far as it could possibly go. Then, suddenly, she seemed to hit
a wall of darkness. Her mind went black, as if someone had
poured a bottle of ink over her window to the world.

"I . . . I must be tired," she said, opening her eyes and
looking at her uncle. "Everything just went dark. It was like
being blindfolded all over again."

Uncle Griffinskitch furled his brow.

"What is it?" Kendra asked. "Is it the future I see? Is the
darkness the City on the Storm? Does that mean we're close?"

"They are your feelings," Uncle Griffinskitch replied. "It is
for *you* to decipher."

"But—"

"That is all I will teach you today," Uncle Griffinskitch
said gruffly. "I will stay and watch the stars. Go to the galley
and find some dinner."

Kendra nodded.

"Just one more thing. Take the boy his dinner when you go below deck."

Kendra felt a tingle down her spine. "The boy" was Agent Leerlin Lurk, a one-time spy who was now their prisoner, residing in a makeshift brig at the bottom of the ship. He was only thirteen years old, but that made him no less intimidating. Kendra had tried befriending him, but her overtures had been met with nothing but contempt.

"It's Jinx's job to look after him," she protested.

"Humph."

So much for that argument, Kendra thought.

A few minutes later, she lingered in front of Agent Lurk's door, steeling herself for her visit with the sulky boy. In one hand was the platter she had fetched from the galley; in the other was her wand. Now, with a gesture of magic, she unlocked the door and stepped into the gloomy chamber. It was in complete disarray and Kendra couldn't help thinking that it looked as if some wild beast was imprisoned there instead of an Een.

"What do you want, Kandlestar?" a voice rasped from a dark corner.

"I've brought you dinner," Kendra said, placing the platter on the floor. "You know, it's not very light in here. Why don't you open a shutter? Or light a candle?"

"If you looked like me, you would not mind the shadows,"

Agent Lurk replied and, as if to prove his point, he skittered into the meager light.

Kendra tried to stifle a gasp. It didn't seem to matter how many times she gazed upon Agent's Lurk face; it was no less startling. Despite his youth, Lurk appeared as vile and ghastly as an ancient crone. Only a few wisps of hair graced his head, not even enough for an Een braid. His ears looked as if they had been nibbled by rats, while his pale, drawn face was marred with bright red scars. One of his eyes was milky white and half-closed; the other was bloodshot and red.

Kendra couldn't help but look away.

"See what I mean?" Agent Lurk wheezed, dropping to the floor to gnaw at his dinner. "The darkness suits me. Now, tell me, girl. Where's my cloak?"

"Your shadow cloak?" Kendra asked in response. "It's safe and sound. Besides, you know it can't turn you invisible in here, anyway. Uncle Griffinskitch cast a spell on this chamber."

"Then why not just let me have it?"

"Because Uncle Griffinskitch doesn't trust you," Kendra told him. "And . . . neither do I."

"That is the first intelligent thing you've ever said," Lurk said between mouthfuls. "I will escape this wretched prison—one day, and disappear as easily as the slither of a serpent's tongue."

"And then what will you do?"

"What I have always meant to do," Lurk replied. "It's the very reason I traveled here from a hundred years in the future. To stop the cauldron from being repaired."

Kendra frowned. "Don't you understand that's what I want to do, too?"

"No," Lurk said firmly. "You will side with Trooogul. This is a fact. The history books speak of it."

"Then you're reading the wrong books," Kendra said hotly. "Listen, I don't care what future you come from, or what you think you know. I will not betray my people. I'm not like you."

"My loyalty is to the Land of Een, I assure you," Agent Lurk intoned. "It just needs a few . . . tweaks. To iron out the wrinkles."

Kendra knew what he meant by "wrinkles." Agent Lurk believed in a pure Een race. As far as he was concerned, the Land of Een would be a far better place if every last Een animal was eradicated. "You're just like Burdock Brown," Kendra snapped. "He's arrogant and misguided—and destroying the land I love."

"Don't fret," Agent Lurk said, slurping down the last of his meal. "The Land of Een faces a threat more severe than Burdock."

"What do you mean?" Kendra asked, plucking at a braid.

"War is coming," Agent Lurk said, wiping a sleeve across his mouth. "The Ungers, the other monster tribes, they will turn their spears upon the Land of Een."

"More history?" Kendra asked, doing her best to keep her cool. "Then rest assured, I will stand with Een. Not against it."

"Funny thing about war," Lurk said. "It makes people do the things they least expect."

CHAPTER 3

The Last Flight of the Big Bang

That night, Kendra found herself plummeting through the darkness. It was the same inky color that she had encountered during her vision on the deck of the *Big Bang*, except now the blackness was in the form of giant, swirling clouds. It was if they were pulling her downwards—and at an alarming speed. She fumbled in her cloak for her wand, but it was missing! In desperation, she spread out her arms, bracing herself for the impact she was sure would come.

And come it did.

Kendra's eyes popped open and she found herself lying on the floor of her cabin. Her bunk, instead of behaving properly and lying beneath her, was sitting next to her.

It took a moment for Kendra to connect her dream to reality. Somehow, she had tumbled right out of bed! In a daze, she sat up, only to suddenly feel the whole ship lurch beneath her. Her wand rattled across the floor and bumped against her leg.

What is it doing on the floor? she wondered. *I left it on the—*

"Kendra!?"

She looked up to see Oki, her best friend, staring at her wide-eyed and confused from his hammock. "What's going on?" the little mouse squeaked.

Kendra heard the long, rumbling sound of thunder. "Storm!" she cried. She picked up her wand and immediately heard her uncle's voice communicating through the magic of the Eenwood. *Kendra! Get up here!*

"Come on!" Kendra told Oki. She rose to her feet, but at that moment the ship pitched so dramatically that she stumbled into the wall.

"Eek! Don't think of rhubarb!" Oki wailed.

Kendra threw him an odd glance.

Kendra! Uncle Griffinskitch's voice urged as she struggled into some clothes.

With Oki at her heels, Kendra dashed to the upper deck to find herself in a swirl of black clouds—only this time, they were real. She could feel the snap of the wind and the hot spit of rain. A flash of lightning clawed at the sky, soon followed by another boom of thunder.

"Uncle Griffinskitch!?" Kendra called into the darkness.

"This way," Oki said, scampering ahead.

Kendra hurried after him, and heard a loud "Humph!"

Oki had charged right into the old wizard, knocking him over as if he was nothing more than a toadstool in a game of Een bowling.

"Sorry!" Oki cheeped, as he tried to help the old wizard to his feet.

Uncle Griffinskitch fired a piercing glare at the mouse then pointed to the sky. "Look!"

Kendra's eyes followed the direction of her uncle's bony finger, but found more darkness. Then the clouds shifted, and she spotted something rising up through the mist.

"What is that thing?" she wondered out loud. "A tree?"

"No," Oki said. "I think it's a tower."

He was right, Kendra realized—though it was unlike any sort of tower she had ever seen before. It had curves and bulbs and a needle-like spire; she was reminded of the whimsical ornaments she and Oki used to hang as children to celebrate Ald Meryn's Eve. Then another tower materialized through the clouds—and another, and another, followed by archways and buttresses until Kendra found herself gazing upon a spectacular castle that somehow seemed as if it was just floating in the sky.

"The City on the Storm," Kendra murmured in awe.

It was still in the distance, but as the ship plowed through the thundering clouds, Kendra caught snatches of other dazzling details—fluttering flags, crenellated walls, even an ornate belfry. *How did they build all of this on the clouds?* she pondered, and then felt a little foolish when, a moment later, she glimpsed the dark outline of a cliff through the mist. The truth was that the entire structure was perched (and somewhat precariously if you asked Kendra) on top of a mountain. But you certainly wouldn't know it at first glance; the clouds made it all seem so magical.

She turned to look at Oki, only to realize that the entire crew was now assembling at the bow. Professor Bumblebean,

the tall and fussy scholar who so loved complicated words, was clutching a large book and beaming ear to giant ear. Juniper Jinx, the grasshopper who served as the crew's soldier, hopped right up to the railing, wielding a sword and two spears (that was Jinx for you; she was always prepared for trouble). Last to arrive was Ratchet Ringtail; the large grey raccoon was fiddling with a pair of Foggle Goggles. You see, not only was Ratchet the captain of the *Big Bang*, but (in his own words) an inventor of extraordinary talent. What this really meant was that he invented with what little magic he knew. His Foggle Goggles were a perfect example. They were supposed to let you see through the fog, but the problem was that they kept, well, fogging up. In truth, many of Ratchet's gadgets didn't seem to quite work out, though ever since he had taken on Oki as a pupil, his success rate seemed to be on the rise.

"My word, the City on the Storm is well named," Professor Bumblebean said. "It seems quite a tempest is brewing here. There is no doubt that we shall soon be drenched in precipitation."

"Or in boredom if we have to keep listening to your nonsense, *Mumblebean*," retorted Jinx.

"I have to agree with Professor B.," Ratchet said, still trying to adjust his goggles. "Clouds are one thing. Wind and lightning are another. We have to find a way to land—unless we want to be ripped to shreds."

"Oh, don't think of rhubarb," Oki squealed.

"Why do you keep saying that?" Kendra asked.

"You know I always try *not* to think of something when I'm scared," Oki explained. "So Ratchet suggested rhubarb. Everything else seems to cause trouble."

"That's a preposterous idea," Jinx grumbled.

"Well, rhubarb is a natural laxative," Professor Bumble-bean mused.

"See?" Ratchet told Jinx. "He's the brains. And he says rhubarb helps you relax."

"Laxative doesn't mean to relax . . . not exactly," Kendra told the raccoon over the rising howl of the wind. "It means to, er . . . well, it helps . . . you know. To go."

"Go where?" Ratchet asked.

"In private, hopefully!" Kendra said.

"Humph!" Uncle Griffinskitch grunted. "We don't have time for this nonsense. Captain Ringtail, turn the ship around and get us out of here."

"What!?" Kendra exclaimed. "The city's in *front* of us!"

"So is the storm," her uncle growled. "If we want to reach it in one piece, we will have to find another—"

Kendra didn't hear the rest of his sentence, for at that moment the ship was clobbered full force by the squall. What had been a sporadic spittle of rain now turned into a bombardment of wet missiles, pounding the deck with such a deafening racket that all other sounds were drowned out. Kendra's clothes were instantly drenched through. Then the ship began to spin and dip.

Quickly, Kendra tucked away her wand and grabbed hold of a nearby rigging line. This was just in time, for now the ship listed at such an angle that her feet were dangling in the air, alongside the cascade of rain sliding down the deck. She clung, white-knuckled, to her rope, desperately hoping the ship would right itself. She heard an "EEEEEEK!" and caught sight of Oki whirling by in a blur of fur. She risked taking one hand from her rope to reach for him, only to have the wind rip her away too. She careened downwards, hitting the railing

on the other of the deck. The ship
tilted the opposite direction,
then back again like a
seesaw, and back and
forth she tumbled,
her hands frantically
trying to find traction
on the slick surface
of the deck.

Now she had no
idea where anyone was. It
was as if they were caught in
a whirlpool, swirling round
and round and plunging downwards at the same time.

Then something walloped them—hard. It wasn't the
storm, Kendra realized, but something with weight, something with intention. The next thing she knew, the long tentacles of some sort of creature were snaking across the deck.
These coiled around the *Big Bang* as if it was nothing more
than some juicy insect, squeezing until the ship's timbers
began to splinter and snap. Whatever it was, it was giant and
green—and attacking in a fury. One of the enormous tentacles slapped Kendra's chest and sent her sprawling across the
deck. As she slid to a halt, she glimpsed Uncle Griffinskitch
flashing his wand to retaliate the attack with a zap from his
staff. As soon as it was struck, the tentacle—all the tentacles,
in fact—suddenly released the ship and slithered away. The
ship plunged towards the ground in a terrifying free fall.

It's like my dream all over again, Kendra thought—but this
time she knew her landing wouldn't be so gentle.

CHAPTER 4

Uncle Griffinskitch Loses His Temper

There is nothing like the sound of a terrible crash. It's a sound that seems to grab you by the pit of the stomach and flip you inside out. The strange thing is that the clamorous pandemonium of the collision always seems to be followed by utter silence, as if the entire world has just suddenly stopped for a moment to stare at the accident, wide-eyed and bewildered, as if to say, *I can't believe that just happened.*

Such was the case with the crash of the *Big Bang*. When Kendra finally came to, it took her a moment to piece together what had happened, as if her memory of the last few minutes had been smashed against the floor—and now her brain had to retrieve the pieces, one by one.

23

Slowly, it all came back—the storm, the crash, even the strange creature. It had been so chaotic, and now it was so quiet. She could hear nothing. Then, in a panic, she thought of her friends. Where were they?

Woozily, she sat up and found herself completely alone in the middle of some sort of vast, tropical garden. Everywhere she looked there were lush ferns, strange flowering plants, and giant trees draped in moss and thick vines. Above her was a canopy of leaves; she couldn't even see the sky. Kendra wiped perspiration from her brow, suddenly realizing how hot and humid it was. An insect hummed past her ear, and Kendra waved it away in annoyance.

I'm in a jungle, she thought. *Maybe I was just thrown free of the ship.*

Sluggishly, she pulled herself to her feet. She was dry enough now and supposed that either the storm had abated or they had crashed beyond its reach. After checking that she still had her wand and that her own injuries were no worse than a few scratches and bruises, she began making her way through the foliage.

She did not have to go far to find the ship—or, better said, what was left of it. Pushing aside a leaf that was the size of a curtain, she found the *Big Bang* lying shattered on the jungle floor, a trail of flattened ferns and chewed-up soil marking its tumultuous skid across the ground. The ship had once resembled a giant bird, but now it was nothing more than a tangled heap of timbers and torn masts. There was no sign of the strange creature that had tugged the ship to its doom.

Kendra gave a braid an anxious yank. "Hello?" she called, cautiously approaching the wreckage.

A small green head popped out from the debris. "Kendra!" Jinx called back. "You okay?"

"Yes . . . but where's everyone else?"

"C'mon," the grasshopper beckoned. "We'll find them."

They wandered around the rest of the crash site and, one by one, found everyone except for Agent Lurk. His cabin, like the rest of the ship, had been torn to pieces, but of the spy himself there was no sign.

"There's more bad news," Jinx announced. "The shadow cloak is missing. It was in the hold next to the galley."

"Then Lurk took it," Uncle Griffinskitch said, stroking his disheveled beard. "He survived the crash, snatched the cloak, and now he is on the loose again—and most likely invisible. We must be alert."

"Well, at least everyone is in one piece," Professor Bumblebean remarked. "For that, at least, we can be immensely grateful."

"What about my ship?" Ratchet moaned, cradling a fragment of the steering wheel. "She's not in one piece! Oh, my beautiful *Big Bang!* You were so young and brave!"

"I'm sorry, Ratchet," Kendra said, clutching his paw.

"She served us valiantly," Uncle Griffinskitch told the raccoon. "You can be proud of her, Captain."

"And you never know," Oki piped up. "Maybe we can fix her."

"Are you crazy?" Ratchet asked. "She's ruined! Look at her! Maybe you have *crashimonia*, Oki."

"*Crashimonia?*" Kendra asked. "What in the name of Een is that?"

"Ratchet and I decided we should try and discover new diseases," Oki explained. "It might make us famous."

"Then you must have *idioticosis!*" Jinx grumbled, shaking three fists at the mouse. "You don't discover a new disease just by using a silly word!"

"Jinx is correct," Professor Bumblebean agreed as he tried to straighten the frames of his spectacles. "The discovery of a new disease involves study and scientific enquiry and—"

"Humph," Uncle Griffinskitch interrupted (to which Oki whispered, "I think he must have *humphilitus,*" forcing Kendra to stifle a giggle). "We don't have time for such ludicrous nonsense," the old wizard said. "The ship will not fly again, that much is certain. Which means we must seek the City on the Storm by some other means."

"How?" Kendra wondered, looking around at the maze of plants and trees. "We don't even know which direction to go."

"I suspect we crashed at the base of the mountain," Professor Bumblebean replied. "Which means there's only one direction for us to go. And that, my dear comrades, is upwards."

"We have to climb?" Oki asked. "That would take forever."

"That may be so, but climb we must," Uncle Griffinskitch said.

The first order of business was to search the wreckage to see what supplies could be salvaged. Kendra was able to find her canteen (still full) and small traveling pouch, along with a few other essentials, including some food. Jinx outfitted herself with a sword and two spears, while Professor Bumblebean was able to retrieve enough books to fill a large pack. As for Ratchet and Oki, they were able to kit themselves with all sorts of gear, but there was one item in particular that caught Kendra's attention. To you or me, the gadget might have

seemed like an old-fashioned radio or record player, but Kendra had never seen such a thing. To her, the device looked like a dome with a series of knobs and switches, and a long trumpet protruding from the top.

"What is that?" Kendra asked.

"It's our recent invention," Ratchet declared. "We call it the Snifferoo."

"The Sniff-a-what?" Kendra asked.

"The Snifferoo," Ratchet repeated. "It records smells."

"Another ridiculous idea," Jinx complained. "Why would you want to record smells?"

"Because it's like Oki and I have *inventimonia*," Ratchet told her. "We just have to invent things; we can't help it! And you just wait—if we ever get back home, this gizmo is going to sell like firecrackers at Jamboreen. I suggest we do a demonstration, Oki. Let's record the smells of this jungle."

"There's just one problem," Oki said, fiddling with the buttons on the Snifferoo. "We're out of space. There's only room for three smells at a time."

"What smells are in there so far?" Kendra asked curiously.

"Well, there's the fragrance from that soap we bought from that peddler in Anse-Maru," Ratchet said. "And then there was the scent of the sea that you so liked, Kendra. Oh—and remember when we ate rhubarb for three days straight and then we all ended up with terrible—"

"DAYS OF EEN!" Uncle Griffinskitch roared, which was something he said when a humph just wouldn't do. "That is quite enough."

Everyone immediately silenced. Unfortunately, this was also the moment that the Snifferoo let out a long and flatulent sound—and the odor to match.

Uncle Griffinskitch's ears (not to mention his nose) turned flaming red, a sure sign that he was angry. Kendra didn't take her eyes off of him, but she made sure to take a quiet step back, putting as much distance as possible between her and the Snifferoo.

"Cease this buffoonery!" the old wizard warned, his face contorting with rage.

"To be fair, Ratchet and Oki's inventions have helped us through all sorts of scrapes in the past," Kendra dared to tell her uncle. "Where would we be without the cloud ship?"

Uncle Griffinskitch leveled a stern glare at her. "Where we are *now* is this jungle," he said eventually. "And if we are ever going to get out of here, we are going to have to stop fooling about and pull together. Now, come! We have a mountain to climb."

CHAPTER 5

Perils and Pitfalls

When life doesn't offer you a clear path, you just have to forge ahead and make your own. There was no trail through the jungle, no signposts or markers, but Uncle Griffinskitch merely humphed and began marching up the nearest slope. The others followed behind in single file, with Jinx coming at the end.

Most everything in the world is large compared to an Een, but the jungle plants were some of the most enormous Kendra had ever seen. The stalks seemed as wide as tree trunks, and they were just as tall too, with their canopy of leaves casting long, dappled shadows. And then there was the cacophony of sounds that came from these shadows: buzzing, warbling, fluttering, and humming—all the sounds of the jungle creatures. Kendra glimpsed multi-colored birds and slippery reptiles, but these kept mostly to themselves. The insects, on the other hand, were all too brazen and it wasn't long before they began dive-bombing the Eens.

"I'll show them who's boss!" Jinx declared as a giant mosquito swooped towards her. With a slash of her sword, she cut the insect in two, leaving a pulpy mess at her feet.

"That's disgusting," Ratchet said. "Besides, how can you kill a bug, Jinx? That could have been your long-lost cousin!"

"Then he should have been more polite," Jinx snarled.

"I do say, Ratchet," Professor Bumblebean remarked. "You should know that the denizens of this jungle are wild, while our dear Jinx here is a civilized inhabitant of the Land of Een. She's of no certain relation to that mosquito."

"Never mind the insects," Uncle Griffinskitch announced. "It is the enemy that can think that we must be wary of."

Onwards they trudged, and it wasn't long before onwards became upwards. Indeed, it soon felt like they were climbing more than walking. Kendra's clothes were soaked through with perspiration and she drank continually from her canteen. Her legs felt like jelly.

"It's times like this that I really begin to miss home," Oki panted. "They don't have heat like this back in Een."

"Except for the hot air coming from Burdock Brown," Kendra huffed. "Don't forget, he's ruling Een like a king and we're wanted fugitives there."

"I suppose," Oki said. "But—and I never thought I'd say this—I think I'm actually beginning to miss my sisters. All eight of them."

For days, their exhausting trek continued. They climbed hour after hour, stopping only to eat or rest. Luckily, they were able to scavenge nuts, seeds, and berries from the jungle and it rained often enough ("We're approaching the City on the Storm, after all," Professor Bumblebean reminded them) that they had a steady supply of water.

On the afternoon of the third day, they found the stone marker. It appeared out of the jungle as a giant face, towering above them with round, vacant eyes and a set of pointed teeth. It looked so monstrous that Oki let out an ear-splitting "EEEK!" and Kendra had to grab him by the tail just to stop him from scampering all the way back down the mountain.

"What an ugly statue," Ratchet remarked. "Why would someone stick it right in the middle of the jungle?"

"A warning," Uncle Griffinskitch explained, leaning heavily on his staff as he stared up at the monument. "It is meant to dissuade us from continuing."

"Ah, yes," Professor Bumblebean declared. "Many cultures erect such ominous idols near their settlements in the belief that they will ward off malevolent spirits."

"So that means we're getting close," Kendra mused, walking slowly around the stone-faced pillar. She couldn't help thinking it looked like an Unger, for it had long tusks and a beard. The plants growing from the top of its head made it look like it had a crop of hair.

"Come. We won't let a little statue deter us," Uncle Griffinskitch said.

"Little?" Oki murmured.

As they continued their ascent of the mountain, they discovered more statues, each identical to the last. After a dozen or so, Kendra stopped counting. Besides, something else had caught her attention; it was the silence. The jungle had gone completely quiet, as if all the creatures had just mysteriously vanished.

Maybe the stone guardians scared them away, Kendra thought.

That's when she was suddenly knocked face-first to the ground.

"What happened?" Oki asked, nearly bumping into her.

"I think something tripped me," Kendra replied, as the rest of the crew gathered around her.

"Like what sort of something?" Oki cried.

"Like a tree root," Kendra said, pulling herself up. "Or a vine."

"I don't see anything," Ratchet said. "Maybe you just have *tripabetes*."

"I felt it," Kendra insisted.

"Humph," Uncle Griffinskitch muttered. "I fear there is a mysterious force at work in this jungle."

As they pressed on, Kendra couldn't help feeling that they were being watched. More than once she thought she spied something slithering away from the corner of her eye, but whenever she turned for a closer inspection she saw nothing but regular jungle plants, innocently standing there. She was beginning to wonder if the jungle was driving her mad.

Then, just when Kendra thought she could take it no more, the jungle broke and the Eens found themselves standing before a wide chasm. On the other side of this gap they could see the continuation of the jungle, rising up the mountain once more; down below there was nothing but swirling mist. Professor Bumblebean kicked a stone off the edge. It rattled off the side of the cliff, but Kendra didn't hear it hit bottom.

"What do we do now?" Jinx asked, peering over the edge.

"We find a crossing," Uncle Griffinskitch said. He wiped the sweat from his brow and began leading them along the edge of the abyss.

Eventually, the gap narrowed and they saw a gigantic tree perched on the edge at such an angle that one of its long roots spread across to the other side. The root was so wide that it made the perfect bridge for the small Eens.

Uncle Griffinskitch stroked his beard. Shuffling forward, he tapped the root with his staff. Nothing happened. He recited a spell, tapped again, and still nothing occurred.

"What are you thinking?" Kendra asked.

"This jungle is fraught with trickery," the wizard replied. "We must be cautious."

"Let me cross first," Jinx suggested.

Without waiting for argument, she bounded along the root to the other side, then came back. "It seems safe enough."

Uncle Griffinskitch nodded, and started leading the small band of travelers across the chasm.

"Don't think of rhubarb!" Oki chanted.

Kendra would have taken him by the paw if she could, but the root was not wide enough to walk two abreast. "Don't worry," she called. "We're almost there."

It was at this very moment that the root began to tremble and quake. It started slowly, so that at first Kendra just extended her arms to steady herself, but then the whole root began to twist and turn. Kendra dropped to her stomach and clung to the bark. The others did the same—except for poor Professor Bumblebean, who tumbled right over the side. It was only at the last moment that Jinx reached out to grab hold of him by the collar.

"Oh, my!" Kendra heard the professor exclaim as he dangled over the chasm.

"I don't think I can hold you!" Jinx yelled, now reaching over with her other three arms to clutch at him. "Drop your pack!"

"My dear Jinx, have you quite lost your mind?" Professor Bumblebean called. "Do you not realize my pack is full of books?"

"And they're HEAVY!" Jinx growled. "So unless you want us to change your name to *Tumblebean*, DROP THEM!"

If the professor had a reply, Kendra didn't hear it—for now the root began thrashing about so violently that it took all her powers of concentration to hang on. She felt like a flea clinging to the end of an Izzard's tail—a very angry Izzard that had decided it was time for a house cleaning. Kendra's canteen spun loose from her belt and she caught a glimpse of it careening into the chasm below. She hugged the bark even tighter, but the next spasm of the root was so powerful that she lost her grip and was tossed upwards in an arc and sent smashing into the ground on the other side of the gorge.

Kendra's whole world was spinning around her, as if she had left her stomach somewhere back on the bridge. Finally, she looked back, but instead saw only the tree root, stretching quiet and still across the chasm. Just like that, it had stopped convulsing—and then, with a queasy, sickening feeling, Kendra realized why. There was no one left to shake off; the entire crew had been thrown into the mist below.

CHAPTER 6

Ensnared
by the
Jungle

We've all experienced those
moments in our lives when we
wish we could just press some
sort of magical reverse button
and make it all go away. Of
course, no such button exists
(unless Ratchet invented
one that we don't know
about) and we must con-
front the reality before us.

Or, in Kendra's case, below
her. Feeling helpless and distraught, she crept to the edge of the
abyss and stared downward. There
was still no bottom to see, only the
swirling mist. How could anyone
survive such a fall?

Maybe Jinx, Kendra thought. *She has
wings. But she was holding on to Professor Bumble-
bean and his heavy books, and if she had let go, then where is she?
And Oki . . .*

Kendra couldn't bear to think of it. She turned around
and contemplated the dense jungle rising before her. If it had

seemed ominous before, it was more so now. What was she going to do?

A loud grunt broke her train of thought. She looked around, but could see nothing but the jungle on one side and the chasm on the other. Then she noticed a vine from a tree near the edge of the gorge, thrashing about madly as if it had caught some sort of prey—except whatever the prey, it was invisible.

Agent Lurk.

Kendra knew it in an instant. That was the slippery spy for you; he was a survivor.

And now I'm alone with him, Kendra thought.

"You might as well show yourself," she declared, stepping forward with some hastily-mustered courage. "I know you're there and, by the looks of it, so does the tree."

Lurk shimmered into visibility, and now Kendra could see that the vine had him ensnared by one bony ankle. He was like a worm on a hook, dangling upside down, and helpless.

"Looks like you could use a hand," Kendra said.

"Go away," Agent Lurk rasped. "I don't want your help."

"You're going to get it anyway," Kendra said. A part of her was tempted to abandon him, but another part—a bigger part—couldn't bear to leave him in trouble. She took a moment to calm her flustered mind, then used her wand to fire a zap at the vine. As soon as it was struck, the vine recoiled, dropping Lurk roughly to the ground.

"Stupid girl," the boy snarled, slowly pulling himself to his feet. "I could have broken something."

"Not your heart," Kendra retorted, staring into his dark hood. "You'd need one first. I don't know how you managed to make it across that chasm when everyone else fell, but if I find out you did anything . . ."

"Like give a certain mouse a push?"

Kendra lunged at Lurk with both fists, striking him in the chest. He was so frail he toppled like a twig, landing right near the edge of the gorge. The danger didn't even register with Kendra; she was so enraged that she jumped on top of him and began battering him with her knuckles.

Lurk just cackled in glee. After a moment Kendra gave up and rolled away, tears pouring from her face.

"I hate you," she spat.

"Then we are even, Kandlestar," Agent Lurk gloated, tugging himself to his feet. "For my loathing for you is deeper than this chasm."

Kendra rose up, pointing her wand right at his chest. "All it will take is one flick of my wrist to send you over; then you can find out just how deep it is."

Lurk chuckled and slowly paced a semi-circle around her. "Go ahead. This jungle is just one enormous death trap anyway. Neither of us will likely escape. Which is fine by me."

"I find that hard to believe," Kendra retorted, turning with Lurk to make sure her wand was still aimed in his direction.

"Look at me," Agent Lurk croaked, yanking down his hood so that Kendra was forced to gaze upon his hideous face. "What do I have to live for? Ha! You should have seen me once, Kandlestar. I was handsome. Strong. Now I stagger across the world, broken and wracked with pain. If you knew what it was like to be me . . ."

"You have only yourself to blame," Kendra said, trembling. "You should not have tried to command your master's magic. That's what maimed you."

"NO!" Agent Lurk roared, his face erupting in a flush of red. "You made this happen. And why? You're jealous of any-

one who gets a scrap of success. You've had everything handed to you, as easy as Eenberry pie! But not me. I wasn't born to some famous magical family. I've had to *earn* everything."

"So have I!" Kendra cried.

"Oh, sure," Lurk snarled. "Your all-powerful mother, Kayla Kandlestar. Your masterful uncle. You were born famous, Kandlestar. But that wasn't enough for you, was it? You had to deny me the chance to study Een magic—you and that despicable little rodent. I could have been one of the most powerful wizards Een has ever known. But you stopped it."

Kendra stared at him, bewildered and angry at the same time. "This is all in some distant future," she said after a moment. "This doesn't even make any sense. You hate me for something I haven't even done."

"*Yet*," Lurk hissed. "You haven't done it yet. But you will."

Kendra finally lowered her wand. "I don't care if you believe me," she said. "I didn't want this to happen to you."

Lurk sneered in response. During this whole conversation, he had been edging away from the chasm, ever closer to the thick of the jungle. And, now that Kendra's wand was no longer aimed at him, he threw up his hood and completely vanished. Kendra could hear him as he rustled through the thick undergrowth.

Instinctively, she chased after him, firing zaps from her wand. By mere chance, one of her bolts stung him right in the shoulder, causing him to turn visible and pitch head over heels across the ground. Kendra grabbed him by the arm and wrenched him to his feet.

"You're coming with me," she ordered. "We're going back to the gorge. We're going to see what happened to them."

Still holding Lurk firmly, Kendra turned around, only to find her way blocked by the jungle. It was as if all the plants had shuffled behind her when her back was turned, except now they looked more dangerous than ever. Some of them were dripping with strings of green drool and reaching with wiggling green feelers. Others had long vines that flickered in and out like reptilian tongues. And there were some that spread their fronds to reveal rows of tiny thorns—*Just like teeth*, Kendra thought with a shudder. It was as if the entire jungle—every flower, fern, and nettle—had just sprung to monstrous life.

"What are you waiting for?" Lurk hissed. "Use your magic!"

Kendra nod-ded. Still clutch-ing Lurk with one hand, she raised her wand of Een-wood with the other and chanted:

Fierce plants, now wither and fail!
Let us free as you recoil and quail!
Bow before me and show safe trail—
So we might pass this treacherous vale.

But the spell was too ambitious, especially for the amount of panic and stress Kendra was feeling at that moment. Nothing happened as the result of her magic—except that one of the plants fired a ball of spit. Both Kendra and Lurk had to duck to avoid it.

"Good work," Lurk huffed. "You've made them angrier."

Kendra slowly let go of his cloak, and stared up at the writhing mass of plants. "We're in trouble," she murmured.

"What now?" Lurk wondered.

"Run!" Kendra screamed.

As if on cue, they both whirled around, only to find more of the strange plant-like creatures writhing towards them. They dashed past—barely—and into more danger. For now the entire jungle seemed alive, with every plant against them, clutching, grabbing, spitting. A green gob exploded at Kendra's feet; when it splattered against her skin, it itched and burned.

Finally, Kendra could run no farther. She stumbled to a halt, hands on her knees, panting heavily. Lurk collapsed to the ground beside her, just as spent. The plants were closing in. The day had waned and the jungle had grown dark; Kendra could no longer exactly see, but she didn't need to. She could hear the creatures smacking their lips, preparing to feast.

"It's like this jungle is just one giant web," Kendra panted.

Lurk nodded, then said with a wheeze, "And we're the flies."

CHAPTER 7

In the Stomach of the Snare

Nothing

unites two sworn
enemies like a common
danger. Only moments
ago, Kendra would have
gladly seen Agent Lurk plummet
into the gorge; now, pitted against
the perils of the jungle, she
clung to the insidious boy
as if her life depended
upon it.

And perhaps it did.

"Any ideas?" Kendra
gasped, still trying to
catch her breath.

"Look," Agent Lurk
croaked, thrusting a crooked
finger past her nose. "Is that a cave?"

A faint glow was shining amidst the
shadows of the jungle. Then another light appeared, and
another, like eyes blinking open in the dark. Kendra's instincts
warned her to flee, but she couldn't help thinking how warm
and inviting those lights appeared.

A thorn gashed her side, causing her to cry out in pain, and that was all the encouragement she needed. She grabbed Agent Lurk by his collar and yanked him to his feet.

"Come on!"

They dashed towards the nearest tunnel, plants snapping at their heels. They charged inside the cave and ran until at last Lurk stumbled, causing both of them to topple to the ground with a surprisingly soft plunk.

It seemed they had escaped the predatory plants. Kendra gazed at her surroundings, only to find herself mesmerized by a pattern of light and shadow. It was beautiful, or at least it would have been if Kendra hadn't felt so drained. She suddenly felt incredibly thirsty, but when she reached for her canteen she remembered that it had fallen into the gorge.

At last, she pulled herself up, and it was at this moment that she discovered how sticky everything was. It was like trying to stand up on a sheet of taffy.

"What in the name of Een is this place?" she wondered.

She plodded ahead, each step punctuated by a loud sucking sound. The cave seemed to branch in every which way, each tunnel pulsating with light. She felt completely disoriented and wasn't even sure which direction they had come from. She trudged towards one of the glowing tunnels, quickly realizing that it wasn't a tunnel at all, but just a thin, sticky membrane that she couldn't penetrate—not with her boot or even a zap from her wand. She touched it with her fingers, only to pull them away in pain. Her skin was inflamed and irritated; it was as if the substance was eating away at her very flesh.

And that's when it dawned on her. "We've been tricked!" she cried, turning back to Agent Lurk, who was still lying on the ground.

"What are you talk-
ing about?" he asked.
"Those creatures outside,
those plants—they were just
the minions," Kendra explained.
"It was their plan all along to herd us
right into the lair of their queen." She
paused and gulped. "Or maybe 'stomach' is
a better way to put it."

Agent Lurk gave a derisive snort. "No
plant could be this big."

"Don't you get it!?" Kendra cried in exasperation. "We're
being eaten alive!"

Lurk struggled to his feet, his face flickering with a fear she
had never seen in him before. But, just as quickly, the boy's
ever-so-familiar sneer returned.

"Fool of a girl," he spat. "Your imagination runs as wild as
an Unger."

"I'm telling you," Kendra said, "it's trying to digest us. We
have to get out of here—NOW." Without waiting to see if he
would follow, she turned and began slogging in the direction
of another light.

It was a dead end, but she could hear Lurk creeping
behind her, like a parasite unwilling to let its host out of sight.
Kendra cast him a sidelong glance, then just moved on to the
next spot of light, only to discover that it, too, was a wall.

"It's one enormous trap," she told Agent Lurk. "Everything looks the same."

They had no choice but to keep searching for an exit. They
staggered onwards, but it was slow going, like walking ankle-
deep in jelly. Along the way they spotted bones and skulls—

all that was left of other hapless creatures that had been lured inside the plant. Kendra's head was throbbing. The spectrum of lights made her dizzy and her throat became so parched that she could barely speak.

Hours passed, but how many Kendra could not tell. Then, at last, Agent Lurk collapsed behind her, striking the floor of the plant's belly with a slurp-like plop. Kendra turned back, tried to pull him up, but she was so drained herself that she merely fell down alongside him.

Kendra let her head fall against Lurk's shoulder. *I can't go on*, she thought.

"I never pushed him," Lurk said suddenly.

"What?" Kendra rasped, lifting her head with all the strength she could muster.

"I never pushed that wretched mouse," Lurk repeated.

"Why are you telling me this now?"

"Because we're dying."

Kendra didn't know what to say. He was right; they *were* dying. She closed her eyes and let her mind melt into semiconsciousness. She thought of Oki and her other friends. She thought of the family she would never find. She thought of Uncle Griffinskitch.

And then she heard the old wizard's voice: *Kendra.*

She perked up, clenching her wand. Had he really communicated with her? She reached out with her mind, as if casting a fishing line. *Uncle?*

We are wizards of Een, came a reply—but she wasn't sure if it was real, or just an echo from the past. Maybe she had just been driven to the brink of insanity and it was all in her imagination. Of course, imagined help was better than none at all; and so Kendra listened again.

We do not see what is ahead. We must feel.

The lesson on the ship. She was thankful for it now. Kendra forced herself to her feet and stared at the glowing lights. It was as if they were taunting her, and she felt dizzy again.

So she closed her eyes and welcomed the relief of the darkness.

"Kandlestar," Lurk said. "What are you doing?"

"You must keep quiet," she told him. "But if you want to live, grab hold and don't let go."

He responded with a grunt of disdain, but only a moment later she felt a tug as he rose and grabbed a corner of her tattered robe.

Kendra focused. At first, there was nothing, just a murky, indistinguishable darkness. She tried to be patient. *Escape,* she thought. *Show me the way out.* And then, ever so slowly, the image of a path began to appear in her mind's eye. She could see it winding through the labyrinth of shadow and light and she strode forward. One step, then another . . . She could feel Agent Lurk clinging to her, but it was a vague sensation, as if she was somehow outside her own body, guiding it from afar. Deftly, she trudged onwards. Her magic was working.

And then, suddenly, there was no more resistance at her feet. Kendra stumbled forward, Agent Lurk still clutching her, and landed roughly on a mossy bed of rock. For a few moments she just lay there, squinting in the sudden bright light and feeling the warmth of the sun on her skin.

We must have passed an entire night inside the belly of that beast, Kendra thought.

Once her eyes had fully adjusted, she climbed to her feet and surveyed their surroundings. They were standing on a shelf of rock, high up the mountain. Nearby was the opening

through which they had escaped; from the outside it looked like a giant green funnel. She supposed it was no different than the one they had entered, except in the dark jungle she had only noticed its glowing, beckoning mouth. As for the rest of the plant, Kendra had a better picture of it, now that she had a higher vantage point. It poked out of the ground like the top of an enormous head, with the snappers, funnels, and other jungle foliage seeming like hair.

That's what attacked our ship, Kendra realized.

She cast a weary look at Agent Lurk. He appeared worse than ever, smeared head to foot with slime and grit, his pale skin raw and red. She imagined she looked just as terrible. But at least they were alive.

"We did it," she said, her voice coming out in a hoarse whisper.

Agent Lurk offered no congratulations. Instead, his expression flared with surprise—then he raised his hood and instantly disappeared.

"Where are you. . ." Kendra started.

But she only needed to turn around to see what had alarmed the cunning spy. Part of the rock face behind her had slid open to reveal a long, dark tunnel and there, standing at its entrance, was a terrifying bird-like creature. It was armed with a spear and saliva was dripping from its beak.

Kendra knew all too well what it was—a Krake, one of the five monster tribes sworn to destroy every last Een. Her mind began to spin. What was a Krake doing here? Wasn't the City on the Storm supposed to be a haven? Or had her brother just betrayed and tricked her? And, still, another corner of her mind thought, *Lurk, you ungrateful snot. I saved your life. And you just fled.*

The Krake charged towards her. Feebly, Kendra lifted her wand, but her strength had all but evaporated, like a drop of water in the desert. Distraught and defeated, she simply fell to her knees and waited for the Krake's fatal blow.

CHAPTER 8

The Kingdom in the Clouds

That's when something surprising happened. The Krake stopped short of her, laid his weapon down, and chirped, "Ooh-cha! Een-cha needee wa-wa!"

"Wh-what?" Kendra croaked.

"Een-cha needee wa-wa," the giant creature repeated.

He pulled a canteen from a strap across his chest and held it to Kendra's lips. A paradise of water flowed down her throat.

"Wh-who are you?" Kendra asked after she had drained the canteen.

The Krake stood erect, raised a claw in salute, and announced, "Captain Sneeedo at-cha servee!"

"Captain? Captain of what?"

"Arazeen!" the Krake cheeped.

"Arazeen?" Kendra mumbled. Had she died after all? In death had she found Een paradise?

Captain Sneeedo, appearing to notice her confusion, said, "You might-cha call it . . . City on the Storm."

"Oh!" Kendra gasped. Then, after a moment, she added, "Krakes live here?"

"Krakezee, Ungers . . . all beasties—and Eeneez too," Captain Sneeedo explained. "Thisee place no like-cha outsidee. Here-cha, Eeneez and beasties all-cha onezee."

Eens and monsters living together? Kendra thought. She looked up at Captain Sneeedo's gleaming eyes. Was this a Krake acting friendly?

"Een-cha comezee," Captain Sneeedo chimed.

Kendra shook her head. "My friends . . . the gorge . . ."

"Ooh-cha! No worry-cha. Comezee."

And then the giant Krake picked her up and cradled her in his claws. Into the tunnel they went, the cool stones offering Kendra instant relief from the sweltering heat of the jungle. Captain Sneeedo waddled up a long flight of stone steps and Kendra noticed that the walls were lined with creeping vines that glowed with hundreds upon hundreds of phosphorescent bulbs, lighting the way as surely as torches.

Eventually, they arrived at a platform overlooking a dark shaft. Captain Sneeedo made a clucking sound and a large, thick vine emerged from below. Kendra cringed; after her adventure in the jungle, she thought the vine might attack them. This plant, however, seemed purely of the friendly variety. As it rose up, Kendra could see many enormous leaves slightly curved, like giant cups. Captain Sneeedo hopped aboard one of these leaves—it was surprisingly strong enough to support them—and upwards they went.

"It-cha long way-cha," Captain Sneeedo told her.

But Kendra was so exhausted that she barely heard him. Before she knew it, her eyes closed and she faded into slumber.

It was Kendra's nose that awoke first. A delicious aroma tickled her nostrils and slowly tugged her into consciousness. When she opened her eyes, she found herself in a large, luxurious bed in an even more luxurious chamber. Bright sunlight was streaming through curtained windows and a gentle breeze ruffled her hair. She had no memory of having been brought here, but someone had obviously helped her bathe and change, for gone was all evidence of her ordeal in the jungle.

Where is that smell coming from? Kendra wondered. She was absolutely famished.

It was at that very moment that a small door opened and there appeared the smiling face of a mole. Kendra could tell he was an Een, for not only was he quite large, but he was wearing a checkered waistcoat, a green smock, and a ridiculously large pair of glasses.

He was carrying a broad green leaf, like a sort of tray, and on it was a steaming hot bowl of porridge sprinkled with what Kendra hoped was Een sugar, and a mug of tea. Her stomach rumbled.

"Good morning, good morning," the little mole beamed, setting the tray down before Kendra. "Tuttleferd T. Thistletoe at your service. But you may call me Tuttleferd."

"I'm Kendra," she replied, instantly digging into the food.

"Nessa will be pleased in the kitchen," Tuttleferd said, his shaggy eyebrows twitching as he spoke. "His Majesty is a fussy eater himself."

Kendra looked up at him and a dozen questions began spilling out all at once. "His Majesty? There's a king here? Is this the City on the Storm? Or am I just dreaming? Have you seen my friends?"

"Oh, my! What a lot of questions!" Tuttleferd remarked, stroking his whiskery chin with a long claw. "Now, don't you fret about your companions. They are trapped in the gorge, but safe enough. Captain Sneeedo has been sent to retrieve them. You'll be reunited with them before long, before long."

"What about the Een boy?" Kendra asked. "He was with me just as Captain Sneeedo found me."

Tuttleferd frowned. "The captain did not mention such a boy."

"He . . . he was frightened, I guess," Kendra said. "He has an invisibility cloak, so he disappeared as soon as he saw the Krake."

"Oh," Tuttleferd remarked. "Then he could be anywhere."

That's what I'm afraid of, Kendra thought.

"As for yourself—well, you have been asleep an entire day!" Tuttleferd declared. "Now, when you're ready, you may get dressed and I'll take you before His Majesty. He's most curious to meet the Een who survived the jungle."

Kendra had finished devouring her breakfast, so it only took her a few minutes to dress in the emerald green tunic that was awaiting her in the wardrobe. She tucked her wand into her belt and was soon ambling alongside Tuttleferd through a tall, arched passageway that was carved with dozens of stone reliefs. It reminded Kendra of the Elder Stone back home in the Land of Een, except that in addition to the faces of Eens and Een animals, there were also many monsters, all gazing out with friendly expressions.

"Welcome, my dear, to Arazeen," Tuttleferd announced. "Or, as you outlanders like to call it, the City on the Storm, though we like to think of it as a kingdom. I suppose it really is just one giant castle, all connected by corridors and bridges, like a honeycomb."

"It's amazing," Kendra said. "How many live here?"

"Oh, hundreds," the mole replied. "You'll see some of our fine citizens soon enough."

He was true to his word, for only a moment later they turned a corner and entered a type of public square where several of the city's dwellers were coming and going. Just like the carvings on the wall, these were a mixture of Eens, Een animals, and monsters—though these monsters were unlike any Kendra had ever seen. They appeared refined and dignified, clothed in elegant robes or with neatly combed fur and manicured nails.

Kendra couldn't help staring, but the truth was that there were far more strange glances cast in her direction. The citizens could obviously tell she was an outsider, and they seemed to pay particular attention to her hair. She wondered if it was because they had never seen anyone with seven braids before. Most Eens wore only one or two—and then Kendra suddenly realized that no one in Arazeen was wearing *any* braids. This wasn't uncommon for Een animals (after all it was rather difficult when you didn't have hair), but was simply unheard of for an Een.

"We do not follow that custom," Tuttleferd replied stiffly when Kendra asked for an explanation.

"But every Een since the time of Leemus Longbraids has worn braids," Kendra persisted.

"Ah, then you have answered your own question," Tuttleferd said. "For we are *not* Eens. We are Arazeens."

They walked past a large fountain that bubbled cheerfully from amidst a bed of the same vibrant, phosphorescent plants that Kendra had noticed in the tunnel shaft.

"They are called lumablooms," Tuttleferd explained. "There are many types of plants in Arazeen, and they provide for all of our needs. The plants give us food (for everyone here is vegetarian—even the Ungers!), clothes, and even transportation, as you witnessed in the shaft."

"But where do all these plants come from?" Kendra asked. "Did you take them from the jungle?"

"No, quite the opposite," Tuttleferd said. "It is our wondrous king. He is a master of gardening, and he designed this entire city. Everything you see here comes from the seeds of his genius."

It's not very Een-like to have a king, Kendra mused as they came before an enormous, ornate door. *Don't they have a Council of Elders here?*

Tuttleferd opened the door and ushered Kendra into the grand throne room that lay beyond. If the rest of the city had been marvelous, then this chamber was even more so. The gabled ceilings were so high that Kendra almost forgot she was still indoors, while the room was so long that she could not clearly see the end of it. Before her stretched a wide green carpet, lined on either side by more of the phosphorescent plants. Kendra noticed that on either side of the chamber there were tall archways that opened to wide stone terraces. She could see billowing clouds beyond; it truly felt as if she was on top of the world.

As Tuttleferd and Kendra continued along the carpet, they passed the strangest assortment of creatures. Here stood an Unger, there an Een, then a Goojun, now a squirrel, an owl, and an Izzard. Kendra assumed that they were courtiers, for they were all dressed in fine clothes. At last, the carpet came to an end and Kendra found herself before a large, ornamental throne carved from green stone. It stood empty, giving Kendra pause to tug on a braid. Tuttleferd turned her gently to the side, where Kendra saw a tall Een standing near one of the open archways. He was staring out at the skies with his back turned, but Kendra could see that he was cloaked in a long, resplendent robe of green and wearing a tall crown.

Then, slowly, the king turned around and gazed upon Kendra. His face was haggard and his lips pursed, as if he was trying to hold in something that he just couldn't quite swallow. He was mostly bald, and had a short beard that seemed as if it had once been brilliant red, but was now flecked with grey. When his eyes fell upon Kendra and her long braids, his brow furled.

There's something familiar about him, Kendra thought.

"King Krimson," Tuttleferd announced. "Here is the girl found by Captain Sneeedo."

"Krimson?" Kendra cried.

"Well—ahem—that's *King* Krimson to you, my dear," Tuttleferd stuttered.

Kendra stared at the king. In that instant she knew the truth. She rushed forward and threw her arms around him.

"Dear girl!" the king cried, fidgeting uncomfortably within her embrace. "Do I know you?"

"You should," Kendra managed to say between sobs of happiness. "I'm your daughter."

CHAPTER 9

A King of Many Moods

It was a dream come true. Kendra's search for the City on the Storm—and indeed her family—had been so long and arduous that there had been those times when she had doubted whether or not she would ever succeed. And all through that time she had been building a dam across her heart to hold back all of her hopes. But now there was no restraining those feelings; the dam burst, sweeping Kendra away in a flood of emotion.

The king—Kendra's father—gazed at her in uncertainty. "In the name of Arazeen," he murmured. He turned to gape at his courtiers, who were whispering in astonishment.

"Your Majesty!" Tuttleferd cried. "Could it be possible?"

Krimson seemed at a loss for words. Kendra saw Tuttleferd give the king an encouraging nod; then, with a deep "ahem," the little mole turned and quickly ushered the courtiers from the royal throne room. Kendra was now completely alone with her father—and she anxiously tugged on a braid.

With a gentle hand, Krimson lifted Kendra's chin and stared into her face. "It *is* true . . . isn't it?" he ventured. "You look just like her."

"My mother?" Kendra asked. "Is she here? And my brother?"

But instead of answering her question, Krimson just pulled Kendra into his arms and hugged her so tightly she could barely breathe. "I did not dare to believe you were alive," Krimson uttered. "The Unger told me as much. But I did not believe him."

"Kiro?" Kendra asked.

At the mention of her brother's name, Krimson's eyes flared with wildness. "His name is Trooogul!" the king roared, pushing Kendra away. "And he is no family to us. He is a traitor—that much is certain."

His anger was sudden and powerful, like an animal that at one moment seems tame and friendly, and the next wild and vicious. Kendra couldn't help but back away in fear. "No . . ." she said, "you don't understand—"

But just as quickly as he had erupted, Krimson regained his composure. The flush of red drained from his face and he gave Kendra an apologetic smile. "Don't . . . don't worry about this now," he said. "You are here. We are together. Oh, child— it's a miracle!"

He offered Kendra a hand and, hesitantly, she took it. He laughed, his green eyes sparkling. Then he led her through the nearest archway and onto the palatial terrace. It was like a garden, with iridescent plants sprouting forth from ornate vases and water trickling from delightfully carved fountains.

"It's beautiful," Kendra said.

"*You* are the most beautiful sight to me," Krimson told her. "You are alive. You are *alive.*" He led her to a nearby stone bench and said, "Tell me everything. I want to know where you have been and how you came here."

Kendra stared at him in bewilderment. Since he had disappeared when she was a baby, she had never known him. Where was she to start?

Krimson seemed to sense her unease and gently squeezed her hand. "I understand," he reassured her. "It's all a bit overwhelming. But tell me, child, where have you been all this time?"

"Here, there . . . everywhere," Kendra said. "I've seen the Castle of Krodos. I've seen the underground kingdom of the dwarves. I've seen the maze behind the Door to Unger. I've even seen the Rumble Pit."

Krimson's eyes flickered with incredulity. "We . . . I . . . have heard rumors," he stammered. "That Unger said as much. But I did not believe him."

"Which Unger? Trooogul?" Kendra asked. "Why didn't you believe him?"

"I thought he was just trying to trick me, trying to tempt my hopes with the idea that you were alive," the king answered hotly. "If I had known it were true . . . well, there's no point in ifs, is there?" He paused and sighed. Then, after a moment, he asked, "Tell me, child, how did you survive such adventures?"

"I haven't been alone," Kendra declared. "Oki's been with me. And Uncle Griffinskitch, and—"

"Gregor?" Krimson said in surprise. "That old fussbottom? He's still alive?"

"Of course!" Kendra said. "I suppose you never really got along with him. But he's . . . well, he's my uncle. He's teaching me the ways of Een wizardry. Just like my mother."

Krimson slouched forward, kneading his forehead with one of his large hands.

"Are . . . are you all right?" Kendra asked.

Krimson nodded and looked at Kendra with a strange expression. She could not even begin to know what he was thinking. "You found the Door to Unger," he said. "You found the Rumble Pit. But how did you find Arazeen?"

And so Kendra told him about the *Big Bang*, and how they had spent months sailing the skies. She told him how they had crashed into the jungle, and how the crew had all disappeared into the gorge.

"Do not fret about that," Krimson said. "The bottom of the gorge is lined with spongy plants. Your friends landed gently enough, I assure you. I imagine Captain Sneeedo will fetch them to the castle by dinner time."

"So . . . so it was you who planted all of those jungle traps?" Kendra asked.

"I did it to protect this city," Krimson replied proudly. "The first few traps are not meant to harm—not really. Just to dissuade any over-curious explorers. But for those who persist . . . well, I'm afraid that's when they meet Mertha."

"Mertha?"

"Yes; the enemy eater."

"She ate *me!*" Kendra cried. "I'm not an enemy!"

And now the look of erratic madness returned to Krimson's eyes. He flew from his seat with such vehemence that Kendra gasped. "Arazeen MUST be protected!" Krimson bellowed. "There are those who seek it with ill intentions! Those who

would destroy what it represents. This kingdom is only for the open-minded. Those who would leave their prejudices behind. If Arazeen is to survive, we must block the outside world."

"I-I don't understand," Kendra stammered.

"Look around you, child," Krimson commanded. "This is Arazeen! Paradise!"

"Paradise?" Kendra asked.

"Yes!" Krimson exclaimed.

He yanked Kendra to her feet and pulled her to the edge of the terrace so that she could see the city stretching before them.

"Here, we are all one," Krimson declared, sweeping his arms wide. "This is the true meaning of Arazeen, Kendra. Unity! Togetherness! Just as the legends say—'In the Days of Een, when all were *one*.' In those times, there were no Ungers, Krakes, Orrids, Izzards, or Goojuns. Just Eens. And then the Wizard Greeve cast his curse upon his brothers. The Eens, just like the cauldron in which that vile curse was brewed, splintered into pieces. But I have fixed everything, Kendra! I have done what the Land of Een and its council of fools could never do!"

He spoke with such passion that his whole body was quaking; even his temples were throbbing. Kendra looked at him in wonderment, then gazed back at the city, taking in the ornate towers and turrets. Down below she could spot cozy squares, gabled galleries, and shady gardens where orchard trees blossomed. It was truly a magnificent place; she could not deny it. Perhaps it really was paradise.

Then she heard a faint rumbling and she looked past the buildings to contemplate the brooding clouds that swirled below the city. The storm was ever present, she realized, so thick and dark that no one in Arazeen could ever glimpse the world below.

Her father touched her shoulder and Kendra looked up to see his glimmering green eyes. One moment he looked crazed, and the next so incredibly kind. She was having trouble sorting him out.

"Kendra," he said softly. "Let me tell you how this all began."

CHAPTER 10

The Story of What Happened to Kendra's Family

There was a tenderness now to Krimson's voice—a tone you know all too well if your parents have ever sat you down to discuss a situation that might be delicate or perhaps just a little upsetting. Even though Kendra had never spoken to her father before this day, she knew enough adults to understand that tone. Her father was going to explain what had happened to her mother, and it wasn't going to be good.

Perhaps Krimson sensed her anxiety. "Come, let us walk," he said.

He took Kendra by the hand, as if she were a small child, and led her across the terrace, down a flight of steps and across a long, graceful bridge. It was a beautiful, picturesque scene, but one Kendra found hard to appreciate.

"Where are we going?" she asked.

"Ah, it is a question I have asked myself many times over these past ten years," Krimson said, with a distant look in his eyes. He paused halfway across the bridge, looked over the side and said, "It was the worst day of my life, when the Ungers captured us in the outside world. I thought they left you to die there in the wild."

"Uncle Griffinskitch found me," Kendra said. "But what happened to *you*? Didn't the Ungers take you to the Door? To throw you in the maze?"

"Indeed," Krimson replied with a woeful look. "But before we reached that treacherous place, we were able to trick our captors and escape into the wilderness. I went a separate direction from your mother and brother, trying to lure the Ungers away from them. But the beasts did not fall for my ruse; in the end your mother and brother were recaptured."

Kendra could feel the pain in his voice. She squeezed his hand tightly and he looked at her with a broken smile. "I did not give up on them," he declared. "I traveled to the Greeven Wastes, surviving merely by my wits and desire to save my family. But I failed, Kendra. I was too late. By the time I arrived at the Door, months later, your mother and brother had already been cast through its terrible gate. As I was to later learn, they were turned into Ungers, and completely forgot who or what they had once been."

"My mother . . . sh-she's an Unger, too?" Kendra stammered.

Krimson nodded sadly.

"What did you do then?" Kendra asked.

"There were other Eens there, imprisoned in the Ungers' dungeons," Krimson replied. "They were doomed to go through the Door at the next ceremony, the so-called 'Festival of Greeve.' Tuttleferd was one of them, you know. I managed to rescue him—and all the others there, too. Over two dozen Eens!"

"Then what?" Kendra asked. "Didn't any of you want to go back to Een?"

"Een is broken, Kendra," Krimson replied harshly. "Any Een who had left had done so for the same reason as your mother and I. To find a new life, free from the Council of

Elders and their closed minds. As for me, I didn't know you were still alive, Kendra. If I had, then of course I would have come and fetched you. But I believed my family was completely gone. And so what else could I do? I led the ragtag group of rescued Eens into the wilderness, away from the Ungers and other beasts who wanted to destroy us. We journeyed long and hard until we found this place, a refuge in the mountains."

"And my mother?" Kendra asked, plucking at a braid. "That's not the end of the story, is it? You know what became of her, don't you?"

Krimson nodded. "After your mother was transformed into an Unger, she was befriended by a powerful wizard of that monster race. He was unlike the other Ungers. He wished to forge a new future, one in which monsters and Eens could live together. He revealed to your mother her true origins and, drawing on the power of his own magic, helped her remember her past. Once she realized that she was really Kayla Kandlestar trapped within an Unger's body, she became determined to find your brother and I. So she set forth with the Unger wizard, scavenging the outside world for us.

"Eventually, they found my secret community of Eens. It was a difficult reunion, but I could see beneath the Unger skin the Een whom I loved so dearly. And so we decided to make the best of things. Together we would build a new future—not only for us, but for all those trapped between the worlds of Een and monster."

"Arazeen," Kendra murmured thoughtfully.

"Yes!" Krimson proclaimed. "It was a marvelous moment in our history—monsters and Eens toiling side by side to carve out a new future on this mountaintop. During this time

the Unger wizard continued to search for your brother; he did not find him, but he sent many others to our sanctuary—monsters who believed in our ways."

"And Eens?" Kendra asked.

"A few," Krimson said. "No one seemed to leave Een after your mother and I. But there were many who had been surviving on their own in the outside world for quite some time. They found a community at last, here, at our castle in the clouds."

"Oroook," Kendra said. "That was the name of the wizard, wasn't it?"

Krimson looked at Kendra in surprise. "How do you know this?"

"He found me," Kendra explained. "Somehow he managed to cross the magic curtain and enter the Land of Een."

"What happened?" Krimson asked intently. "Why did he not bring you here?"

"He died," Kendra answered under the weight of her father's gaze. "He was terribly injured when he found me. His last words were to urge me to seek the Door to Unger."

"Why would he send you there?" Krimson cried.

"It was the prophecy," Kendra said. "He knew I was the one who could destroy it."

Krimson slowly nodded. "And you did destroy it, didn't you?" he murmured. "Now it all begins to make sense. Oroook must have learned of your existence during one of his many journeys in the outside world. We—your mother and I—did not know any of this. But when news reached us about the destruction of the Door, your mother raced to that nefarious place to see it for herself."

Kendra could guess the next part. "I know what happened!" she said excitedly. "She must have found Kiro! And that means we can all be—"

"NO!" Krimson screamed in sudden outburst. "They are lost to us, Kendra. They are gone."

"How? I don't understand."

Krimson did not answer. Instead, he turned and walked the remaining length of the bridge, his hands now clenched in tight fists. Kendra scrambled after him.

"Wait!" she cried.

But he did not even turn to look at her. He walked briskly down another flight of stairs, entered a doorway in a turret, and began navigating his way through the network of passages within the castle city. He moved with certain purpose, and Kendra had to race to keep up with him. Through this doorway and that Krimson strode, sometimes unlocking doors with a key that he withdrew from a chain around his neck. Eventually, he came to a halt before a wooden door that was only large enough for an Een. Kendra's father placed his hand upon the handle and whispered, "In the Days of Arazeen."

With a creak, the door swung inwards and Krimson led her into a small, circular chamber. Light filtered in through a pair of narrow windows. Kendra looked about the room to discover books, planting pots, and an assortment of gardening implements. A workbench lined one wall; here were parcels of seeds, more pots, and vials that bubbled with colorful liquids.

It's like a wizard's den, Kendra thought. *This must be where he works on his magical plants.*

Krimson stroked one of his long sideburns and stared at Kendra, as if weighing something in his mind. Then he made sure the door was shut firmly behind them and said in a hushed tone, "You are my daughter. So you deserve to know what became of your mother. And I will tell you—on this condition. After today, we shall never discuss her again. Do you agree?"

He was speaking like a king now, as if negotiating some sort of new law or treaty. But Kendra knew she had no choice. She needed to know the truth. Yanking fiercely on a braid, she nodded.

"Very well then," Krimson said. "I shall tell you the fate of your mother, the infamous Kayla Kandlestar."

CHAPTER 11

The Heart of an Unger

If Kendra's father had seemed upset before, he was even more so now. He looked pale and drawn as he moved a stack of books from an armchair and let himself fall heavily into it. He gestured for Kendra to take a nearby stool, but instead she simply sat at his feet.

Krimson let out a heavy breath. "Do you know what's happening down there, in the outside world? There is a war between the monster tribes."

"Yes . . . I know," Kendra said. "I've seen it first hand. What does that have to do with my mother?"

"I shall come to that," Krimson replied. "First, you must understand something about your mother. You see, after she realized that she was not actually an Unger, she forsook her monster name. Everyone in Arazeen knew her as Kayla Kandlestar. She was a powerful symbol for our people. She may have looked like a monster, but she had the name of an Een—she was two races in one body. Arazeen in every true sense. And Kayla Kandlestar is the name she took with her when she left Arazeen to seek the remains of the Door to Unger."

He paused and swallowed hard. Kendra watched as his eyes darted uncomfortably about the dark recesses of the chamber. "Kayla—your mother—returned to the ways of Unger," Krimson said at last.

"What do you mean?" Kendra asked.

"She reclaimed her monstrous name," Krimson replied, speaking with such bitter contempt that spittle flew from his lips. "Shuuunga, they call her. The Unger witch. She is like the rest of them now, those monsters of the outside world, mad with desire to rebuild the cauldron of Greeve."

"That's impossible!" Kendra cried. "You must be mistaken! Why—"

"It is true!" Krimson yelled, thumping a fist against the arm of his chair. "She salivates to resurrect the curse. Listen, Kendra, she did find Trooogul out there in the ruins of Greeve's temple. I don't know what passed between them, but I did not hear from your mother for many, many months. Then, one wild night this past December, she returned to Arazeen carrying the fragments of that vile cauldron. She told me we must find the missing pieces and rebuild it!"

"But why?" Kendra persisted. "I don't understand."

Krimson hesitated, his temples twitching as he gazed at Kendra. "Because," he said eventually, "she, too, wishes for Arazeen. Oneness! Only she would achieve it by turning us into *them!* If only she would have accepted the ways of this kingdom. *My* way. The way of peace."

Tears began rolling down Kendra's cheeks. It wasn't supposed to be this way. She had spent so long searching for her family, so many years dreaming of the moment when they could be reunited. But now, gazing upon her father, it seemed impossible.

"I attacked the witch and tried to seize the cauldron," Krimson continued. "But she is more powerful than I. She escaped into the jungle. And now . . . well, the Ungers have all but won the monster war. Word has reached me that Shuuunga's army has collected every fragment of Greeve's cauldron—all except one."

"Kiro has it," Kendra said.

Krimson glared at her. "Trooogul, you mean? No. He only *thinks* he has it. He brought that dark Shard here one tempestuous night, just a few weeks after your mother came, claiming he was my son—"

"He is," Kendra interjected. "I have met him. He's Kiro. And he knows it."

Krimson flinched and for a moment it seemed as if he would erupt again. But then he seemed to swallow his anger. "He may have once been your brother, Kendra," Krimson said, leaning forward to stare into her eyes. "But no longer. He only came to Arazeen because he expected to find the witch here, with the rest of the cauldron. I tried to convince him to abandon his quest, to join Arazeen. But Trooogul has chosen the ways of the Unger witch. When this became clear to me, I stole the Shard and replaced it with a counterfeit. He only thinks he has the real one."

"He's more clever than that," Kendra said. "He wouldn't fall for such a trick."

"He did," Krimson assured her. "The Unger has no magical ability. And the Shard's iniquitous power only comes to life when touched by a wizard."

Or a wizard-in-training, Kendra thought, remembering her own experience with the Shard. "But where is Trooogul now?" she asked, looking anxiously back at her father.

Krimson shrugged. "What do I know? He left to rebuild the cauldron with the rest of his monstrous brethren."

"Won't he discover your deception? Won't the Ungers come to retrieve the real Shard?"

"They can try," Krimson declared icily. "We have the jungle on one side, and a vast ocean on the other to impede them. With my defenses—which you, Kendra, have seen first hand—Arazeen is impregnable. If the Ungers attempt an assault on this city, they will fail."

Kendra hoped he was right. "Tell me," she said after taking a deep breath. "Where is the Shard now?"

Krimson stroked his sideburns again, then turned to pick up a simple pot of soil. He turned it over on his workbench and there, resting amidst the dirt, was the Shard from Greeve. In spite of herself, Kendra gave one of her braids a fretful tug. The Shard looked so small and harmless, just a single wedge of blackened stone. It was hard to imagine that it could be the key to anything—let alone resurrecting a spell that could obliterate an entire race.

"You must not touch it," Krimson warned, "for it is the darkest magic."

"I know it," Kendra said earnestly. "And that's why you should destroy it."

"I have tried to do so, but in vain," Krimson said.

"Then throw it from the mountain! Let it drop into the sea!" Kendra urged.

"NO!" Krimson shouted. "It must not leave Arazeen; we cannot risk it being found by the Unger witch."

"How would she find it?" Kendra demanded. "It would be impossible."

"Shuuunga is powerful," her father rebuked. "Remember: she was taught as an Een by your uncle, then as an Unger by Oroook. She must not be underestimated. No, the only place the Shard is safe is here, under *my* watch. For if she gets her claws on the Shard, she will be able to rebuild the cauldron. Then Arazeen will be destroyed."

"And the Land of Een, too," Kendra said.

"Een?" Krimson said bitterly. "They have destroyed themselves already. They have closed themselves to the monster world, ignored their connection to them."

Kendra looked at her father in horror. "So you just give up on everything? On Een? On Kiro? On Mother?"

Krimson's face was livid with rage. "She has given up on me!" he roared. "She has given up on herself! She is a monster now, Kendra, in the truest sense of the word. She . . . she would stay one of *their* kind, not only in shape and form, but in her very heart. She has forsaken me. She has forsaken all of us!"

His whole body was trembling as he turned and stormed back into the corridor. Crying, Kendra stumbled after him.

"What do you know of heartbreak?" he demanded, whirling to confront her. "Your mother is lost to me, Kendra. Your brother, too. They have chosen their path—and it is against us. But now you are here, Kendra. You and I, we are family. We are together. And we can be strong. Together, we can defeat the dark Ungers."

Kendra wiped a sleeve across her tear-streaked face and stared at her feet, remembering her mother. Even though Kayla Kandlestar had disappeared when Kendra was a baby, they had met during Kendra's time travels. Kayla had been such a fierce, powerful woman. It was hard to imagine her as a villain. It was even harder to abandon her.

"I know what you are thinking," Krimson accused. "You harbor a notion that you can save them. But you cannot. That is but a child's dream." His eyes had that feral, raving look in them again, as if he had been overcome by another bout of madness. "Your mother and brother have chosen their side. Now, you will have to choose yours."

Kendra didn't know what to say. She just stared at her father in complete bewilderment.

"Either you are with me or against me," he said firmly. Then he clasped his hands behind his back, turned, and slowly walked away.

CHAPTER 12
The Would-Be Princess of Arazeen

"**I'm** stuck between the shadows and the night." It's a famous Een saying, one that Kendra herself had never really understood until this very moment when she found herself speaking it out loud in the gloom of the passageway.

How can I choose a side? Kendra wondered. *Either way, I turn against my family.*

Her mind reeling, she shuffled down the corridor with the vague hope of navigating her way back to the guest chambers. She had gone some way without seeing a soul when a large, greenish Izzard trundled around a corner and nearly crashed right into her. Kendra was still trying to grow accustomed to living in a city full of monsters and she couldn't help emitting a little shrick. After all, the Izzard looked all too menacing; he had reptilian eyes, crooked fangs, and a long tail that twitched back and forth like a whip.

But if Kendra was startled, then the Izzard seemed even more so. Eyes wide with fear, he dropped to his knees and bowed his head.

"Wh-what are you doing?" Kendra asked, tugging on a braid.

"Yousssa daughter of kingsssa," the creature sibilated in reply, a long tongue flickering out as he spoke. "Ziiinga bow beforesssa Princesss Star!"

"Princess!?" Kendra blurted, trying to ignore the rather foul odor of the Izzard's breath. "I'm not a princess! I'm a wizard's apprentice, I'll have you know, and—"

She didn't have a chance to finish her sentence, for at that moment Tuttleferd appeared. "Ah, there you are, Princess!" the little mole exclaimed, performing his own gracious genuflection before Kendra. "Don't mind Ziiinga! I'm afraid that you've become quite the celebrity throughout Arazeen, quite the celebrity indeed."

"I don't want to be a celebrity," Kendra growled.

"Not to fret, not to fret," Tuttleferd chimed. "Come; Captain Sneeedo has returned from the jungle with your friends. I've taken the liberty of moving your belongings from the humble chamber you slept in before. You will now stay in the royal apartments in the North Tower."

"You call that humble?" Kendra asked.

"It was hardly fit for you, Your Highness," Tuttleferd remarked. "Not to worry, not to worry—all your friends have been given suites nearby. You can spend a little while with them now; tonight there will be a great feast to celebrate the return of His Majesty's daughter—wondrous news, wondrous news indeed!"

Everyone they encountered on the way to the North Tower bowed and made such a fuss that Kendra began to wish that she had a shadow cloak of her own.

"They love you," Tuttleferd beamed. "You are like your name, Princess Star; a twinkling light in the night. A sign of hope."

"How do you figure?" Kendra asked.

"Why, you will one day wear your father's crown," Tuttleferd explained. "You will be queen."

"I'm not going to be a queen!" Kendra cried in exasperation. "Doesn't anyone seem to understand that I'm a sorceress?"

"I would think being a queen would be more desirable, more desirable indeed!" Tuttleferd said in a reproachful tone.

Kendra sighed and fiddled with a braid. *Thank Een that Lurk's not here,* she thought. *He thought I was famous before? This would really boil his blood.*

Of course, there's nothing to make you feel more like yourself than meeting old friends, and when at last they drew near the entrance to the North Tower, Kendra's heart sang to see Oki and Ratchet awaiting her. She rushed ahead and embraced them so tightly that Ratchet gasped, "I think I have *squeezeareah!*"

"Ah, a happy reunion," Tuttleferd declared. "But come! Let me usher you to your royal chambers, Princess."

The little gray mole now held open a tall and regal door, at the same time giving another bow. Kendra rolled her eyes and quickly steered her friends into the small waiting room on the other side.

"I will leave you for now, Princess," Tuttleferd informed her. "But do not worry; I will send someone along shortly to help you dress for the feast."

"I *am* dressed," Kendra told him, but the cheerful mole-servant had already closed the door.

"Is it true?" Oki asked Kendra. "Your father is here? He's the king? That means you are a princess!"

"Don't you dare think of calling me that," Kendra said.

"These Arazeen folk have been treating us like we have a bad case of *royalitis,*" Ratchet said. "They've bathed us, brushed our tails—they even ran a comb through your uncle's beard. Don't mention it to him—he's a bit snarly about it."

"Just a bit?" Kendra asked. "And the gorge? No one was hurt?"

"It was just like landing on rhubarb jelly," Oki explained. "Soft and delicate."

"Is there even such a thing as rhubarb jelly?" Kendra asked.

"I don't know," Ratchet replied thoughtfully. "But there should be!"

They now walked through an archway and found themselves in a grander space, a sitting room furnished with sofas and chairs and lit with the glowing lumablooms. One wall was accentuated with tall, glass-paned windows, while the others were decorated with enormous paintings. Kendra had never found herself in such an opulent space. For a moment, she just stood there, turning and staring.

"Humph. I prefer the comforts of an old hollow tree."

Kendra knew the humph, of course, but when she turned she barely recognized the refined and fashionable Een standing before her. Uncle Griffinskitch was still mostly beard, but he had been trimmed, combed, and preened to glow. Bows adorned his whiskers, and he was wearing a robe to match. Kendra had never seen her uncle look so fancy—and he appeared none too happy about it.

Kendra suppressed a smile and scampered across the enormous chamber to hug him. Jinx and Professor Bumblebean were standing there as well, both just as beautified.

"They tried to put blush on my cheeks," Jinx grumbled. "BLUSH!"

"Well, I do say, we must do our best to acquiesce to the customs in this marvelous realm," Professor Bumblebean proclaimed. "And it seems we are to receive the royal treatment, all thanks to our young Kendra here. Or perhaps, I shall call her Princess Star?"

Kendra sneered at him then looked earnestly at her uncle. "So much has happened," she said. "You would hardly believe it."

"Humph," Uncle Griffinskitch said, but it was a quiet, gentle sort of humph, the kind that meant: "Tell me."

And so tell him she did. The old wizard took her by the hand and led her to a quiet corner of the grand room, where they could talk in private. Her stories began spilling forth, as if she were a cliff and the words the waterfall; more than once, Uncle Griffinskitch had to ask her to slow down. Kendra decided to just start from the beginning, and tell him about encountering Agent Lurk and surviving the monstrous plant.

"What became of the boy afterwards?" Uncle Griffinskitch asked intently.

"I don't know," Kendra answered. "He disappeared."

"We must not lower our guard then," Uncle Griffinskitch warned. "Now, tell me about your father."

With an anxious tug on a braid, Kendra described her reunion with the temperamental king, of his deception with the Shard from Greeve, and of the rift between her family. During all of this, Uncle Griffinskitch listened without interruption, though he fidgeted uncomfortably during many parts, especially those that related to Kendra's mother, his own sister.

"Kiro and my mother aren't out to betray Een," Kendra declared at the end. "They can't be. I won't believe it."

"Belief can be a powerful ally," Uncle Griffinskitch said solemnly. "But it can also blind us, Kendra."

"What are you saying?" Kendra demanded. "Do you share my father's opinion in all of this?"

"I didn't say that, did I?" Uncle Griffinskitch growled. "But if your mother is now Unger—"

"Inside, she is still Een," Kendra interrupted. "My father said so himself. It's just that he's so . . . so . . ."

She felt herself beginning to tear up and Uncle Griffinskitch placed his hand upon hers. "Kendra," he said soothingly. "I may have not always seen eye-to-eye with your father, but I'm sure of one thing. His love for your mother runs as deep as the roots of the great tree of Een. I now fully understand the sense of grief that struck me the moment I stepped foot in this city. It seems to course through the walls, rumble through the passageways. Your father's heart has been shattered. You must try to understand what he is going through."

Kendra stared at the floor and fussed with a braid. "He doesn't seem to understand me at all."

"Humph," Uncle Griffinskitch murmured, his voice filled with a hint of sadness. "That is family for you," he said gently. "Especially ours."

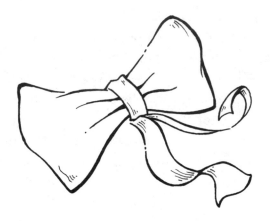

CHAPTER 13

The Girl Who Had Never Seen Een

There is a great deal of pomp and ceremony that comes with dining with a king. Kendra herself had little experience with such affairs, and so it was with surprise that she found herself whisked away that afternoon by a retinue of royal attendants. Within their clutches, she was measured, mapped, and made up.

"We'll have to do something about this wretched hair," scowled the head attendant. Her name was Fayda and if she was stingy with her smiles, she was less so with her opinions.

"I'm keeping my braids," Kendra proclaimed, jerking away from Fayda's hands, only to bump into the prickles of a hedgehog who was busily measuring her waist.

"Arms out, Princess Star," the hedgehog fussed. "Your gown must fit perfectly."

"Why can't I just wear my robe?" Kendra wondered.

"Your Highness, if you could focus," Fayda sighed. "We *really* must fix your hair."

"The braids stay," Kendra insisted. "At least some of them."

"The king will not like it," Fayda scorned, but she said nothing further on the subject.

In three hours, the ordeal was over and Kendra was finally pushed before a tall mirror. She gasped when she saw her reflection; indeed, she could hardly recognize the girl staring back at her. She was dressed in a dazzling patterned gown that curved out like a giant bell (*How am I going to walk in this thing?* she wondered). As for her hair, this was now stacked in a high nest of braids, while two longer plaits hung on either side of her face.

It was at this moment that Tuttleferd appeared, beaming behind his large spectacles. "Ah, you look very regal, Your Highness, very regal indeed," the mole said. "Come, let me escort you to the feast."

Only a few minutes later, Tuttleferd ushered Kendra into the royal dining hall, and she was greeted by a fanfare of trumpets. Stretching before her was the longest table she

had ever seen and all the courtiers now stood and bowed. Kendra had to desperately fight the temptation to yank on a braid. Instead she just looked nervously about the hall. It was an enormous, opulent place, much like the royal throne room, gabled on either side with tall archways that led to outdoor terraces.

Tuttleferd nudged her along and Kendra soon found herself at the far end of the table where, to her great relief, she found her companions. At the very head of the table, sitting in a throne-like chair, was her father. His expression betrayed none of his earlier anguish. Rather, he looked the perfect picture of a king, regal and composed. Tuttleferd pulled back a chair and gestured for Kendra to sit. Awkwardly, she took her place.

"Wow!" Oki told Kendra. "I hardly recognize you."

"Don't worry; it's the same old me," she assured him. Then she felt her foot knock against something under the table. "What is that?" she asked.

"The Snifferoo," Ratchet replied. "We thought we might be able to record some smells during dinner."

"Just don't cause trouble," Kendra warned.

"As you wish, Your Highness," Ratchet quipped.

Kendra made a face at him, then turned to marvel at the table. It was decorated with a long green runner, beautiful vases filled with flowering plants, and many gleaming candelabras lit with lumablooms.

Krimson now stood, cleared his throat, and proclaimed, "Welcome, all, to the grand feast to celebrate the return of my beloved daughter, the one you know as Princess Star."

A round of applause erupted from the table. Feeling her face flush with embarrassment, Kendra began to sink in her chair, but a stern look from her father inclined her to stand and bow her head in acknowledgement.

Thankfully, this moment quickly came to an end, for now an army of attendants began scurrying forth with bowls of steaming hot soup. Kendra breathed in the tantalizing aroma and realized she hadn't eaten since breakfast. She tucked in and finished the soup at a speed that was likely inappropriate for a princess. Thankfully, the soup was just the first of many delectable dishes. There were salads seasoned with roasted nuts, succulent vegetables glazed in honey and garlic, and mounds of mashed yams. And then there was dessert, which consisted of all sorts of iced treats, sugary cakes, and scrumptious pies.

"Whatever is in these pies?" Ratchet wondered out loud. "They're delicious."

"Those, my friend, are rhubarb pies," Krimson said. "They're rather a specialty here."

"Oh, good," Ratchet remarked. "At least I'll be able to go."

"Go?" Krimson inquired. "And where will you go, kind fellow?"

"Oh, in private—not to worry," Ratchet declared, which caused Kendra to give him a kick underneath the table.

When dessert was finished, Krimson stood once again and this time announced, "And now for a bit of entertainment. I present to you Charla Charmsong. She will delight you all with her wonderful rendition of *I Dream of Clouds*."

The dinner guests turned their attention to one side of the chamber where there appeared a little Een girl wearing a simple blue frock and a matching flower in her hair. Kendra guessed she could be no more than seven or eight years old. Bashfully, the child clasped her hands in front of her, but when she began to sing all trace of self-consciousness vanished. Indeed, she sang with such beauty and confidence that Kendra was instantly captivated.

Alas, the song came to a finish all too quickly. Kendra stared at the child in stupefied wonder while the rest of the chamber applauded enthusiastically.

"Charla is a very important person," Krimson informed Kendra. "She was the first to ever be born in Arazeen."

"She has never been to Een?" Kendra asked.

Krimson's expression turned dour, but Kendra realized at once it was not due to her remark, but to a truly dreadful smell that was suddenly wafting across the table. She turned in her seat to find Ratchet and Oki frantically fiddling with the Snifferoo.

"That was the wrong switch!" Oki cried.

"I think I know how to work my own mach—ugh, that does smell terrible!"

"Eek! That was the play switch!"

Kendra began to gag. Frantically, she reached for a napkin and tried to mask the smell.

"What in the name of Arazeen is that abominable stench?" demanded Krimson.

"Well, er . . ." stammered Ratchet, "that is what a mouse smells like after three days in the jungle without any soap."

"Why would you record such a thing?" Kendra cried.

"Er . . . science?" Ratchet offered.

"You idiot!" Jinx snapped. "I've had it with your Stinkeroo."

"For your information, the correct name is Snifferoo," Ratchet declared.

"Ugh!" Kendra groaned. She now didn't care what was appropriate for a princess; hastily, she pushed back her chair and fled to the terrace. Even as she did so, she could hear the entire dining hall erupt in commotion. That was Ratchet for you, Kendra decided; if there was one thing he was good at inventing, it was trouble.

Night had fallen and Kendra sat on one of the stone benches on the terrace, breathing in the fresh air and staring up at the moon that hovered in the cloudy night. She could smell a hint of rain, but she supposed it often smelled like that in the City on the Storm. Before long, she caught a movement from the corner of her eye and whirled to find the Een girl, Charla, peering at her from behind one of the large plants that stood on the terrace.

"Come now. Don't be shy," Kendra told her, coaxing her forth with a wave of her hand.

The girl took a cautious step forward. "You're beautiful, Princess Star."

Kendra laughed. "You should have seen me three days ago when I was trapped in the jungle."

"Did you really survive Mertha?" Charla asked, sidling next to Kendra on the bench.

Kendra nodded.

"Then you really *are* a wizard. King Krimson says wizards have dangerous thoughts. But you don't look dangerous."

Kendra laughed again. Whatever shyness the girl had demonstrated earlier had now completely evaporated.

"I would like to be a wizard. Maybe you could teach me," Charla declared.

"Well, I'm only an apprentice myself," Kendra told her. "And I don't think there's any Eenwood here. How would you get a wand?"

"What's an Eenwood?" Charla asked.

"You don't know?" Kendra asked in surprise. She reached into the folds of her gown and withdrew her wand.

"Oh," Charla said. "It's pretty."

"You can touch it."

Charla ran her hand over the bumpy wood. "It doesn't exactly feel magical."

"They're tricky things," Kendra admitted. "But after a while it becomes a part of you. Well, when you see the great tree of Een, then there is no doubt about the magic."

"The great tree?" Charla asked.

"You really don't know anything about the Land of Een, do you?"

Charla shook her head.

And so Kendra told Charla tales of the Land of Een. She told her of the Whispering Grove where the great tree of Een stood in all its majesty. She told her of the legend of Hag's Claw and the story of the Shivering Wood. She told her about Leemus Longbraids, the first Elder of Een, who had built the magic curtain and cherished the animals of Een. Charla listened intently to every word.

Kendra was just about to begin the story of Leemus Long-braids and the one-eyed dragon when Krimson suddenly appeared on the terrace.

"Ah, Charla, here you are," the king spoke. "Your mother seeks you. It is late, after all."

Charla rose from the bench and curtsied before the king. Then, bidding farewell to Kendra, she scampered off.

Kendra rose and stared at her father. She wondered if he had heard her telling stories of Een. She half-expected a scolding, but Krimson only said, "You look lovely. A true princess of Arazeen." Then he wandered away, back towards the dining hall.

Kendra stared down at her gown and then at the wand she still held in her hand.

Pretty trinkets and clothes, Kendra thought. *They're no match for the simple beauty of Eenwood.*

CHAPTER 14

A City Under Siege

Intuition. We all have it, but it's a particular specialty of Een wizards. And it's why Kendra bolted upright in her bed, only a few hours later, to tug anxiously at a braid. It was still dark outside, but she knew, *just knew,* that something was wrong. She dashed across her chamber, flung aside her window drapes, and gazed out with suspicious eyes. The North Tower was at the back of the city; before her stretched the rest of the castle kingdom. But she could see nothing— just the intermittent twinkle of a lumabloom lantern here and there. Arazeen was at peace, asleep on its bed of storm clouds.

Then, suddenly, the silence was pierced by a distant, panicked shout; only a moment later a clang from the bell tower rang across the city. Instantly, the lumablooms in Kendra's room flared to life and began flashing brightly in alarm.

Kendra turned and rushed to the large wooden wardrobe that stood in the corner of her bedchamber. "Isn't there anything here without frills and bows?" she wondered out loud as she began rummaging through the closet. "Where in the name of Een is my robe?"

She finally found it in a bottom drawer, tucked away as if it had been shunned by the other garments. And perhaps it had; for even though it had been laundered and patched since her adventure in the jungle, it still looked shabby.

Such is the life of a wizard, Kendra mused as she donned the threadbare robe. Then, as she tugged on her boots, she glimpsed herself in a nearby mirror and realized that she was still wearing her new hairstyle.

No time to change it now, Kendra thought. *Besides, maybe this style befits a sorceress as much as a princess.*

There was a frantic knock on the door. Kendra turned, but before she could answer, the door flung open and in scuttled a distressed Tuttleferd.

"Your Highness, I must take you to safety," the mole urged.

"Why? What's going on?" Kendra asked, tucking her wand into her belt.

"Well, ahem," Tuttleferd stammered. "It's just a minor alarm, I'm sure, just a minor alarm."

"Is that what you call it when your entire city is under siege?" came the sound of a gruff voice.

Kendra and the mole both whirled around to see the hunched form of Uncle Griffinskitch standing in the doorway.

"We're under attack?" Kendra asked.

"W-we don't know that!" Tuttleferd spluttered. "It could be a wayward explorer. It could be—"

"Ungers," Kendra said grimly, her intuition giving her another solid boot.

"Aye," Uncle Griffinskitch affirmed. "They've come for the Shard." Then, with a sweep of his beard, he turned and whisked away.

Kendra gave Tuttleferd a worried glance. Then, with the mole on her heels, she chased Uncle Griffinskitch into the corridor, only to find the rest of her companions assembled there. They were all standing at attention, as if ready for war— but Kendra couldn't help thinking they made an unlikely platoon. After all, Jinx was the only one who had any conventional weapons; she was armed with a sword, a battle-axe, and two spears. Ratchet and Oki, on the other hand, were each wearing utility belts loaded with all sorts of canisters and pouches (containing their infamous magic powders, Kendra guessed) and, of course, they were carrying their beloved Snifferoo. As for Professor Bumblebean, he had nothing more than a large book tucked under one arm.

"What's all this?" Tuttleferd demanded.

"We're going to help defend the city," Jinx declared.

"We have Captain Sneeedo and the guards for that!" Tuttleferd cried. "We need to find safety; it's the king's orders!"

"Humph!" Uncle Griffinskitch grunted, which pretty much summed up what he thought of the king's orders. "Come, let us make haste to the ramparts."

"Oh, dear," Oki moaned as the old wizard began leading them down the tower's spiraling staircase. "Don't think of rhubarb. Don't think of rhubarb!"

"Everything will be okay," Kendra told the mouse, grabbing his paw, though the truth of the matter was that her own stomach was reeling with anxiety.

They were soon in the heart of the city, where they found themselves amidst complete pandemonium. The warning bell was now clanging without pause and Arazeen citizens were dashing this way and that, wailing in panic and clutching important valuables as they sought refuge.

Uncle Griffinskitch navigated the chaos of the city surely and briskly, and eventually they arrived at one of the broad outer walls that skirted the castle. The sun was just beginning to peek over the horizon, and in the dull light Kendra could see dozens of Arazeen soldiers assembling on the ramparts in grim anticipation of attack. Most of these soldiers were of the monster variety, though Kendra noticed some Eens and Een animals as well. Whatever their race, all were either armed or manning strange-looking cannons. Captain Sneeedo waddled along the line of soldiers, clucking commands. He showed no surprise when he spotted Kendra and her friends; he merely gave them a slight nod before continuing on.

Tugging on a braid, Kendra leaned over the bulwark. She could only see a short way down the cliffs before they disappeared amidst the seemingly ever-present layer of dark and broiling clouds. These now emitted a slow and thunderous rumble, like a hungry stomach. And then Kendra heard something else: a distant *clink-clink-clink:* the sound of metal on rock coming from beneath the tempest.

"They're climbing," Uncle Griffinskitch surmised.

"I dare say, they must have some wonderful technology at their disposal," Professor Bumblebean remarked. "These cliffs must be hundreds of leagues high and yet they attempt to scale them in this inclement weather!"

"I'm so pleased you're impressed by our attackers, *Burble-bean*," Jinx growled. "Maybe you can cheer them on once they reach the top. But be quick about it; they'll probably want to trample you."

"Eek!" Oki squealed.

"As for you," Jinx snarled, turning on the little mouse, "you need to calm down."

"It's not his fault," Ratchet interjected. "He's got a bad case of *eekitis.*"

"He's going to have *knucklemonia* if he doesn't shush it," the grasshopper retorted, waving a fist in Oki's direction.

"Don't worry," Ratchet told the mouse. "We've got plenty of *Itch Twitch.*"

"*Itch Twitch?*" Kendra asked.

"One handful and you'll want to climb right out of your own skin," Ratchet explained.

"I sure hope it works on Ungers," Kendra murmured.

"That's a good point!" Oki cried. "We've never tested it on anything other than . . . well, er, *me.*"

"Well, we have the Snifferoo—and we know *that* works," Ratchet said.

"And how's that idiotic invention going to help us against an army of Ungers?" Jinx demanded.

"Ungers have noses, same as anybody," Ratchet said. "We've got a couple of stinks on this baby that could curdle milk!"

Jinx scowled. "Listen, *Freak* and *Eek*, why don't you find some real weapons?"

Kendra was just about to say something in Ratchet's defense, but at that very moment her father stormed onto the rampart, his face blazing with fury.

"KENDRA!" he thundered. "What in the name of Arazeen are you doing here?" He turned and fired a glare at Tuttleferd. "I told you to take her to safety."

"I insisted, Your Majesty, I insisted," Tuttleferd said in a fluster. "But—"

"Krimson!" Uncle Griffinskitch said and Kendra's father turned to him with a growl.

"That's *King* Krimson to you, old man," Kendra's father snapped. "Whether you like it or not, I'm in charge here."

Uncle Griffinskitch leveled a long and steady glare at the king. "I am not interested in sparring with you, *Your Majesty*," the old wizard countered. "There are hundreds of Ungers scaling the cliff face and if you are to repel them you will need all the help you can get. Including the help of Een magic."

Krimson looked at Kendra. "I won't endanger you, child. I already thought I lost y—"

But then Captain Sneeedo suddenly squawked in alarm and everyone looked over the wall to see the first of the Ungers appearing out of the mist. The great beasts might have been rocks themselves, such was the texture and color of their skin. They were heaving themselves upwards, using their massive three-fingered claws or pick-axes and other devices that bore into the rock. Some were even using long ropes with grappling hooks attached to the ends. It made them look like spiders, skittering in for the kill.

Impatiently, one of the Arazeen soldiers fired a cannon and Kendra watched as a blob of green goo hurtled towards the scaling attackers. It was the same substance found within

Mertha, she realized—but this blob missed the target completely, splattering harmlessly on the rocks.

"Ooh-cha!" Sneeedo cried.

Then Kendra heard another voice boom across the sky. It was her father; he had climbed up a flight of stairs to stand on a higher parapet to gaze upon his soldiers. Even from this distance, Kendra could see that his face was as red as fire.

"Hear me now, warriors of Arazeen!" Krimson proclaimed. "This is our city! Our paradise! We are Arazeens—and we shall not let these dark Ungers take us!"

In response to this impassioned speech, the Arazeen soldiers raised their weapons and whooped with a startling war cry of their own. Kendra grimaced. The last thing she felt like doing was cheering. Throwing up—maybe.

She peeked over the wall again, only to feel a spear whistle past her head. The Ungers were almost upon them! Captain Sneeedo's soldiers began firing their cannons with full force. Uncle Griffinskitch joined them, raising his staff to unleash a crackle of lightning; his shot struck an Unger right between the eyes and with a grunt the poor fellow went tumbling into the clouds.

Kendra looked at her uncle in panic. *What about my mother?* she asked through her wand. *And Kiro? What if they're here? We can't harm them. We can't—*

She didn't have a chance to finish her thought. For at that moment, the first flurry of Ungers came spilling over the wall.

CHAPTER 15
The Ungers Attack

These Ungers were nothing like the ones Kendra had come to know in Arazeen. Indeed, the Arazeen Ungers were refined and dignified. They wore fancy robes, and their hair was slicked with oils and perfumes. They spoke in gentle grunts and moved with grace. The attacking Ungers—why, these were wild and savage, like the kind Kendra had met in her adventures in the outside world. They had tangled hair, gnarled claws, and crooked tusks. Battered pieces of armor covered their thick hides, while their faces were streaked with war paint or etched with tattoos. Some bore gruesome scars, while others were missing tusks. Yet all of them wielded weapons: crude, brutish implements of war—spiked clubs, double-bladed axes, or barbed swords.

Then came the Unger war cry. It began as a deep, rumbling roar, then quickly crescendoed into a shrill howl, an unearthly sound that made Kendra's feet beg to whisk her away. But there was nowhere to flee now; the Ungers were simply everywhere, swelling onto the ramparts in unimaginable numbers. If they had looked like spiders during their climb—well, now it was an infestation.

Kendra!

Uncle Griffinskitch's voice reached through her wand to snap Kendra from her stupor. She blinked and looked up to discover an enormous Unger looming over her. She had never seen an Unger so ferocious—he had three tusks, all jostling for space in his giant mouth. With a blistering roar, the brute lifted his deadly weapon.

She didn't wait for Three Tusks to land his blow; she tucked and rolled through the gap between his spindly legs, crashing back-first into the crenellated wall behind him. She felt a sudden tug on her robe and realized that one of the Ungers who was still on the cliff face had snatched her from behind! He began to pull her over the edge, but her uncle suddenly appeared to fire a zap of magic over her shoulder. She heard a squeal of pain and the Unger released her—and just in time, for now Three Tusks had turned around and was swinging again. Kendra ducked and scampered away from his murderous assault.

She was surrounded by the havoc of battle. She could hear squawks, grunts, and the clang of metal against metal. Her nose twitched with the smells of perspiration and blood. From the corners of her eyes she caught snatches of the close-quarter fighting. Captain Sneeedo cawed and snapped as he bravely held his ground. Uncle Griffinskitch was a blur of beard as he fired lightning zaps from his staff. Jinx pinwheeled through the throng, slashing with four weapons at once. Oki and Ratchet were casting pawfuls of *Itch Twitch* and Kendra could only guess what else. She even saw Professor Bumblebean thwack an Unger right on the head with his heavy book.

There was no sign of her father, but Kendra didn't have time to worry; Three Tusks was after her again. In a panic, Kendra fled, only to crash right into Tuttleferd. They both went sprawling across the stones, with Tuttleferd ending up right at Three Tusk's feet. The mountainous Unger lifted his club and chortled in delight at the prospect of such an easy victim. Quickly, Kendra found a spell inside her mind and issued an invisible wave from her wand that pushed Tuttleferd out of the way, just as the Unger's club crashed to the ground.

Three Tusks snorted in fury. Kendra fired a crackle of lightning from her wand, but the zap didn't even stun him. He charged at her—only to come to a screeching halt. His eyes watered and his nose wrinkled in disgust. Then he dropped his weapon and began to gag.

Kendra smelled it too—it was a horrendous stench, something she couldn't even begin to describe. Quickly, she clutched her robe to her nose in a vain attempt to muffle the smell. Then Ratchet appeared, proudly carrying the Snifferoo, with Oki fast on his heels. Each of them was wearing a strange sort of homemade mask.

"Where did you discover that nauseating odor?" Kendra gasped.

"Let's just say that we discovered the beastie bathroom in Arazeen," Ratchet explained. "And, as far as I can tell, rhubarb pies do NOT agree with your average Krake stomach."

"I think I'm going to vomit," Kendra wheezed, as she scurried over to poor Tuttleferd and pulled him to his feet.

"Princess," Tuttleferd wailed, "we simply must find safety!"

Kendra barely heard him. Looking over the mole's whiskery head she could see Three Tusks pick his weapon back up and shake his head, as if to clear it. In the early morning breeze, the stench from the Snifferoo was already beginning to dissipate and now Three Tusks stormed forward for another round.

Kendra misfired a weak and pathetic bolt from her wand that bounced harmlessly off the ground. Then, from behind her, a chunk of broken rock hurtled through the air and struck

Three Tusks right in the chest, causing him to stagger backwards. Kendra heard a war whoop and knew in an instant that it was Jinx to the rescue.

"Why don't you pick on someone your own size?" the grasshopper growled as she shot towards him.

Three Tusks just chuckled at the sight of such a tiny foe, but before he could event react, Jinx seized the tail of his long beard and bounded right overtop his head to stand behind him. Using her immeasurable strength, she yanked the Unger by his beard then leapt out of the way to watch him stumble backwards, desperately flailing his giant arms. Then the Unger's heels struck the edge of the wall; for one desperate moment he fought for balance—then plummeted over the edge, into the abyss.

Kendra stared at Jinx, wide-eyed, and yanked on a braid. "Thanks," she said.

Jinx didn't even answer. She had already returned to the fray.

When you're in the thick of a storm, it's hard to measure just how much rain is falling. Battle is no different. Kendra was fighting so fiercely with each Unger that lurched towards her that she had no sense of the overall attack. She had no way of knowing that the Arazeens were outnumbered at least two to one by the Unger force. Slowly and surely, the defenders were pushed back from the walls, but it wasn't until that moment when they were fighting amidst the very splendor of the city that Kendra realized they were in trouble. No longer were they battling on the ramparts; now they were ducking and dodging behind pillars, fountains, and lush lumabloom vines. The Ungers had even assembled crude catapults and were hurling large rocks at the towers. There could be no denying that the attackers were winning.

Kendra eventually found herself all alone in the rubble of one of the city squares, fighting out of pure desperation to survive. Her muscles ached, her brain throbbed, and she had a gash across one cheek. Wisps of smoke began to sneak across the square and Kendra realized that parts of the city were on fire. Then the twisted shape of an Unger emerged through the haze, lunging at her with his blade. Then, suddenly, he stopped short.

"Little Starzum?"

"Kiro?" Kendra gasped.

"Itzum Trooogul!" came the harsh reply.

Kendra blinked through the stinging smoke and stared at him in bewilderment. Could it really be her brother? She hardly recognized him! In the months since she had last seen him, he had grown bigger and stronger, his arms and torso rippling with muscles. As for his face, it was streaked with war paint and blood, further disguising the features she had once known so well. But she knew his eyes. Those hadn't changed at all and now they were looking at her with a mixture of emotions: concern, anger, and confusion.

"What Eenee dozum withzum hairzum?" Trooogul demanded in his deep, gravelly voice.

"My . . . hair?" Kendra reached up to touch her head, remembering that her long protruding braids were no more.

Both she and Trooogul had changed and it made her heart throb with fresh feelings of missing him. But seeing him stand before her, wearing a soldier's paint, and carrying a soldier's weapon . . . it made her feel something else too: a swell of rage.

"You told me to come here!" she cried, reaching out to strike him with one of her tiny fists. She landed the blow right on his chin, but it was like punching brick. "Why!?" she demanded. "So you'd know where to find me? To destroy me?"

Trooogul's nostrils flared. "Nozum! Trooogul no thinkzum Ungers need return. Trooogul just wantzum Eenee be safezum!"

"And how did that work out for you?" Kendra snapped, massaging her now throbbing hand.

Trooogul slammed one giant claw against the ground. "Nozum time for arguezum. Wherezum old Eenee hidezum Shard?"

"Our father, you mean?" Kendra retorted.

Trooogul growled—and even though Kendra knew him so well, loved him so deeply, she couldn't help feeling anxious. Trooogul paced in front of her, the long hairs on his back bristling in rage. "Old Eenee betrayzee Trooogul—and Eeneez too," he uttered. "Youza no listenzum to crazy Eenee. Givezum Trooogul Shard! Trooogul savezum Eenzum."

"Y-you're the crazy one," Kendra mustered. "Why do you want to rebuild the cauldron? So all of us can turn into monsters? Is that it? You can't be an Een again so no one can?"

Trooogul opened his mouth, as if trying to speak, but no words came out. Then he lowered his giant face so that he was looking her right in the eye. Kendra could feel the heat radiating from his body, smell the sweat from his battle. "Trooogul no canzum explainzum," he said at long last.

"Why?" Kendra asked quietly.

But before he could reply there came a low, guttural growl from the other side of the square. Kendra felt her skin prickle and a chill scurry down her neck; it was the unmistakable sound of something on the hunt. She looked into Trooogul's face to see his eyes flicker with apprehension. Kendra peered around his massive body. The growl came again, this time followed by a loud thwack, like wood striking stone, and the smoke snaked away to reveal the hulking form of another Unger—but unlike any that Kendra had ever seen before.

"Shuuunga!" Trooogul rumbled under his breath. For a moment Kendra thought he had just uttered some sort of Unger curse, but then he added, "Thatzum why Trooogul no can explainzum. Shuuunga."

Not a curse, Kendra realized.

A name: Shuuunga, the Unger witch.

Her mother.

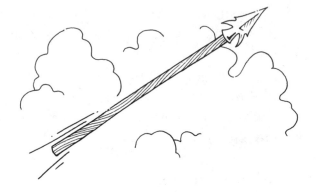

Darkness Falls

She was fierce, wild, and magical all at once—but that's where the similarities ended between Shuuunga and the beautiful Een woman who had once been Kendra's mother. Simply put, Shuuunga was hideous. Her face was long and sallow, punctuated by dark tattoos and a pair of sharp fangs that jutted from the corners of a festering scowl. A mane of thick hair covered her head, while her hunched and misshapen body was draped with a long, tattered cloak, the color of charcoal. Her limbs might have been tree branches, for they were crooked and covered in knots, and she had giant, bony claws for hands. One of these tightly clenched a tall wooden staff that was adorned with rattling beads and red feathers.

Just the sight of her filled Kendra with one thought: danger. Instinctively, Kendra looked for a place to hide. But Shuuunga had already spotted her prey. Lurching across the square, she swept past Trooogul, snatched up Kendra, and lifted her high into the air.

Kendra lost herself in the witch's reptilian eyes. *What is she feeling?* Kendra yearned to know. She could not tell if it was love, contempt, or something else.

But the witch's expression defied understanding, and now a growl escaped her throat—a soft, threatening sound that caused her yellow-gray lips to curl and reveal a flash of pink gums. "Wherezum Shard?" she rasped.

"I-I don't have it!" Kendra stammered.

"Tellz Shuuunga!" the witch implored. "Youza must!"

Looking over the witch's bent and crooked frame, Kendra saw her father standing at the far end of the square. With his robe in shreds and his face splattered with the tests of battle, he looked more deranged than ever.

Still holding Kendra, Shuuunga made a slow and ponderous turn to confront the king of Arazeen. She took one look at him and snorted in disdain.

Krimson's eyes blazed. "You twisted, demented dragonspawn," he spat. "Put down my daughter!" Then, picking up a discarded Unger weapon that was lying at his feet, Krimson charged, all his pent-up madness erupting in a single moment of absolute fury.

Shuuunga didn't move—and she didn't need to. In an instant, Trooogul pounced between them, lifting his own deadly weapon in defense of his mother. He was much bigger than his father, but Krimson had rage on his side. He bowled the young Unger over and thrust his toothy sword at Shuuunga's chest. Surprised, the witch used her staff to brush away his assault, and in doing so was forced to drop Kendra to the ground. The Een girl landed hard on her heels, and immediately had to duck to avoid a vicious swipe of her father's sword. Trooogul scrambled to his feet and leapt back into the fight.

Stunned by the barbarity of their fight, Kendra backed away. Countless times she had dreamed of her family becoming one again . . . but she could never have imagined this catastrophe.

I have to get away, Kendra thought, clutching at her braids.

Tears gushing down her cheeks, Kendra turned and scrambled across the square—but she only managed a few steps before she tripped and went skidding across the ground. She quickly rolled to her feet and spun around in a crouch. There had been nothing in her path. Whatever had caused her to stumble was invisible.

Agent Lurk.

She didn't have to see the treacherous spy to know it was him. He had a way of turning up at the worst possible moments. Blindly reaching out, Kendra grabbed hold of him.

"Let me go, girl!" the odious boy crackled as he winked into visibility.

"Where have you been?" Kendra demanded.

"Here, in *paradise,*" Lurk retorted. "Biding my time."

"For what?" Kendra asked.

Lurk's face flickered with smugness.

Kendra pulled him closer. "For what, I said."

Then, suddenly, the sound of the clanging weapons ceased and Kendra glanced up to see her entire family staring at her and Lurk. "Youzum, Eenee!" Shuuunga growled, pointing a crooked claw at them. "Youzum havezee Shard!"

Kendra shook her head. "I told you, I don't—" Then she looked at Lurk, and suddenly realized the witch was talking about *him.* "How did you get it?" Kendra hissed. But she didn't need an answer. She knew it instinctively. Lurk had been there, concealed by his cloak, when her father had divulged the Shard's hiding place to her. And, of course, he had decided to steal the dark stone for himself. He had probably spent the rest of the time waiting for the opportune moment to slip away from the city—but the Unger assault had put a kink in his plan.

But none of that mattered now.

"We have to get rid of the Shard," Kendra told him.

"NO! It's mine!" Lurk cackled. Yanking free of Kendra's grip, he sprinted away.

Kendra sped after him. Behind her, she could hear Shuuunga joining the chase. But Kendra couldn't worry about the witch; she had to catch Lurk first. The Een spy now turned invisible again, but Kendra had his trail; she could see objects toppling and clouds of dust and ash form as he scrambled through the blazing ruins of the city. She chased him under a fallen column, then through a crack in a wall. These were places much too tiny for Ungers to squeeze through and Kendra heard Shuuunga grind to a halt behind her. It wouldn't stop her entirely, Kendra knew, but at least it would slow her down.

Kendra turned a corner to find a dead end. In front of her was a wall and, beyond that, only sky. They had reached the outer edge of the city. She still couldn't see Lurk, but she didn't need to. She could hear him gasping from his run and knew he was standing against the wall. She heard him shuffle, as if to make another break for it, and Kendra quickly stepped to block him.

"You're trapped," she declared.

Agent Lurk turned visible and glared at her like a serpent. "Leave me be, Kandlestar." He clambered up onto the wall itself to stand precariously at the edge. Kendra knew he was trying to scare her, but she wasn't going to be deterred.

"I won't hurt you," she said, slipping her wand into her belt. Then she cautiously climbed up alongside him. She glanced down to see the precipice at her feet; one wrong step would mean plummeting into the ocean, countless fathoms below.

"We need to destroy the Shard," Kendra urged. "Just throw it over. You said yourself you didn't want the cauldron rebuilt."

Wheezing, Lurk reached into his robe and pulled out the black wedge of stone. "I *don't* want the cauldron repaired," he said, a crazed expression on his pale face. "But I don't need to destroy the Shard, either. I will keep it. I'll use its power for myself."

"There's no magic left in your heart," Kendra told him. "Maybe once, but not now. And that means the Shard won't work for you."

"NO!" Lurk shouted, cradling the Shard to his chest. "It *will* work. It *has* to work. I will coax the darkness from it."

Kendra grabbed him by the robe and they began to tussle. "Let go of me!" Lurk screamed.

Then he lifted his gnarled hand, the one holding the Shard, and walloped Kendra directly between her eyes. Lurk might have had no magic left in his heart—but Kendra did, and the moment the Shard touched her flesh, an excruciating pain flared across her face. She screamed in agony. It felt as if her eyes were on fire. She could see nothing but bright pinpricks of color swirling around a plane of black.

Then there was another sensation: the feeling of air rushing all around her. In horror, Kendra realized that the force of Lurk's blow had sent her careening over the side of the wall. She could hear the boy shriek; because she had been holding him, he had been pulled over, too.

Only a moment later, they landed amidst a leafy cushion: the boughs of a tree jutting sideways from the cliff. The tree instantly began to bow beneath their weight, causing them to slide along its spindly branches towards the abyss. Screeching, Lurk clutched at Kendra's robe. Then there was a ripping sound and in the next instance he was gone, his wail fading into the distance. The tree, now relieved of its extra burden, snapped upwards and Kendra found herself pitched through the air in the opposite direction. She tumbled across a hard and flat surface. Miraculously, she had been tossed back into the castle, though she realized this was a different, lower level of the city, beneath the ramparts where she had confronted Lurk. Her ears were now bombarded by the sounds of riotous cries and clanging metal. Here—wherever exactly here was— the battle between the Arazeens and Unger soldiers was still raging.

Kendra knew she had to find safety, but the torment blazing across her face was overwhelming. Gasping in unbearable pain, she tried to blink, but she could find nothing ahead but an impenetrable darkness.

"Help me!" she sobbed in panic.

Then a weapon crashed to the ground nearby, a jolt that forced her into action. Moaning, she dragged herself on knees and elbows across the ground, flinching at every sound around her.

She bumped into something. Reaching with a trembling hand, she felt the texture of wood, then the round shape of a knob. It was the door to some sort of cabinet or cupboard. Prying open the door, she crawled inside and curled into a ball. Her hands found her wand and she pulled it close to her chest.

Uncle Griffinskitch, she pleaded through the magic Eenwood. *Help me. Help me.*

But no reply came—just the violent clamor of war.

CHAPTER 17

A Vision of Een

Consumed by her pain, Kendra slipped away into fever. If you have ever had a fever yourself, then you know all too well what a strange experience it can be. Everything blurs together in a delirious daze until it's hard to know what is real and what is fantasy. Kendra's dream felt real enough, like all dreams do. It began with her spinning through a whirlpool of darkness and hearing the voices of those she loved. Here was a "Humph," then an "Eek," and an "I do say." Jinx growled, and then Ratchet piped up, "Don't worry, Kendra. We just need to work out the kinks." She heard her brother call out in his Een voice: "Little Star." But Shuuunga roared and chased him away. At last there was another voice, one that sounded all too familiar to Kendra, though she had trouble placing it. "Come, Kendra," the voice beckoned. "There's something you must see."

Kendra now felt as if she was standing in some sort of tunnel. Everything around her was still dark, but in this dream world, she couldn't feel the pain from her injuries. "Come," the voice said again, so she moved towards its sound. Then she saw something gleaming in the distance and she hurried ahead.

Slowly, out of the darkness, a shape emerged. It was a throne, tall and magnificent, though Kendra realized she was approaching it from behind. *How strange!* she thought. All around her was a plain of black, but she could see the throne perfectly. She paused a short distance away, and now the throne began to rotate until the tall and royal figure of her father came into view.

"We must protect ourselves from the outside world," he proclaimed, banging a fist on the arm of his throne. "We must preserve our kingdom! We must preserve . . . "

". . . Een."

It was a new voice. Kendra blinked, only to realize that her father had shimmered away—and in his place was someone that caused Kendra to gasp: Burdock Brown. It took a moment for Kendra to recognize him, for the would-be emperor of Een was grotesquely fat. He had not neglected to eat since she had last seen him! Indeed, at this very moment, he was stuffing a large piece of frosted cake into his mouth. But other than his rolls of flabby flesh, there could be no mistaking Burdock. He still had his single snarling eyebrow and long pointed nose. He was wearing a lavish robe and on his flat head sat a heavy crown with sharp spikes. In one hand was what Kendra thought to be a scepter—until she realized it was actually Burdock's wand of Eenwood, which he had fitted with a golden claw to increase its length.

"That's cheating," Kendra told him. "A wand grows with your understanding of Een magic."

Burdock didn't answer. And now the blackness that was surrounding the two of them began to dissolve and Kendra could see trees and pathways and buildings appear against the backdrop of a dull spring afternoon. Kendra plucked at a braid. She was now in the Land of Een, or at least what the Land of Een had become under Burdock's rule.

How did I get here? Kendra puzzled, cautiously turning in a half-circle. She was in Faun's End, the largest town in Een. And yet it was hardly how she remembered it. The shops looked dilapidated, many of them even boarded up. A crowd

of Eens was assembled in the square, but these were a melancholy bunch. Where were the sights, sounds, and smells that made Faun's End so famous? Where was the delicious aroma of Gilburt Green's Eenberry pies? Where was the ever-familiar hum of Luka Long-Ears the tailor?

Come to think of it, where are any of the Een animals? Kendra wondered.

Then she spotted the Elder Stone. It stood in the near distance, but it had changed too! It had been capped with tall spires and flags. Once the hallowed and humble meeting place of the Elders of Een, it now looked like some sort of royal castle.

"What have you done?" Kendra demanded, turning to glare at Burdock.

The hunched and hideous Een glared back, but it was as if he was looking right through her. Kendra lifted a hand and waved it in front of him.

Then a group of cloaked Eens assembled behind them. They were all dressed in long scarlet robes, their faces hidden by hoods of the same color. Each was holding a short wand of Eenwood—*They can't be more than Teenlings,* Kendra thought. *Burdock has finally dissolved the Council of Elders and replaced them with this lot.*

Then one of the figures in red announced, "The court of Burdock Brown, Royal and Supreme Emperor of Een, is now in session. Bring forth the prisoners."

Kendra turned around to see Raggart Rinkle, Captain of the Een Guard, marching into the square. In one hand he held his sword; in the other he was holding a chain attached to a long line of animals, all shackled together. When he neared the throne with his prisoners, he yanked on the chain, causing the animals to tumble to their knees. "Ye shall bow before His Majesty!" Captain Rinkle cackled.

"And you too, Rinkle!" Burdock snarled. He flicked his wand and a long crackle of lightning shot out, like a whip, forcing the bedraggled captain to drop to one knee. "That's better," Burdock chuckled, now taking another gluttonous mouthful of his cake. "So tell me, what are the crimes of these dangerous scoundrels?"

Kendra cast her eyes upon the row of Een animals lying miserably in the dust at Burdock's feet. They hardly looked dangerous. In fact, most of them looked to be nothing more than children—and scrawny, undernourished children at that. There was a hedgehog, a toad, an owlet, an otter, a rabbit, and two tiny little mice.

That's when Kendra gave her braids a sudden tug—for at once she recognized these mice as Oki's littlest sisters, Opi and Oji. Why, they were only Eenlets!

"This is ridiculous!" Kendra shouted, yanking out her wand and brandishing it at Burdock. "Listen up, you overfed windbag. If you don't release them right now I'll zap you all the way to the Wishing Falls!"

But Burdock didn't respond. And it was at that moment that it began to sink into Kendra that no one could see or hear her. She waved her wand at the chains that bound the animals, but it had no effect. Frustrated, Kendra marched up to Rinkle and directed

125

a strong, swift kick at his ankle. But her foot merely passed right through him. It was as though she was a ghost.

What in the name of Een is going on? Kendra asked herself.

"My men and I found these critters in hiding, avoiding their service to the throne," Captain Rinkle declared.

"Don't you mean *slavery?*" Kendra retorted in disgust.

Burdock, of course, didn't hear her. He banged his clawed staff against the ground and bellowed to the crowd, "Do you see what we have here?! These critters have shunned their duty to you and me, the True Eens. They hide in the shadows while the rest of us toil to improve the prosperity of the Empire."

Kendra scanned the crowd. No one said a word; their faces were pale and drawn, their expressions impassive. "Is this what prosperity looks like?" Kendra shouted in vain. "Is it?"

"And so we shall punish these abominations of nature," Burdock continued. "I hereby declare that these ungrateful runts be sentenced to hard labor in the Dragon Jaw Salt Mines."

It was at this moment that a crumb of cake happened to roll from Burdock's chin and land on the ground next to little Opi. Kendra watched as the mousling furtively snatched the morsel—but she didn't eat it herself; she passed it quickly to her sister.

"Oy, what's this?" Captain Rinkle growled, leaning down to glare at Oji. "Have you stolen food from His Majesty?"

"We're starving!" Opi squeaked. "You've taken away our parents, and all our sisters, too."

"That's because they are enemies of the crown!" Burdock snapped. "Your whole family must pay for your brother's treachery. He should have never sided with the Kandlestar girl."

"Oki'th not a treacher-er!" Oji boldly spoke up. "He'th a hero!"

"SILENCE!" Burdock roared, and now he snapped his wand-whip so that a beam of lightning snaked out and struck Oji, causing her to tumble backwards and drop the tiny crumb.

"Tell me," Burdock said, wriggling out of his throne and waddling forward, "where do you find such impudence, to steal from the Emperor of Een?"

"Pl-please, Your Majesty!" Opi stammered, cradling her sister close. "It's my fault. I took the crumb. We're so hungry."

"And you will be hungry yet!" Burdock yelled as he took what was remaining of his cake and hurled it into the ground. Then he zapped it with his wand, turning it to dust. "Bah!" he snarled. "I will not let these wretched rodents anywhere near the royal salt mines. They'll lick the walls dry."

"So what do we do with 'em?" Captain Rinkle asked uncertainly.

"We shall adjust their sentence," Burdock said, glowering at the two mice. He turned to his horde of red-cloaked judges. "You are the Red Robes, my trusted magistrates. What say you?"

In unison they each pointed a finger at the animals then, as if in one voice, proclaimed, "EXECUTION!"

"No!" Kendra screamed as a collective gasp came from the Een spectators. Kendra clutched at the children's chains, but once again her hands floated right through.

"The judges have spoken," Burdock said. "See—I leave it to the Eens. And the Eens say 'death.'"

"No, they don't!" Kendra yelled. "They just do your bidding!"

Even more surprising was the fact that Captain Rinkle seemed to be on her side. "But they're just Eenlets," the scraggly captain stammered. "Surely—"

"Do you dare defy me?" Burdock screamed.

"I-I'm just sayin' . . . well, I won't raise a sword to 'em, that's all," Captain Rinkle replied.

"Then you will not have to," Burdock said. For a moment, Captain Rinkle looked relieved. Then Burdock added, "After all, a sword isn't much good in the salt mines!"

"What!?" Captain Rinkle cried.

Cackling, Burdock snapped his plump fingers. Two of his Red Robes stepped forward, relieved the captain of his weapon, and escorted him away.

"That's settled," Burdock growled. Then he snapped his fingers again, and another of his constables appeared at his side. "Ah, Falsto—perfect lad for the job. Tomorrow, at noon, we shall execute these worthless prisoners, right in this square, for all to see. Not just the mice. The whole lot of them! Until then, take them to the dungeon."

Falsto nodded, picked up the end of the chain that was attached to the Een children, and headed out of the square.

"Court dismissed!" Burdock proclaimed.

CHAPTER 18

The Knights of Winter

Dream or not, Kendra felt she had to do something to help Oki's little sisters and the rest of the children. She didn't seem to be able to affect the world around her, but at least she could move. And so she bustled after Falsto and the prisoners as they headed towards the Elder Stone—and Burdock's dungeons.

"Please!" Opi wailed. "Won't you show us any mercy?"

"If it's Mercy you need, then it's Mercy you shall have!" came a cry and Kendra instinctively ducked as a blur of feathers zoomed from one of the nearby bushes and dove straight at Falsto.

"Ahh!" the constable screamed as a long sharp beak struck him in the head. His hood fell down and now Kendra could see that he really was not much older than herself.

As for the blur, it was a hummingbird.

Falsto fired at the little bird with his wand, but she easily dodged his attacks. And then came the reinforcements bursting from the bushes: a rabbit, a squirrel, and an enormous badger with grizzled fur. Each of these creatures was armed with weapons and, realizing that he was outnumbered, Falsto let out a little shriek then turned and fled down the path, back towards the town square.

"Who are'th you'th?" Oji asked in bewilderment, staring at her rescuers.

It was a question Kendra wanted to ask too, and now the hummingbird flittered above the children's head and said, "I'm Mercy Moonwing! And this here is . . . er . . . Poopoo?"

"It's *Paipo*," said the rabbit in an annoyed tone.

"And Joymus," the squirrel added. "Can't you remember anything, Mercy?"

"Oh, my mind turns to mush when I'm flustered," the hummingbird said sheepishly, casting a weary glance at the large and intimidating badger.

"Thunderclaws," he snarled, showing sharp teeth. "Timmons Thunderclaws."

"Oh, of course!" Mercy said.

Paipo sighed. Then she produced a ring of keys from her belt and quickly freed the children from their chains.

"Now follow me, little ones," Mercy urged.

She led the way back into the bushes and everyone followed, including Kendra. Here, hidden beneath the bush was what appeared to be an ordinary rock. Mercy tapped her beak three times against the rock, and it opened inward to reveal a dark tunnel.

"In we go!" the hummingbird chimed, hustling the children downward. Paipo, Joymus, and Timmons followed, and then Kendra slipped through just as the rock closed, wondering at the same time if she might have just been able to walk through it.

Timmons lit a lantern, casting a faint light in the cramped hole. Kendra knew they had entered one of the many secret tunnels that ran beneath Faun's End. She herself had once used them to escape Burdock's men.

"Come," Timmons commanded.

Taking lead of the band, he turned and shuffled into the darkness. He was so large that his broad shoulders kept scraping against the ceiling, causing clumps of soil to fall on top of them—well, at least everyone except Kendra.

Eventually, they reached a wall of rock. It appeared as if they were at a dead end, but then Timmons called out, "The forest birds sing in December."

With these words spoken, the rock shifted to reveal a small cozy cavern, furnished with a few simple comforts. As Kendra followed the others inside, she was surprised to see more Een animals poking their heads from the shadows. They cheered when they saw the Eenlets.

"Oh!" Opi cried in wonderment. "Where are we?"

"You are safe now," Mercy told the little mouse. "Welcome to the underground resistance! You're under the protection of the Knights of Winter."

Then a small door opened from the side of the cavern and there appeared a little old Een woman. She had long white braids, and she was dressed all in white, too. Even though the cavern was quite dark, she seemed to shine like a snowflake on a winter's night.

"Winter Woodsong!" Kendra cried.

She suddenly realized that the familiar voice she had heard at the beginning of her dream belonged to the old woman. *Did she somehow call me here?* Kendra wondered. Kendra wasn't sure how a thing would be possible—but if anyone could do it, it was Winter. After all, she was a powerful and wise sorceress. It was one of the reasons she had led the Council of Elders for so many years—until Burdock had taken over Een for himself.

"You'th suppothed to be dead!" Oji stammered.

"Show some respect," Timmons snarled.

"Oh, it's quite all right," Winter Woodsong said, hobbling along with the help of her long white staff. "The mousling is right. I *am* supposed to be dead. But you, my dear little creature, are supposed to be a slave of Burdock. So I suppose neither of us is playing her role correctly."

"Elder Woodsong faked her own death in order to fool Burdock," Mercy explained to the children. "She's the one who formed the underground resistance, to help the Eens against Burdock and his 'Red Robes.' But come, my little dears. You have suffered much—let us fill your bellies."

A murmur of delight came from the Eenlings, who were now ushered away through an adjoining tunnel. Soon all the animals dispersed, leaving behind only Kendra and the old woman.

"Now what?" Kendra wondered aloud, tugging on her braids.

"Now we shall speak, my young wizardess," Winter answered, the lines on her face dancing as she spoke.

"You can hear me!?" Kendra cried. "Can you see me too?"

There was a twinkle in Winter's eye. "You have seen what you must," she said. "Now it is time to return to the darkness."

Then the old woman turned and tottered back through the doorway from which she had come. Kendra followed her, only to hesitate at the entrance. She could see nothing ahead except an empty blackness.

"Do not be afraid," came the sound of the old sorceress's voice.

"But I *am* afraid," Kendra spoke into the tunnel. "It's . . . it's so very dark ahead."

"The darkness is your teacher, Kendra. Not your master."

"What do you mean?"

A pale, trembling hand reached out of the doorway, beckoning her. Kendra fiddled with a braid, unsure. But she trusted Winter implicitly, so at last she stepped forward until she was completely enveloped in darkness. It was just like the beginning of her vision; she couldn't see a thing. She couldn't even see Winter, not for all her whiteness.

"Come now," Winter Woodsong coaxed, leading her further into the tunnel. "You are a sorceress of Een. What is darkness to you? You do not need your eyes to see."

"Yes, I do," Kendra insisted. "Everyone does. Even you, Elder Woodsong. Even you."

"And is that your dream, Kendra?" Winter chastised. "To be no better than me? Won't you be something more than those who have gone before you?"

"But you are Winter Woodsong!" Kendra cried. "No one is more powerful than you."

"My season is coming to an end. And I need you, Kendra. Een needs you. You must come home, Kendra. You must."

Kendra could now feel a quake beneath her feet. It felt like the thunderous beating of a thousand hearts, but it was not a good sound. It filled her with terror. "What is that?" she asked anxiously.

"War," Winter replied gravely. "They are coming. All the monster tribes, thousands strong. They come to trample Een into dust, and we will be no more. Unless you come."

Kendra remembered Agent Lurk's words aboard the *Big Bang*, before they had crashed. He too had told Kendra that war was coming to Een. "What can I do?" Kendra asked. "I'm only an apprentice."

"You will become more powerful than you have ever dreamed. If you let yourself."

"You're not making any sense," Kendra said. "How?"

But Winter was fading from her now; this Kendra could sense. Indeed, the whole tunnel was closing in and it felt as if she was somehow being squeezed out.

"Remember, Kendra. The darkness is your teacher. Not your master . . ."

Most of our dreams slip away into oblivion. If we remember them at all, we are left only with mere snippets. As for Kendra, when she returned to consciousness, she had no recollection at all of her vision of the Land of Een. It was locked inside her, like a forgotten treasure. All that mattered to Kendra was the present moment—the throbbing in her head and the intense burning pain across her face. And the darkness. She was surrounded by it and it took a few seconds of panicked disorientation for her to remember that she had taken refuge in some sort of cabinet.

She needed to get out! She needed to see the light. There was not a sound to be heard, filling Kendra with hope that the battle for Arazeen had finally ended. She fumbled in the darkness for the cabinet door, only to find it stuck. She tried mustering some magic from her wand, but the words just fluttered away; she was in too much pain to think. Finally, she shifted her position and kicked open the cabinet.

As soon as she tumbled out, fresh breeze soothed her burning face. She began to crawl, but still, there was nothing to see. Only blackness. Kendra blinked, but she might as well have been in a cave. And that's when the horrible reality of her situation dawned upon her.

She had lost her eyes.

Now, and forever more, she was blind.

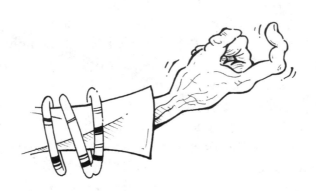

CHAPTER 19

The Story of the Wizard Who Fell

Now you know, dear reader, about Kendra's loss, the one introduced at the very start of our tale. It was nothing trivial, like a trinket or a charm. Her loss was devastating—and permanent. As she lay in the smoldering ruins of Arazeen, Kendra could do nothing more than sob.

Then she heard: "Kendra!"

It was Ratchet. A moment later, she felt the large raccoon pick her up and cradle her in his arms.

"I've got you. Don't worry. The Ungers have retreated, Kendra. They're all gone."

"But I can't—"

"Shhh," he said. "I'm here. Oki, too. Everything's going to be all right."

She could almost believe him. Feeling safe for what seemed like the first time in forever, she clutched the raccoon's soft fur and disappeared into unconsciousness.

When Kendra next awoke, her pain was mostly gone. She touched her face and found the skin smooth and soft. Her burns, she knew, had been healed by her uncle's magic.

And yet she still could not see.

A gentle breeze played upon her cheek and she heard the familiar flap of curtains. She realized she was back in her bedchamber in the North Tower, which had been fortunate enough to survive the Unger attack.

Then her nose detected a familiar scent: Uncle Griffinskitch. Strange—she had never thought of him in terms of smell before. But it was as sure and strong as the lines of his face. He smelled like a tree, strong and oaky.

"Kendra?" he asked.

"My eyes!" she moaned. "Why haven't you fixed them?"

"I have tried, Kendra. But you were struck with the Shard, the darkest of magic."

"So?" Kendra cried. "Don't you remember the peryton? He was wounded by the Shard too—but you gave him back his wings and antlers."

The old wizard squeezed her hand. "The peryton had stumps for wings, stumps for antlers. There was something to grow. But your eyes . . . I cannot explain it. They are there, but not there at the same time."

Kendra felt a lump form in her throat. She didn't need to ask him to explain further. She knew what her eyes looked like. She had seen them in her ancient, future self—they were empty and white, as if bleached of all color. Plus, the Shard had touched her directly; she had experienced the full wrath of its power.

"Kendra," Uncle Griffinskitch said gently. "There are other ways to see . . ."

"No lessons now!" Kendra cried, rolling away from him. "Just leave me alone."

For the next several days, Kendra remained in bed, staring into the abject darkness that had become her world. Her friends and family came and went, but Kendra, inconsolable, slipped into silence and was only vaguely aware of them. Once so full of fire, she now felt as meek as a candle in a tempest. Her days became a blur of experiences; the touch of Oki's paw, the taste of soup forced upon her by a fretful Tuttleferd, the sound of her father's anxious pacing on those rare occasions when he ventured into her chamber.

"All these years without knowing her," she overheard him say to her uncle one afternoon when they thought she was sleeping. "And now this tragedy. How can I be a father to her? I don't even know where to *start*."

"Humph," her uncle had grunted. "The point is to start."

But Kendra could hardly blame her father for his discomfort. The fact of the matter was that she felt just as awkward about their relationship.

He cares at least, Kendra thought.

It was more than she could say for her mother. The only thing *she* seemed to care about was the Shard. Over the past few days, Uncle Griffinskitch had told Kendra the story of the battle. Shuuunga had razed half the city trying to find the Shard, but once realizing it had disappeared over the wall with Agent Lurk, she had simply retreated down the cliffs with her army.

To continue her obsessive hunt, Kendra supposed. *She didn't stick around to see what happened to me. And how will she find the Shard, anyway? Surely it plunged into the ocean below Arazeen. Or perhaps it was dashed to pieces against the rocks, along with Lurk.*

Kendra wasn't sure what had become of Lurk, but even if he had met his doom, she found it difficult to find sympathy for him. After all, he had destroyed her eyes and, as far as she was concerned, he deserved his fate. But such dark thoughts did nothing to help Kendra's mood—indeed, they only served to send her swirling ever deeper into a vortex of despair. No one could cheer her, not Ratchet, or even Oki, who spent hours by her side.

"Why don't you find something better to do?" Kendra growled at the mouse one afternoon.

"I'm not going to abandon you," Oki declared. "You've never abandoned me."

"There's nothing wrong with you," Kendra snapped.

"Nothing at all," Oki piped up. "Unless you count the *eekitis, clumsabetes,* and the dozen other things that Ratchet likes to point out every day."

"Those are just stupid, made-up diseases," Kendra snarled. "I have a real problem, in case you haven't noticed."

"Humph!" Uncle Griffinskitch grunted as he entered the room. "Leave, Oki," he said, marching forward. "Let me talk with your *friend* in private."

Kendra heard the mouse slink away. Then her uncle said, "Rise, Kendra. We are going for a walk."

"I think you are confused, Master," she retorted. "I can't walk."

"Do you not have feet beneath you? *You can walk.*"

Then Kendra felt her blankets being yanked away. "I'm only wearing my dressing gown!" she protested.

"Never mind. No one is about."

Taking Kendra by the hand, Uncle Griffinskitch pulled her from the bed and led her out of the chamber. Kendra's heart began to flutter. "Where are you taking me? I want to stay here. I can't see!"

Uncle Griffinskitch ignored her. Then, on the way through the door she bumped hard into the frame.

"Ouch!" Kendra yelped in frustration. "See!? I'm useless."

Uncle Griffinskitch only acknowledged the mishap with a grunt and continued to lead Kendra down the corridor. Before long, Kendra smelled fragrant lumablooms. Next, came a warm breeze ruffling her hair, and she knew they were outside, standing on one of the many terraces that jutted from the tower.

"Take me back," Kendra implored in a panic. "Who else is here?"

"No one," Uncle Griffinskitch replied. "Everyone is hard at work. There is much to repair. Your father is intent on restoring the city to its former glory. To rebuild it. Just as you, Kendra, should rebuild."

Kendra clutched at her hair. It was a mess, but she still found a braid that offered suitable distraction.

"Listen," the old wizard said. "You say you saw yourself in the future. Who was that future Kendra? A broken-down old woman, blind and weak? Or a strong and powerful sorceress?"

Kendra grimaced. Her future self had seemed powerful, but . . . how could that be possible while being so . . . so . . . blind?

Uncle Griffinskitch sighed. "Kendra, did I ever tell you the story of the wizard who fell?"

"I don't recall you telling me *any* stories when I was an Eenling," Kendra said.

"Well, I shall tell you one now," he said. Then, before Kendra could object, he launched into his tale. "Long ago, before you were born, Kendra, there lived an Een wizard of significant talent. He could make the stars dance in the skies and the trees bow along the forest paths. Yet, with this power, came an insatiable hunger for prestige. More than anything, he desired to sit on the Council of Elders. But the elders refused him. For one does not earn a seat on the council by simply having talent. One earns it by attaining something much more elusive. A sense of inner understanding. A sense of . . ."

"Arazeen?" Kendra guessed, in spite of herself.

"Yes," Uncle Griffinskitch affirmed. "Arazeen. Something that the arrogant wizard did not understand. He was too obsessed with his stature. So when he heard that a fire lizard had nested in the mountains south of Een, he decided to snatch one of its eggs. In the wizard's mind, such a feat would capture the elders' attention, and they would not be able to refuse him.

"And so the wizard journeyed to the south, across the River Wink, through the Shivering Wood, and into the Mountains of Thune. For several days he climbed those treacherous peaks, and at last he reached the top."

"And did he find his prize?" Kendra wondered.

"Aye. There, sitting amidst a nest of ash, was the most beautiful egg he had ever seen—blazing red, like coal in the fire. But when he reached for the treasure it was so hot that it caused the wizard to yelp and lose his footing. He tumbled down that mountain and crashed into the rocks below. His bones were shattered, his body broken, and there he lay in anguish and pain."

"So he died?"

"He should have," Uncle Griffinskitch said. "But his old master, a powerful sorceress in her own right, found him there. Though she used all of her magic arts to nurse him back to health, he would never be the same again. Left hunched and crippled, the wizard who had once arrogantly strutted the streets of Faun's End was now forever doomed to hobble them bent nearly in two, as if trapped in a perpetual bow."

"What are you trying to tell me?" Kendra demanded. "That I'm like this blowhard wizard? I'm sorry—having a bad back just isn't the same as being blind."

"Perhaps not," Uncle Griffinskitch grunted. "But that is not the point of the story."

"Then what is?"

"That it was only in this crippled state that the wizard lost his arrogance and began to understand the mystery of Arazeen. Then, and only then, was he called before the elders. 'You looked to the mountaintops for a treasure, only to find it buried within,' they told him. And so, at last, he joined the Council of Elders."

"And he lived happily ever after?" Kendra mocked.

"No!" Uncle Griffinskitch exclaimed, thumping his staff against the ground. "That is not the end of his story. It is just the beginning. Don't you see? The wizard's greatest moments came not before his fall, but after."

Kendra pulled hard on one of her braids. "This is just the type of fairy tale that adults tell Eenlings," she said.

"It is no fairy tale," Uncle Griffinskitch said brusquely. "The story is a true one."

"I've never heard of it," Kendra retorted. "Who was this 'arrogant' wizard anyway?"

For a moment Uncle Griffinskitch didn't reply. Then at last, he gave Kendra a simple "humph"—and shuffled away.

There was a lot in that humph, Kendra knew. She could decipher it perfectly. It said: "It was me."

CHAPTER 20

An Aura of Sorcery

And so Kendra
returned to living her
life. She left her room.
She sat in what remained
of the gardens of
Arazeen and listened
to Ratchet and Oki
share progress reports
about the new cloud
ship they were building.
("It's smaller than the *Big
Bang*," Ratchet described.
"But she'll be great for short
expeditions.") She let Charla, the little
Arazeen girl, braid her hair and help dress
her in the pretty garments that her father
insisted she wear each night to dinner. She
decided to keep her new hairstyle. It matched
the fancy dresses and, after all, seven carefree braids just
didn't seem to suit her any longer.

As you can imagine, it was not an easy time for Kendra.
Anyone who has experienced an injury, like a broken limb, has
an inkling of Kendra's frustration. There are moments when

you just want to rip the cast or sling from your body and hurl it across the room. Kendra, however, had no such option; she was left to fumble through a permanent, claustrophobic darkness. During the worst moments, she descended into anxiety. What would become of her? Would she remember what her friends looked like? Would she remember the size and shape of things? Would she remember what her favorite color green looked like? Could she even have a favorite color anymore?

Uncle Griffinskitch scoffed at such thoughts. As far as he was concerned, what was important was what she could see from the inside. He decided Kendra must return to a steady regiment of meditation and the young apprentice soon found herself sitting hour after hour on the scarred and broken terraces of Arazeen, focusing on the magic of Een with her gruff master.

But it wasn't so bad. In the past, meditation had often bored Kendra to tears; now she found herself looking forward to the certain calm she could discover during these moments. You didn't need your eyes to meditate; in fact, when it came to meditating, Kendra felt herself on equal footing as everyone else. And, floating away in her mind, she didn't feel claustrophobic at all. She felt free.

It was during one of these sessions that Kendra suddenly sensed her uncle's staff flying towards her face, as if to strike her. She couldn't see his staff, of course, not exactly—but she knew, just knew, that the blow was coming. And she instantly ducked.

"What are you doing?" Kendra growled.

"Testing your vision."

"Is that meant to be some sort of cruel joke?" Kendra snapped. "You could have hurt me."

"It is no different from our training on the ship," the old wizard said. "Before you lost your eyes, you were learning to hear, smell, and even see by your feelings. You were able to run obstacle courses blindfolded."

"That was completely different!" Kendra cried. "I could just tear off the stupid blindfold if I wanted. Now I'm blind *for real*. I can't even—"

She didn't have a chance to finish—for at that moment she had a sudden feeling that something was hurtling towards her face. Instinctively, she raised a hand to catch what turned out to be a small stone.

"You threw that," she accused Uncle Griffinskitch.

"Humph," he grunted. "And *you* caught it. Seems to me that you are not so blind after all. Tomorrow we begin our wizard matches again."

"More obstacle courses?"

"Aye," the old wizard said. "But I doubt you will find them much of an obstacle at all."

It was like the old days that Kendra had spent aboard the *Big Bang*, training with her uncle. Now, however, the old man seemed to push her even harder—as if her blindness was somehow an advantage instead of a hindrance. Kendra grumbled, but of course that got her nowhere.

The weeks passed and, slowly, Kendra improved. Each day she became a little bit quicker, a little bit keener, a little bit stronger. And more confident too. Soon, she could eat and bathe and dress without assistance. She could even find her way through the rubble of Arazeen.

Then came the day that Oki came to visit Kendra and she sensed him before he even reached the door. She wasn't sure how she knew it was him; she just knew.

"I just felt his presence," she told Uncle Griffinskitch afterwards. "You know Oki; he's like a little tumbling waterfall, all full of excitement and agitation."

"You are learning a new way to be in the world," Uncle Griffinskitch explained. "Your eyes no longer work, and so your wizard's senses are taking over. You saw Oki by his *zeen.*"

"His what?" Kendra asked.

"His zeen," Uncle Griffinskitch repeated. "It's an aura, a type of energy, that emanates from all things. The walls, the plants . . . yes, living things . . . *especially* living things. We each have our own unique zeen, like a fingerprint, except it's a feeling that we project in front of us. You might see it in your mind like a symbol, with a shape and a color. You said Oki was like a waterfall. Well, that's his zeen. With practice— and patience—you will become expert at detecting these zeens."

He was right. She soon began to sense everything just as her uncle had explained. It was like her mind was a canvas, her surroundings the paint, and her feelings the brush. What was "painted" depended on the situation—or the person. Oki might have been like a waterfall, but Ratchet seemed more like a corkscrew, orange and vibrant. Professor Bumblebean was like a cube with soft corners, while Jinx gave Kendra the impression of something sharp and hot. As for Uncle Griffinskitch . . . well, he was hard to define. Even when it came to a feeling, he still seemed mostly beard.

One afternoon, she detected the old wizard's whiskery zeen as she was strolling through the ruins of the city—it was her uncle, sure enough, but he seemed ruffled and anxious. Maybe it was the person next to him—for whomever it was projected a zeen so strange that it caused Kendra to stop in her tracks. It felt like she was in the presence of a flower, but one that had been deprived of water for so long that it was now drooping low to the ground.

Kendra quietly moved towards the two zeens. Clutching her Eenwood and focusing her mind, she tried to pick up the conversation from afar. She heard her uncle first.

"She is advancing," the old wizard said.

"As much as she can, I suppose," came the reply—and Kendra realized at once that it was her father.

Then Uncle Griffinskitch spoke again. "Krimson, you don't understand. A power has been unleashed in her."

Kendra started. Were they discussing *her?*

"What are you talking about?" Krimson demanded. "Make sense, will you?"

"She is stronger than her mother at the same age," Uncle Griffinskitch insisted. "Stronger than *me.*"

"Ha! Fancy you admitting that!"

"Well, I am admitting it!" her uncle growled. "And you should admit it too. Have you seen her wand? It grows long. Longer than it should be for someone her age."

Kendra fingered her Eenwood. She couldn't see its length, of course, but she could feel it. She had indeed sensed it changing over the past few weeks. But was it really that long? She ran her hand along its handle, trying to estimate its length.

Almost as long as my arm! she realized. *When I first got it from the Een tree, it wasn't half this length!*

"But . . . but she is just a child," she heard her father sputter. "And she's . . . she's . . ."

Blind, Kendra thought. *Just say it, Father.*

"Do not underestimate her," Uncle Griffinskitch declared (Kendra could imagine him wagging one long bony finger as he spoke). "She has a gift. Any good wizard knows to trust his or her feelings. But we are constantly dis-tracted by our eyes. Ken-dra has no choice; she can rely only on her feelings . . . and it's caus-ing her to advance beyond all expecta-tion. She is bound  for something . . . triumphant. This I have suspected for a long, long time. But now I know it."

"I will not allow her to leave this city, if that's what you're suggesting," Krimson declared. "She shall never slip away from me again."

"Humph."

"And what is that supposed to mean, old man?"

"It means the choice may not be yours."

"Whose then? Yours? I'm her father."

"And I am her master!" Uncle Griffinskitch boomed. "But I cannot control her, Krimson. No more than I could control Kayla."

"Do not utter that name to me," Krimson warned. "Ken-dra shall be nothing like her mother, if I have anything to say about it."

"Which you don't," Uncle Griffinskitch declared. "Nor do I. Kendra's power is blossoming. It glows brighter than one of your lumablooms. Soon, nothing shall contain it. Not you, not I, nor the walls of this city—no matter how high you rebuild them."

Kendra found herself tugging on a braid again. Could it be true? Was she really becoming as powerful as her uncle suggested?

She shook her head, trying to chase away such notions. Ever since she had been a child she had looked outward, towards adventure. She had been so sure of her dreams! She had wanted to explore the outside world. She had wanted to find her family. But now she wasn't so sure. What had her dreams brought her?

Just disaster, Kendra despaired. *Perhaps my father is right. Stay in Arazeen. Stay safe. What's in the outside world for me? My mother hates me, my brother, too. I'm considered an outlaw in the Land of Een; they'd just as soon bind me with chains. I'm better off here.*

But, as Kendra was to soon learn, it's hard to give up on our dreams. And, sometimes, when you've worked so hard to chase a dream . . . well, eventually, it comes chasing after *you.*

CHAPTER 21

How Kendra Remembered

Kendra charged towards her uncle, wand in hand, hurling spells. On this day, the old wizard had decided to use a bridge as the arena for their obstacle course. It was so damaged and ruinous that it required no preparation, for it was sprinkled with fallen stones from the once-magnificent towers above and pitted with gaping holes. The railings on either side had been so smashed by the Unger attack that the few portions left standing seemed like busted teeth.

Yes, there was danger everywhere, but at this moment Kendra was undaunted. Her mind was in a zone, sharp as an Unger sword; she could feel everything before her as plainly as if she could see it.

Or perhaps better.

Uncle Griffinskitch fired bolts from his staff; she deftly sidestepped them. He threw stones and the fragments of broken lumabloom pots. She ducked and dodged, avoiding every missile.

Then, just like that, she reached him. She sensed the surprised wizard lift his staff to fire—but Kendra beat him to it. A light zap from her wand sent him tumbling to the ground with a satisfying "oomph."

Gasping, Kendra collapsed against a broken stone. During the moment, the victory had seemed so easy to achieve—but in truth it had taken such extreme focus that she now felt as if she might pass out from the exertion. Then, as she slowly regained her strength, something occurred to her. "Did you go easy on me?" she asked suspiciously.

"Humph. Certainly not."

"I bested you then? For real?" Kendra asked.

"Indeed."

"I . . . I can't believe it."

"You should," her master said. "You are powerful, Kendra. And you have taken one step closer to understanding the mystery of Een magic. It's a step that most wizards don't take until much later in life."

"How can that be?" Kendra wondered. "I mean—shouldn't I be . . . I mean, *I'm blind.*"

"Days of Een!" Uncle Griffinskitch exclaimed. "Tell me, why is it that you so steadfastly refuse to understand that your blindness is not an affliction? It is a gift! Listen: The darkness is your teacher, Kendra. Not your master."

Kendra felt a shiver go down her back—for at that moment something clicked inside of her. "What? What did you say?"

She fell to her knees, overwhelmed by the memory that was taking shape in her mind. At first it was blurred and watery, like trying to see through a window in a rainstorm. But then it was as if someone had wiped the glass clean, and everything came into focus.

She remembered Burdock on his throne. She remembered Opi and Oji and the other Eenlet prisoners. She remembered the Knights of Winter Woodsong.

But, most of all, she remembered the old sorceress herself and her chilling words: "The darkness is your teacher. Not your master."

"Kendra? What is it?" Uncle Griffinskitch urged.

"I . . . I remember," she murmured.

"Remember what?"

"Een!" Kendra exclaimed, anxiously yanking a braid. "It's in terrible danger."

"How do you know?"

"I . . . I have seen it," she explained. "When I lost my eyes, I had . . . some sort of dream. It's all coming back to me now! I went to the Land of Een. I spoke with Elder Woodsong."

"An out-of-body experience," Uncle Griffinskitch said. "It must have been induced by the terrible pain you were in."

"So what I dreamed really happened?" Kendra questioned. "What about Elder Woodsong? How could she speak to me?"

"Her magic is powerful," Uncle Griffinskitch explained. "Somehow, she knew how to find you there, in your state of pain. Humph! She *always* knows."

"Burdock is ruling Een as an emperor," Kendra said. "The land is in shambles. And the Unger armies—the armies of *all* the monsters—march upon it. Elder Woodsong . . . she told me I must return to Een. But what can *I* do?"

"Humph," Uncle Griffinskitch grunted thoughtfully. "Whatever you can—that's the simple answer."

"It's safer here."

"But not necessarily better," the old wizard replied. "We must return to Een, Kendra. It is time . . . but first . . . first, we must speak to your father."

Kendra clutched at a braid. "He will be furious."

"Don't worry," Uncle Griffinskitch said. "I will fetch Professor Bumblebean and the others; we'll face him together. Go to the throne room and wait for us."

Kendra lingered awkwardly at the open archway that led to the throne room (the door, once so magnificent, had been ripped from its hinges during the Unger attack and had yet to be replaced). Her father's voice boomed all the way from the other end of the cavernous room, where he was discussing the city's repairs with his courtiers.

Then her father suddenly stopped and said, "Daughter! Why do you loiter at my doorway? What is it?"

"I'm just waiting for Uncle Griffinskitch," Kendra called back. "We . . . we need to speak to you. Alone?"

"Do not stand there, muttering at me from the other side of the castle," her irritable father barked. "Come forth, child. Whatever you need to say, you can say now—and before the court."

Kendra plucked at a braid.

"Come, child! I am busy!" Krimson snapped.

There was no use in stalling. She took the long walk to the throne, feeling the eyes of the entire court upon her.

"Tell me," her father said once she was before him, "what is so important?"

Kendra could hear the impatience bubbling beneath his surface. Resisting the temptation to tug again at her braid, she stammered, "I . . . I . . . it's time to leave Arazeen, Father."

"I see," he bristled. "And may I ask why? And to where?"

Kendra drew in a long breath. Just where was Uncle Griffinskitch, anyway?

"Speak, child!" Krimson cried.

"Een," Kendra replied. "It's in terrible peril, Father. Burdock Brown has declared himself emperor. He has outlawed all magic and enslaved the Een animals."

No one said anything, but Kendra was sure at that moment that she heard her uncle's voice urge through her wand: *Keep going!*

So she did. "There's something more," she said. "The monster armies are amassing. Soon they will attack, just as they attacked this city, but in far greater numbers. They will obliterate Een!"

Now the courtiers erupted into chatter, but Krimson himself still said nothing. He tapped his fingers against the arm of his throne, and Kendra could sense him flaring with temper.

"How do you know this?" he asked at last.

"I had a . . . vision," Kendra explained. "I have seen it."

"But you . . . you cannot see," Krimson said, confusion in his voice.

"I have seen with *this,* Father," Kendra said, tapping her temple.

"It was just a nightmare, child," Krimson said. "Nothing more. Think about it! Een is protected by the magic curtain. No monsters can break through."

"The witch will do it!" Kendra exclaimed. "Just like Oroook once did. It's real, Father! We must go! Een needs us!"

"US!?" Krimson exploded. "Us, you say? Tell me, child—what concern is Een to *us*? We are Arazeens. This is our world. What happens beyond it is of no concern to us."

"But—"

"You are going nowhere, Kendra," Krimson decreed. "I am your father, and you will do as I say. You will stay—here, in this haven."

"Is that what you call it? A haven?" Kendra cried. And at that moment her immutable spark flared to life. All through the past months, all through her blindness, it had been flickering dully. But now it erupted. "Look at me, Father!" Kendra shouted. "I have no eyes. And yet you are the one who is blind! You think this is some sort of paradise? It's an illusion. You hate Een for closing itself from the outside world; and yet you've done exactly the same thing. You've tried to hide atop your mountain. And what has it gotten you? A pile of broken stones."

"We are rebuilding!" Krimson bellowed. "Listen to m—"

But now Kendra's spark was inflamed; nothing could put it out. "No!" she retorted, pacing before his throne. "You must listen to me. You clothe me in pretty gowns, tell me I'm a princess! A princess of what? This place is broken, Father. Just like Een. Where

Burdock rules with his heart of rock. Where the homes of Een animals burn. Where an army points its spears. Do you truly want *Arazeen?* Oneness? Then let us rejoin Een."

"Aha!" her father cried. "And what of the Ungers and Goojuns and the others of this kingdom? Where will they go? Shall they be invited to sit in the Elder Stone?"

Kendra said nothing.

"Of course not," her father said. "I see that you do not have all the answers, after all. Just the fiery temper of your mother. My duty is to *these* people. I will not take them across the world just to endanger them for a hopeless cause. If you go, you go alone."

"Not quite alone," came Uncle Griffinskitch's voice from behind Kendra. "I shall accompany her."

"And me!" came a squeak.

"You have my sword, Kendra," Jinx added.

"And my Snifferoo," Ratchet chimed. "Not to mention our new cloud ship."

"My word, you can certainly count on me," Professor Bumblebean declared.

Kendra smiled. *Perfect timing*, she thought, and then wondered if her uncle had planned it that way all along.

But Krimson was not so moved. "Bah!" he cried, slamming his fist against the arm of his throne. "Ingrates! All of you! You dare to leave? Then leave. But be warned . . . leave and you shall never return."

"You banish us?" Uncle Griffinskitch asked.

"You banish yourself," the king snapped. "You found Arazeen and yet you choose to leave it."

"Then so it will be," Kendra said. "But you are wrong about one thing, Father. I haven't found Arazeen. I'm still searching."

And with these last words, she bowed her head then turned and marched from the throne room—hoping to escape before he might see the tears that were beginning to sneak from the corners of her sightless eyes.

CHAPTER 22

Skyward Once More

Good-byes are rarely happy; they're even worse when no one is there to see you off. This was something Kendra realized all too sharply on the morning of her departure from Arazeen. She had hardly expected a farewell party, but a quiet word from her father would have been nice. After all, three days had passed since their confrontation (it had taken Ratchet and Oki that long to put the final touches on their new cloud ship)—wasn't that enough time for her father's anger to soften?

Apparently not; as Kendra trudged onto the terrace that served as the ship's landing pad, she could detect no hint of the tempestuous king. With a sigh, Kendra climbed aboard the ship that Ratchet had affectionately dubbed the *Little Bang*. The name suited it, Kendra decided, for she could instantly tell it was much smaller than its predecessor. There wasn't even a lower deck—just a few storage compartments and a maintenance hatch to access the mechanical workings of the ship.

"It's going to be a cozy ride," Ratchet admitted as he bumped into Kendra. "We might end up with *squishitis.*"

"Or *get-on-my-nerve-itis,*" Jinx growled. "Everyone better learn to hold their tongues for the next few weeks." Kendra knew this was directed at Professor Bumblebean.

"Humph," Uncle Griffinskitch grunted. "Let's tarry no longer. Captain Ringtail, prepare to lift—"

He was interrupted by a shout of "Wait!" Kendra detected Tuttleferd and Charla hurrying across the terrace towards them and she quickly clambered out of the ship to meet them.

"I could not persuade your father to come," Tuttleferd panted. "But please do not think ill of him. He loves you, very much indeed. But he's been through such an ordeal. I do not think he can bear to witness your departure."

"He could join us," Kendra said. "You all could. What do *you* think, Tuttleferd? Don't *you* want to return to Een?"

Tuttleferd fiddled uncomfortably with his giant spectacles. "I owe much to your father," he said eventually. "My life, in fact! So I must stick by his side, surely I must, Your Highness."

"Just Kendra," she replied. "I'm a princess of Arazeen no longer."

"To me you will be, ever more," the mole beamed with a sniffle.

"I wish I could come with you," Charla said. "I want to see all the magical places in Een."

"Perhaps one day," Kendra said, kneeling down to hug her. "Now, you take care of old Tuttleferd. Don't let him get too flustered!"

Then, with a final wave, Kendra returned to the *Little Bang*. As the ship lifted into the sky, Kendra leaned over the railing and sent out one last feeler for her father. For just the slightest moment she thought she sensed him. Was he standing at one of the tower windows? Then a gust of wind pulled the ship away and Kendra's focus, like the balloon that carried them, drifted away.

"Do you think I'll ever see him again?" Kendra asked Oki.

"I hope so," the little mouse said. "I hope I see my family again."

"You will—and before long," Professor Bumblebean declared. "By my calculations, we should arrive at Een in approximately fifteen days."

"To think it took us months to reach Arazeen," Oki said.

"Only because we had to scavenge the world to find it first," the professor said. "Now we can navigate the return trip by an undeviating course."

For the next few days and nights, they sped across the skies without incident. They made stops to forage for food and to stretch their legs, but they slept on the ship, curling up together on the open decks. It was not completely uncomfortable—though somewhat cold.

Then, one bright afternoon, as Kendra meditated amidst the cramped confines of the deck, she felt a frantic, chaotic energy call to her from the distant ground below. A myriad of textures and colors whirled in her mind, and she could hear the bubbling of pots, the clink of metal coins, and the chatter of voices, hundreds strong. She could smell spices, perfumes, and that pungent, unrelenting stench that one always finds on a hot day in a narrow city street. And there was something else . . .

"Where are we?" Kendra asked, standing up.

"I do say," Professor Bumblebean chimed, rustling with a map, "I believe we are approaching the town of Trader's Folly. From what I've read, it is like one giant bazaar."

"What's so bizarre about it?" Ratchet asked.

"Not bizarre—bazaar, like a market," the professor explained. "Though I'm sure it is also quite peculiar. Why, it's populated with gnomes, centaurs, goblins, and the like."

"Eek!" Oki exclaimed. "Then we should just stay up here."

"No," Kendra said quickly. "We . . . should land."

"Why?" Uncle Griffinskitch asked intently.

"I . . . I'm not sure," Kendra admitted. "Something—or someone—is down there that we . . . I . . . need to find. I can't explain it exactly."

"There is no need to," her uncle said. "Trust your instincts. Ratchet?"

"I'm already making preparations to land," the raccoon said. "Come on, Oki. Let's perch this bird."

"Oh, bother," Oki worried. "Do not think of rhubarb. Do *not* think of rhubarb."

Ratchet landed on the far side of a wooded hill near the city, so as to keep the ship safe from prying eyes. Uncle Griffinskitch cast a simple charm to further protect the vessel, and then the crew set off on foot.

As Kendra trudged down the long gentle slope towards Trader's Folly, she reached out with her magic and tried to create a mental map of the city. It was a near impossible exercise. Trader's Folly was simply enormous, though not tall and built up like a regular city. There were no towers or spires, no central castle or hall. Instead it was spread out, flat and far-reaching, arranged into haphazard streets that were filled with the zeens of countless creatures.

Kendra felt a stir of anxiety. She had grown so confident plodding through the confines of her father's city—but now she was about to enter an unfamiliar realm. If you have ever tried to learn a new language, then you know exactly how Kendra was feeling. It's one thing to practice in a classroom, but quite another to try it in the real world.

Uncle Griffinskitch seemed to sense her panic. *Stay focused,* he said through her wand. *You can do this. It's just a matter of filtering through all of the information. It will get easier.*

Okay, Kendra replied meekly, though with each step she felt even more bewildered. The city seemed like a maze in her mind; it invoked in her the feeling of a beehive. Beehives, however, don't have centaurs to guard the gates—which is exactly what Kendra and her companions found as they reached the city walls. These were huge and magnificent creatures, which Kendra could tell from their zeens. But they weren't exactly friendly.

"Little small for elves," grunted one of the centaurs.

"That's because we're Eens," Jinx retorted.

"A talking bug, is it—and one with a sword?" mused a second centaur. "Well, you'll have to leave your weapons here. This is a place of bartering. The only battles that will be waged beyond these gates are the ones with your wits—and your tongues."

"Oh, Jinx will still win then," Oki whispered to Kendra.

Jinx reluctantly handed over the weapon. "I better get that back on the way out," she grumbled.

"Old man, what is that stick?" the first centaur asked Uncle Griffinskitch. "It looks like a club or some item of enchantment. You will have to leave it here."

"Humph. This old thing?" Uncle Griffinskitch asked. "This is merely my cane. Surely you wouldn't deprive a crippled old man of his walking stick?"

The centaur seemed to consider this for a moment. He must have decided that Uncle Griffinskitch didn't look very formidable, for then he said, "Very well. But I see the girl has one too. Are you going to tell me that she also requires a cane?"

"In fact she does," Uncle Griffinskitch declared. "Look at her eyes. She is blind."

"Her stick is a little short to do the job of a cane," the second centaur said.

"Then perhaps we'll procure a new one for her in the market," Uncle Griffinskitch said. "For now, I beseech you to let her keep it."

The centaur gave a snort, and Kendra heard a creak as the gates to the city opened before them.

"Very well then," the beast snorted. "Keep your wits close, and your purses closer. Welcome to Trader's Folly!"

CHAPTER 23
A Hive of Trade and Trickery

Most of us have been to a flea market, antique store, or junk shop at one time or another. They are the types of places you visit on a weekend with your grandfather or aunt to rummage through secondhand curios and trinkets from ages past. They are often cluttered, dreary places, where everything is coated in a fine layer of dust. But there was nothing dreary about Trader's Folly. Indeed, it was a wild, chaotic place—like a flea market that had bumped into a circus.

To begin with, there were no people in Trader's Folly—no human people that is, but all the races that one could have found in the old days, before the world forgot its magic, such as dwarves, elves, fauns, and many others. And then there was the sense of impermanence to the place. There were no actual buildings, just stalls, tents, and otherwise empty lots with platforms. Kendra had the sense that someone might clap his hands and then the whole city would just pick up and leave. And, lastly, there were the wares for sale; these were stacked and stuffed, piled and plied in every nook and cranny of the bustling town. If you could imagine it, it was for sale.

Kendra felt completely disoriented. Her nose and ears were working overtime, and so were her feelings. Now that they were inside the city walls, she was bombarded with thousands of zeens; for a moment she thought she might suffocate. She bumbled into a vase (that strangely seemed to bumble back) and was yelled at by an ornery merchant.

"It's too much," Kendra told her uncle. "Maybe we better return to the ship. Where it's safe."

"Humph," came the wizard's terse response.

So onward they went, Kendra now clutching tightly to Oki's paw. With every step, there was something new to experience. One section of the market seemed to sell mostly food, strange dishes such as apple core pie, pickle juice pudding, and banana peel custard. But not all the treats were horrible; Oki described some of them as looking simply delicious, like the great puffs of cloud candy. ("Be careful," Kendra heard the merchant warn a customer. "Eat too much and you'll float away.") There were stalls that sold lizard eye soup, spider-on-a-stick, and barrels brimming with spices that at one moment would cause Kendra to inhale with delight and the next to pinch her nose in disgust.

"We should have brought the Snifferoo," Ratchet told Oki.

And then there were the performers and entertainers: escape artists, card-trick magicians, illusionists, battle-axe

swallowers, scorpion jugglers, fire dancers, and pipe players who charmed two-headed cobras.

"That's a large rat ya have, girl," one of the snake charmers called to Kendra as she and Oki passed by. "How much ya want for him?"

"I'm not a rat!" Oki wailed. "I'm an Een!"

"And he's not for sale!" Kendra added.

"Too bad," the snake charmer said. "He'd make fine dinner for me snake."

"Eek!" Oki squealed, pulling Kendra away.

"Ear hair too short?" an old gnome hag beckoned from a nearby stall. (Uncle Griffinskitch humphed; Kendra knew his ear hair was quite long enough already.) "How about my hair-lengthening cream? Works on nose hair, too! Buy now and get a free tin of wart-grower! Or do you smell too fine? Then buy my ode of swill and swine. Guaranteed to keep the ladies away!"

"Maybe I should get that," Ratchet said. "Girls are always after me."

"Humph," Uncle Griffinskitch grunted. "Next time, just turn on your Snifferoo, Ringtail—the infernal odors in that contraption would chase away a cough."

Kendra laughed, finally beginning to feel less bewildered. As she relaxed, she could detect distinct zeens amidst the hubbub, and her surroundings made a bit more sense.

They continued on, with Oki describing flying rugs, exploding baskets, and miniature hats.

"What's the point of these hats?" Jinx grumbled. "They're too small to fit even me—and look at this! They're all identical."

"Why, they grows to fit yer head—and yer personality," explained a merchant who skittered over to greet them. "Jus' try one on—you'll see."

Professor Bumblebean decided to oblige, picking up one of the thimble-sized hats and placing it on his head. Oki explained to Kendra how the tiny scrap of cloth spun around on the professor's head, then suddenly sprouted into a three-cornered hat with purple trim.

"I would have thought it would be square," Jinx remarked.

"My word, I love it," the professor declared. "And it fits perfectly! But, alas, I have nothing to offer in exchange."

"Now who comes to Trader's Folly with empty pockets?" came a voice from the adjoining stall.

Kendra was struck by a vivid zeen. It evoked in her the feeling of being stuck in a giant pool of syrup.

"It's a sphinx!" Oki exclaimed.

Kendra had once seen a picture of a sphinx and she remembered that it had the elegant face of a woman, the torso of a lion, and the wings of an eagle. She wondered if this sphinx looked the same, but before she could ask Oki, she heard the creature prowl up and announce, "Today, my friends, is your lucky day."

"I very much doubt that," Uncle Griffinskitch grunted. "We'll be leaving now."

"Be not so hasty," the sphinx mewed sadly. "I only wanted to offer you an opportunity to earn your hat. It involves a simple game of wit."

"Oh?" Professor Bumblebean perked up.

"Indeed," the sphinx said. Then Kendra felt a swish of her tail and it seemed to her as if Professor Bumblebean's zeen had suddenly turn rigid. It was as if he was under some sort of trance.

Never get involved with a sphinx, Uncle Griffinskitch warned Kendra through her wand. *We will have to see how this plays out—and perhaps come to the professor's aid if he fails to best her.*

"We shall have a duel of riddles," the sphinx informed Professor Bumblebean. "If you win, I'll give you the gold for the cap. But if I win, you can provide me with my afternoon snack."

"We just said we have no money," Ratchet said. "How could we possibly feed you?"

"Oh, we'll sort something out," the sphinx assured. "Now . . . the first turn goes to me." She seemed to take a moment to size up Professor Bumblebean, as if deciding how much she'd like to toy with him. Then at last she asked, "How far can a sphinx walk into the desert?"

"That's impossible to answer!" Oki cried. "How large is the desert?"

"Silence!" the sphinx hissed. "No questions or discussions! The riddle is only for your friend."

"I do say," the professor said, "it's not a complicated conundrum. The answer is quite simple, really. Of course, one can only walk halfway *into* the desert—after that, you are walking *out*."

"Very good," the sphinx purred, though Kendra noticed a hint of irritation in her voice. "Now give me your riddle— once I solve it, we can move to the next round."

"Here's a test for you," Professor Bumblebean said cheerfully. "If you wish to discover what I am, first look to the beginning of *everything*. Then take the last bit of *time*. Lastly, finish in the middle of an *end*—and then you will know me forever more."

For a long while the sphinx said nothing. Kendra heard her flick her tail then give her head a scratch (with a hind leg, Kendra guessed).

"Well, what's your answer?" Uncle Griffinskitch demanded.

"Fie! It makes no sense!" the sphinx yowled. "Tell me the answer."

"Why the answer is *Een*," Professor Bumblebean announced triumphantly. "That is what I am; indeed, that is what we all are."

"I've never heard of your race," the sphinx said. "I say 'no fair.'"

"And I say the match is over," Uncle Griffinskitch said with a thump of his staff. "Give my friend his gold, and let us be."

"Wow," Kendra gasped a few moments later as they ambled down the street. "You actually defeated a sphinx, Professor! *A sphinx!*"

"Why, thank you for your praise," Professor Bumblebean said. "I tip my new hat to you, Kendra!"

They encountered many other items of enchantment as they wound their way ever deeper into the market. One stall sold mirrors that showed you from the back, even though you looked right at it. ("Not much use to me," Kendra said— "Never mind, who wants one?" Jinx growled. "I never knew I had all those speckles on the back of my head!") Another stall sold flying brooches, but after taking a closer look Oki declared that they were tiny pixies chained by their ankles and made to flutter around the wearer's chest.

"That's awful!" Kendra said. "They should be free."

"I'm not so sure," Oki said. "One of them snapped at me."

"You know, I've been think-ing," Ratchet declared as the group paused to rest in the middle of a square. "We could make a fortune here."

"What do you have to sell?" Jinx asked. "Your ideas are ludicrous. Ridiculous. *TER-RIBLE.*"

"Did I hear right?" a goblin asked, marching up to the raccoon. "Are you sellin' ter-rible ideas? Tell me what you've got."

"I got a truck load!" Ratchet said. "How about dragon dentistry?"

"Ooh!" the goblin exclaimed, and tossed down a coin.

"What!?" Jinx snorted. "What sort of dimwit would—"

"I want a bad idea, too!" someone else cried. "What else do you have?"

"Two-for-one dinners for chimeras," Ratchet replied, scratching his whiskery chin. "Someone's going to be left out!"

More coins fell.

"Come on, help me out, Oki," Ratchet urged.

"Er . . . optometry for gorgons?" the little mouse squeaked.

"Why that's a simply atrocious idea!" someone else exclaimed. "Here's ten gold coins."

They were soon inundated with the sound of clinking coins. But then, just as quickly as it had begun, the auction came to an end, for someone down the street yelled, "Rhymes for sale! Get 'em by the bale!"—and all the customers scampered off to buy a piece of verse.

"Ridiculous," Jinx sneered, kicking at the mound of gold. "This town must be full of idiots."

"How are we going to carry all of this?" Oki wondered.

"Humph," Uncle Griffinskitch grunted. "I guess you will have to buy a sack."

CHAPTER 24

Tea with Effryn Hagglehorn

Ratchet's sack was so heavy that he could barely carry it. He begged Jinx to lend her strength, but the irritable grasshopper only crossed her arms and said, "It will all be gone within the hour anyway. We'll turn the corner to find some huckster selling exploding booger buns or something just as absurd and you'll spend the whole load in one go."

"I'm more sensible than that," Ratchet defended himself.

"Humph," Uncle Griffinskitch grumbled. "Let me remind everyone that we came here for a purpose. Kendra, any idea yet why you were drawn to this place?"

"No," Kendra admitted. "But there is . . ." She paused, trying to concentrate, but it was so very hard amidst the buzz and bustle of the market. "I'm sorry," she said after a moment.

175

"I can't make sense of anything in this place. Maybe I've just led us on a wild Eenberry hunt."

"I doubt it," Uncle Griffinskitch said, as Kendra heard him scratch his beard. "Come, let's see what else we can discover in this den of peddlers."

They hadn't gone very far (past a gambling pit where Oki described a gang of surly centaurs placing bets on a fight between a cockatrice and a basilisk) when Kendra heard an all-too familiar voice that caused her to stop in her tracks. It was loud and nasally and was singing a strange song:

> *Is there a pixie nesting in your nose?*
> *Perhaps a wart that grows and grows?*
> *Well, don't just cry and wail and mourn!*
> *Buy the cure from Effryn Hagglehorn!*

"Oh!" Kendra exclaimed. "Is it really him?"

"It is," Oki said, a hint of trepidation in his voice. "He has a stall right across the street."

Effryn Hagglehorn was a faun that Kendra had met during her journey to the Door to Unger. He was a traveling peddler of magical goods and, while he was rather harmless, he wasn't exactly what you would call trustworthy. Which was exactly the sense Kendra got from his zeen. It was like a giant blob of jelly that might slip right off your toast the moment you weren't looking.

"Trader's Folly is the perfect fit for Effryn," Kendra said. "How does he look?"

"Just the same," Jinx piped up. "Scruffy."

Kendra laughed. She remembered that Effryn Hagglehorn was indeed scruffy, which was mostly due to all the hair that covered his body. He had whiskery eyebrows, bristly ears, thick sideburns and a bottom half that was all goat, complete with a tail. Then Kendra sensed a zeen next to the faun and she realized at once that it was Effryn's steadfast companion, the enormous snail known as Skeezle. She had never known what to make of the giant mollusk. He seemed intelligent enough, but he never spoke. As far as Kendra could tell, he was content just to cart Effryn's caravan of magical wares across the countryside—and to sleep, which was exactly what he seemed to be doing at the moment.

"Perhaps it's Effryn I sensed aboard the ship," Kendra told Uncle Griffinskitch.

"I suppose we must go speak to him then," the wizard said wearily.

They had not even reached Effryn's stall, however, when an angry gnome barged up and began screeching, "I want my money back, you cheatin' goat! You sold me this ointment to stop my son from complainin'!"

"And it's guaranteed to work—or I'll be shorn!" Effryn brayed.

"Look! It turned him into a purple toad!"

"Oh! She just pulled him out of her pocket," Oki whispered to Kendra. "He's purple all right—and warty."

Effryn, however, did not seem the least bit flustered. "Well, he stopped complaining, didn't he? Don't worry, he'll return to normal by next full moon. Besides, no refunds, returns, or exchanges without official, itemized receipts."

"But you don't give receipts," the gnome mother protested.

"Then you and your son better hop along!" Effryn declared. "Now who's next? Step right up and discover the curio, charm, or cure that's right for you! What will it be? A hippogriff hiccup? A sip of skarm slime? The wink of a cyclops eye? Or—"

"I'll take it all. Everything!" Ratchet exclaimed, marching up and throwing down his sack of gold. "It sounds MARVEL-OUS."

"Why, barber my beard!" Effryn cried. "If it isn't my old friends, the Eens!"

With a bleat of delight, the portly fellow waddled up to Kendra and wrapped his chubby arms around her. "Now lather my lice—you've all grown up, my dear. Look at your hair and—oh, my—your eyes!"

"I am blind," Kendra said simply. "Don't bother trying to sell me a cure. There is none."

"The Shard," Effryn whispered in awe.

"Yes," Kendra said. "But how did you . . ."

"Powerful dark magic that Shard is," the faun said. "Come, you must tell me about it. Skeezle can mind the shop while we have some tea. Bring that gold, Ratchet, my good fellow. We'll decide just how many of my charms you can buy in a few moments."

"All of them!" Ratchet insisted.

"Fool!" Jinx hissed. "There's no such thing as the blink of a cyclops eye. He's a cheat!"

"You shave me to the shins," Effryn said to the grasshopper. "As a matter of fact, I *do* have the blink of a cyclops; it's good for curing bad tempers, you know."

Jinx snorted as Effryn led them past a yawning Skeezle and into a small room behind the wooden stall. This was a humble place, which, as Oki explained to Kendra, contained just a cot and small stove. Effryn hastily found a few empty crates and containers and flipped them over to make some makeshift seats for the Eens. Effryn himself sat on the cot and put the water on to boil.

"Now, what kind of tea will it be?" he asked. "Moonseed? Squid ink? How about essence of phoenix ash? That one's a bit spicy."

"You wouldn't happen to have dandelion?" Uncle Griffinskitch inquired.

"It's a little on the pedestrian side, but anything for an old friend," Effryn said. "Now, tell me all that's happened."

Together, they related their adventures; Effryn listened intently, only breaking attention long enough to pour the tea and serve biscuits. When the story was done, he gave a low whistle. "Well, that certainly explains a lot," he said.

"What do you mean?" Kendra asked.

"Do you have any idea what's going on up north?" Effryn asked. "I've just been there—but it was getting too dangerous for this faun, so I trotted to safer regions! Ha—I never thought I'd say Trader's Folly was safe. Why, this is the place where hucksters get huckstered. Stay away from the sphinx, by the way; she'll—"

"To the point, if you please," Uncle Griffinskitch grumbled.

"No need to get your knee hair in a knot," Effryn said. "Well, I've only been in Trader's Folly for a few days. And all the way here, what do I see? Wanted posters." Kendra now heard him rummaging about. "I think I plucked one from up near Lonesome Fang. I'm sure I have it somewhere. Just a minute—oh, here it is."

He handed it to Kendra, but she didn't need her eyes to know whom it depicted. Just touching it sent a chill down her neck.

"Lurk," she said.

"So, he is alive," Uncle Griffinskitch said. "And he surely still has the Shard."

"Not for long, if the Ungers have anything to do about it," Effryn ventured. "Those beasties are scouring the land for him. Look at the reward they've offered. Enough gold for a faun to spend the rest of his days frolicking in clover. And now it's gone beyond the beasties. Why, there are bounty hunters everywhere, searching for that boy. Beware of them hunters. Especially that Irko Vex."

"Irko Vex?" Kendra asked. "Who's that?"

"Terrible scoundrel," Effryn replied with a tremble in his voice. "He's got powerful magic. And an odor to boot, or so I've heard. I sure wouldn't want to be this Lurky fellow. Not with what those Ungers got in store."

"Why—what will they do to him?" she asked intently.

"They've played the thunddrum for him," Effryn said faintly.

"The thunddrum?" Professor Bumblebean asked. "My word, what is that?"

"It's the 'thunder beat' of the Unger drum," Effryn explained, his tail twitching so nervously that it swatted Kendra's leg. "Traditionally, they use it on the hunt, when they're in pursuit of dangerous prey. It means 'no mercy, no quarter.' It means that once they catch you . . . well, let's put it this way—there's no magical charm what can put you back together afterwards."

"Shuuunga," Kendra announced. "This is *her* doing. She commanded the thunddrum." And now Kendra's mind drifted away with thoughts of the ruthless witch. An image emerged in her mind of her Unger hunters ripping apart Trader's Folly. *But why here?* Kendra wondered. And then she imagined the deep and sonorous thump of the Unger drum. It was so loud and felt so real that it caused her to reach up and yank a braid.

And that's when she realized she wasn't just imagining the sound of the drum. She was foretelling it. "Uncle Griffinskitch . . ." she murmured. "I can hear it. The thunddrum!"

She could almost feel the stare of his piercing blue eyes. "What do you mean?"

"They're here. The Ungers! In Trader's Folly."

CHAPTER 25

Terror in Trader's Folly

There is something primal and magical about the beat of a drum, something significant that reaches down to the core and shakes you to the bones. It's a sound that can fill you with wonder and awe—and sometimes fear. Kendra's magic had helped her hear it before anyone else, but now the sound reached the ear of every soul within Trader's Folly. At first, the long and ponderous beats had to compete with the cacophonous chatter of the market, but soon all other sounds faded into silence, bowing before the mighty call of the drum. For a moment no one seemed to move and no sound other than the thunddrum could be heard—not a call, cough, or clink of a coin. Everyone was frozen, just listening to the drum.

Then chaos erupted. The beat of the drum ceased, followed by a shout, then a scream, and the sound of wood being wrenched to pieces. (*That would be the gate,* Kendra thought.) Then came more panicked screams, followed by crashes and clangs as the makeshift stalls began to topple beneath the fists of the Unger hunters. A flood of panic was gushing through the streets—and it was headed straight towards the Eens.

"Horns and hooves!" Effryn bleated, jumping up so quickly that Kendra heard him knock something over. "They'll flatten the whole city!" The portly faun was soon dashing about on his nimble feet, cramming belongings into various satchels and crates.

"What are you doing?" Kendra asked.

"I'm leaving!" Effryn replied. "Ungers are bad for business."

"Eek! Don't think of rhubarb!" Oki squealed.

"We're leaving too," Uncle Griffinskitch declared. "If anyone gets separated along the way, do not linger; just meet back at the ship. Now come, Eens!"

"Farewell, Effryn," Kendra said, quickly hugging the faun.

"Foam my fleece!" Effryn fretted. "For folks so small, you sure bring enormous trouble!"

Oki grabbed Kendra by the hand and pulled her away. Uncle Griffinskitch led them out the back of Effryn's little room, through an adjoining stall and into another street—if you could call it a street at all, for now it was choked with collapsed walls, broken tables, and merchandise that had been trampled into the dust by the feet of fleeing creatures. If Kendra had once pictured Trader's Folly as a beehive, then now it was a beehive that someone had poured boiling water overtop—leaving the colony frantically abuzz.

To Kendra, it was all just a fluster of feelings. Then she discerned another type of feeling moving through the swarm of panic. It was a feeling of hostility, and the image of running her finger across a sharp and jagged saw blade appeared in her mind.

"Ungers!" Oki shrieked.

"Come, Eens, this way!" Uncle Griffinskitch beckoned. "Ratchet! Leave behind that infernal sack of gold! It's slowing you down."

"But I was going to buy—"

"You masked muffinbrain!" Jinx barked at Ratchet. She snatched away Ratchet's sack, swung it round her head with her mighty arms, then heaved it right at the oncoming Ungers. Kendra could hear it strike one of the beasts with a heavy clinking thud and drop him to the ground, as sure as any cannonball.

"There!" Jinx growled at the raccoon. "It just bought you your life! Now, c'mon!"

Oki clutched Kendra's hand tightly, and they scampered away through more rubble, darting this way and that. Kendra could hear the ferocious Ungers tearing through the wreckage behind them, which only caused to increase her panic. It was one thing to duel her uncle in a controlled obstacle course; it was quite another to navigate through a maze of toppling stalls and fleeing creatures, even with Oki to guide her.

"Look out!" Oki suddenly cried, pulling Kendra out of the way of an oncoming creature (it sounded like a centaur). Both of them hit the ground rolling; then Oki snatched Kendra by the sleeve and whisked her under a tilted beam of wood and into a wrecked stall. In the next instant, Kendra heard the heavy feet of Ungers rumble past.

"Where are the others?" Kendra gasped after a moment.

"Nowhere I can see!" Oki cheeped, so close to her that she could feel the tickle of his whiskers.

"Okay . . . okay," Kendra murmured. "We'll meet them at the ship, just like Uncle Griffinskitch said. Right?"

"But how are we going to get out of here? There are Ungers everywhere."

Kendra wasn't sure. Her heart was racing like a river and her mind was exhausted. How could she focus amidst this havoc? But they seemed safe enough for the time being, so she clutched her wand and took a moment to settle her mind.

Uncle Griffinskitch? she called out.

No reply.

Then she sensed something: some terrified creature was nearby. She could see his zeen, which appeared in her mind like a hard and chiseled stone. *Another Unger?* Kendra wondered. No, it was something else. Someone small and good at hiding . . .

Kendra reached out and grabbed Oki. "He's here." She turned and began scuttling on her hands and knees through the rubble.

"Who?" Oki cried, scrambling after her. "Where are you going?"

"Don't you get it?" Kendra asked over her shoulder. "Why are the Ungers here? Why did they play the thunddrum?"

"Er . . . to get us?" Oki offered in reply. "To rip us to shreds and show no mercy. You know, all that stuff Effryn said."

"The thunddrum isn't for *us*, Oki. It's for Lurk. And that means one thing."

She felt Oki's zeen flicker with anxious realization. "Oh! That's who you sensed aboard the ship."

"Exactly. Come on; I have to find him."

They crawled onwards, squeezing past overturned crates and slanted timbers. In the background, Kendra could still hear the clamor of the Unger attack, but Lurk's zeen was growing clearer inside of her, calling her forth as surely as metal to a magnet. They soon came upon another ruined stall. Oki explained that the roof had collapsed at an angle, forming a small wedge of darkness.

"A good place to hide," Kendra declared as she and Oki wormed their way inside. "Especially if you're small, like an Een."

A hiss greeted them.

"He's here!" Oki cried. "But he's invisible."

"It doesn't matter," Kendra assured her friend. "I can see him."

And it was true. In a way, she *could* see him, for his shadow cloak could shield his body, but not his zeen, allowing Kendra to feel his presence all too clearly. Kendra shuffled forward, blocking any possible escape route. Then, over her shoulder, she said, "Oki, go keep a look out. I want a moment alone with him."

"But we should be making our way out of here," Oki protested.

"And we will—in a moment."

She heard the little mouse scurry away to take up position near the opening of their hidey-hole. Kendra took a deep breath and let her feelings settle upon Lurk. All this time, all through the months of dealing with her blindness, she had hated Lurk. Meeting him again, she thought she would hate him even more. But instead she was struck by something that completely surprised her. It was his zeen—for now, with her eyes no longer in the way, she could see him truthfully, for what he was on the inside. He had always pretended he was as hard as stone, but now she could see the cracks in his hard demeanor and, shining through them, were slivers of gold. He wasn't some ball of pure evil. In fact, he was really nothing

more than a terrified boy, exhausted and malnourished from weeks of being on the run from Shuuunga's hunters.

"I don't hate you," Kendra announced.

"Pah!" Lurk spat. "I hate *you*, Kandlestar. How ironic; all the world hunts me—and yet the one who can't see me at all is the one to find me."

"I can still see. I can see right inside of you. You're lonely . . . and frightened. And I know what that's like, that's for sure."

"I'm nothing like you," Lurk balked.

"Except we're both broken."

"Only your eyes, you spoiled brat! For me it's my whole body. I'm hideous."

"Not to me, not anymore," Kendra insisted. "That's not how I see you now."

"Hear my voice," Lurk wheezed. Then he placed his fingers on her wrist. "Feel the gnarled shape of my limbs. There is more than one way to know my deformity."

"You don't frighten me," Kendra said.

"Pah!"

"Do you still have it? The Shard?"

There was no response; that meant yes.

"Come on—you're coming with us," Kendra said.

"No, I'm not. I don't need you."

But he said nothing more as Kendra took him by the hand and led him out of the debris, into the remains of Trader's Folly.

CHAPTER 26

In the Clutches of Irko Vex

The city had quieted. From time to time a squeal or a shout could be heard in the distance, but it was more like the aftershocks of an earthquake—still dangerous, but far less dramatic. Oki offered to take Kendra's hand and guide her, but she was already holding onto Lurk with her left hand, and she needed her right for her wand.

"I'm okay," she told the mouse. "My mind is more focused now. I'll lead the way. Just stay alert."

Kendra reached out with her magic, mapping out the ruins before her by how she felt about them. Then she began navigating what remained of the city streets.

"How about Ratchet and the others?" Oki asked, as they scrambled through a gaping hole in the city wall.

"They'll be at the ship," Kendra said confidently. "Do not fret. We did it!" Then her nose wrinkled. "Wait a minute . . . what's that sm—"

Something suddenly looped over her head and fell onto her shoulders. It was like a magical, electrified rope that was now quickly tightening around her neck. Desperately, she raised her wand, but nothing came from it—not even a fizzle.

"EEK!" Oki squealed. "It's—"

"Irko Vex!" Lurk gasped and Kendra could tell by her companions' voices that something had clamped around their necks, too.

"Who?" Kendra wheezed. Her magic thwarted, she brandished her wand like a club of wood, trying to smite her attacker.

"That's the game ye want to play, eh?" came a snarl. Then something heavy and hard struck her head, sending her into darkness.

Groggily, Kendra came to. Her head was throbbing, but she could tell she was in some sort of cart rumbling across a rugged terrain; her whole body was bouncing up and down. She could hear the snort of the horse that was pulling them along, and smell him too. And there was another, fouler odor.

Irko Vex, Kendra thought. *He's that bounty hunter Effryn warned us about.*

She cast out with her feelings to get a better sense of him—only to feel nothing. Then she realized she still had the magical collar around her neck. Somehow, it was completely negating her powers. It was just like when she had first been injured. Without her Een magic, she was truly blind.

"Oki?"

"Oh!" he cried. "Thank rhubarb, you're awake. You have quite the lump on your head. How do you feel?"

"Like I was run over by a dragon," Kendra replied, slowly sitting up. "Where's my wand?"

"Vex snatched it," Oki said.

"He didn't need to," came Lurk's voice from her left. "It won't work with these cords around our necks. His magic thwarts us! Not even my cloak will function."

"And the Shard?" Kendra asked.

"It's concealed within my cloak," Lurk said. "Though not for long."

"What is that supposed to mean?" Kendra wondered.

"Where do you think this wretched bounty hunter is taking us?" Lurk groaned. "He is delivering us to the Unger war camp! Do you know what they'll do to me?"

"Yes," Kendra realized. "And they'll take the Shard and then . . ." She didn't want to think about it. "We have to escape before that happens," she declared. "Where are we, anyway?"

"Headed north," Oki answered. "I don't know where, exactly. I've already searched every crack and corner of this cart to see if there's a way out. But no luck."

"What about this Irko Vex? He must be close—I can smell him."

"He's up top, driving this cart," Oki said. "But there's something else you should know about him. He's . . . he's . . . well, he's Pugglemud."

Kendra had to fight a reflex to gag. She knew Pugglemud all too well—as you do, too, if you have followed Kendra's past adventures. Pugglemud was a dwarf, though perhaps he was also part chameleon, for he was ever changing his appearance and slipping into a new career. During the time that Kendra had known him, Pugglemud had been a treasure hunter, a king, the captain of a pirate ship, and even ringmaster of a circus. It was no surprise to Kendra that the rascal had now reinvented himself as a bounty hunter. Still, one thing was a constant with Pugglemud—he was an irritation, like a mosquito that refused to stop buzzing in your ear.

And, oh, how Kendra wanted to swat him. As far as she was concerned, his new alias was perfect. "Vex," she muttered in disgust.

"He looks the same," Oki told Kendra. "Bushy red beard, long nose, and greasy clothes. But he's got all of these tools and contraptions, like these long rods with magical nooses at the end of them. That's how he ensnared us. Everything he uses seems to block Een magic."

"I know, I can't feel anything about that scoundrel," Kendra said.

"I've been keeping a look out for any sign of the *Little Bang*," Oki said. "But nothing yet. Oh, I hope they're coming."

"And I hope they're careful," Kendra said. "They have no idea about Pugglemud's magic!"

They bumped along for several hours until Pugglemud finally stopped for the night. Kendra heard him set up camp, bustling about and humming a cheerful song. Eventually, he approached the cart. His stench reminded Kendra of the jar of canned Eenberries she had once found in the root cellar back home. The seal had broken, allowing a skim of green mold to form along the top. The smell had almost made her vomit.

"Ah, it's me old friend, Kendra Kandystar, don't ya know," Pugglemud chirped. "You and yer friends goin' to fetch me a fair pile o' gold—tee hee!"

"Isn't it dangerous to be working for the Ungers?" Kendra asked. "You once enslaved hundreds of them in your mines."

"Oh, that wasn't me, don't ya know," the repugnant dwarf chimed (and Kendra could imagine him winking). "That be old Reginaldo, crafty king o' the dwarves. Me? I'm jus' a humble bounty hunter. By the way, what happened to yer peepers?"

"My eyes?" Kendra asked. "That's no concern of yours, Pugglemud. Rest assured, my blindness doesn't stop me from seeing the repulsive, snot-nosed creature that you are."

"No need to compliment me," Pugglemud said. "And that's Vex to you, anyhoo. Best bounty hunter ya ever know'd."

Kendra snorted.

"Well, caught you, didn't I?" Pugglemud said. "All them beasties were jus' rippin' the market ta pieces and I says to meself, 'Vex, you jus' let 'em do all the chasin', sit outside and bonk them varmints on the head when they scurries out.' And who should come

a-scurryin', but you lot. Tee hee! I struck the mother lode. Three Eenies!"

"Well, at least you've learned to count," Kendra retorted.

"Hardy-har-har," Pugglemud sneered. "Well, ya oughta laugh now, cuz soon enough yer gonna be meetin' that Unger witchy. And I'll get my gold. Tee hee! Now—here's yer grub. It's all ya get."

He pushed some bowls through the bars of the cart, then turned and pranced away, which Kendra could tell not only by the sound of his footsteps, but by the fading of his stench.

"Whew!" Oki gasped. "He's sure got a bad case of *stinkatitis*. I bet the Snifferoo would explode if I tried to record it!"

"I'm glad you can find humor in our impending doom," Lurk growled, as he slurped back his bowl of gruel. "Ridiculous rodent."

"And you're clearly not getting over your bout of *creeples*," Oki said boldly, only to have Lurk utter a threatening hiss in response.

"Stop it!" Kendra said. "None of this is going to help."

She sighed and sipped from her bowl. It didn't taste as terrible as she might have suspected. Then she heard a loud growl come from Lurk's stomach.

He's still hungry, she thought. *When did he last properly eat?* "Here," she said, forcing the bowl into his clammy hands. "You have the rest of mine."

"No thanks," he said tersely.

"Just take it," Kendra commanded in her best Uncle Griffinskitch tone.

After a moment of hesitation, she heard him gulp down the contents of the bowl. "Y-you," he muttered afterwards. "You should not treat me this way."

"Why?" Kendra asked. "Because of what you did to me?"

Lurk only responded with a grunt.

"The thing is . . . I . . . I . . . did the same thing once," Kendra stammered. She was thinking of how she had once injured her friend, the peryton, with the Shard. She hadn't meant to—but what did that matter? Had Lurk meant to take away her eyes? How could she blame him for something she herself had done? The only difference was that Uncle Griffin-skitch had been able to heal the peryton; she and Lurk . . . well, they would never be quite the same.

"As I said before," she told the boy. "We're more alike than you know."

CHAPTER 27

Into
the
Unger
Camp

For the next
three days, the
prison cart rattled
across the rugged
landscape. There was
no sign of the *Little
Bang,* and Kendra and
Oki began to worry that
something had hap-
pened to their com-
panions. Without
Kendra's magic,
they had no way
of knowing.

All during this
time, Pugglemud con-
tinued to treat them
horrendously. He carried
a long rod and often used it to prod
them, taking extra delight in making Oki squeal.

During one such incident, Lurk suddenly lunged in front
of Oki and cried, "That's enough, you dim-witted dunce of a
dwarf!"

"Want ta play hero, do ya?" Pugglemud roared, jabbing Lurk so hard that the frail boy pitched backwards. "Ack! I can't wait ta get rid of the lot of ya. Yer more trouble than yer worth, don't ya know."

"Th-thanks," Oki told Lurk as soon as the dwarf had stamped away.

"Why did you do that?" Kendra asked the boy. "I thought you hated us."

"I . . . I just didn't want to hear him squeal any longer," Lurk retorted. "It's annoying."

He retreated to his corner to sulk and Kendra felt her heart soften even more towards him. At this moment she didn't need her magic to see his true self show. "Your gold's beginning to slip out," she murmured.

"What?" Lurk snapped.

But Kendra didn't reply.

It was on the morning of their third day as Pugglemud's prisoners that they entered a wide valley and first heard the boom of the Unger war drums. At first the noise was distant and dull, but as they drew ever closer, the thuds grew louder and deeper, until the valley walls echoed. Even though it was not the thunddrum beat, it was no less terrifying, for it was rapid and intense and made Kendra think of being chased. *Pah-pah-pah, pah-pah-pah-POOM! Pah-pah-pah, pah-pah-pah-POOM!*

"Don't think of rhubarb!" Oki fretted.

"The drums are not for you," Lurk said with an inconsolable whimper. "They are for me."

By afternoon, they could smell the camp. It gave off a putrid, rotting stench that was stronger than even Pugglemud's.

Then, just as the sun was starting to sink in the sky, Oki reported that the camp itself had finally come into view. In a fluttering, anxious voice, the mouse described a vast area stretching before them, where thousands of Unger soldiers scuttled amidst tusk-shaped tents and flickering campfires.

"I can't even see the end of them," Oki gasped.

As they approached the edge of the camp, a massive Unger sentry stomped across the field and brought the cart to a halt. "Youzee, dwarf!" the Unger growled over the roar of the drums. "How darezum approachee camp of Unger?"

"Because I'm Irko Vex, friend of yer witchy, don't ya know," Pugglemud brazenly replied. "And I got a special treasure for her . . . now lemme through so I can gives it to her—and then she can gimme gold. Tee hee!"

The guard peered into the cage; Kendra could tell by the smell of his pungent breath, which caused her to recoil. But the beast wasn't interested in her. Kendra heard him jab at the curled up little ball that was Agent Lurk, causing the boy to unfurl with a shriek.

"Itzum thiefzum!" the Unger exclaimed.

Lurk scampered behind Kendra and Oki, as if somehow they could protect him.

"Thiefzum must gozum Shuuunga," the Unger declared. He clutched at the reins of Pugglemud's horse (which, Kendra could tell by its whinny, was quite spooked) and escorted them into the camp. As they went, Kendra heard startled snorts and gasps from the Unger throng.

"It's a nightmare!" Oki squealed.

Kendra squeezed his paw and fumbled for the words that might calm him. But nothing came to her; the truth was that she was just as frightened. "Just tell me what you see, Oki," she begged.

"Claws and tusks and weapons of steel!" Lurk answered for the mouse. "Everywhere!"

All three of them huddled together in one corner of the cart, and now Kendra found that she was holding Lurk's hand, too. As they left behind the perimeter of the camp, the sounds of the war drums faded to a grumble. Here were the less savage beasts—the elders of the mighty army.

Before long, they came to a stop.

"There's a ring of tall standing stones in front of us," Oki relayed to Kendra. "They're massive, like tusks of rock, and all arranged in a circle."

"We must be at the heart of the camp," Kendra said apprehensively.

"This is where it will happen," Lurk wheezed. "This is where they'll kill me."

"Try to be calm," Kendra said. "We don't know what—"

She didn't finish her sentence, for at this moment another Unger came lumbering towards the prison cart, and Kendra knew who it was, even without her magic. She knew him by his smell and the sound of his grunt.

"Trooogul!" she blurted.

"Whatzum . . . howzum . . ." the Unger stuttered. Then his tone changed as he addressed Pugglemud. "Dwarfzum! Youzum should bringzum only thiefzum! Whyzum others?"

"They got in the way, don't ya know," Pugglemud declared boldly (though Kendra could hear a slight tremble in his voice). "Besides, a little bonus fer ya."

"Returnzum to postzum!" Trooogul barked, and Kendra guessed he was addressing the sentry who had led the cart.

"Giving orders now?" Kendra asked Trooogul after she heard the guard leave. "You've really worked your way up. A reward, I suppose, for your loyalty to . . . *her.*"

"Youzum!" Trooogul snarled at Kendra, now plunging his massive face before the cart so that Kendra could feel the full force of his breath. "Whyzum leave city? Shouldzum stayzum there! With kingzum!"

"I don't have to explain anything to you!" Kendra snapped. And now she stared defiantly in his direction with her blank eyes. She couldn't see his reaction of course, but she could hear his murmur of shock and—a moment later—feel the touch of a leathery finger against her chin as he reached through the bars of the cart to tilt her face towards him.

"Little Starzum," he groaned. "Whatzum . . . whatzum is thizum?"

"This is the hand of your dark magic, my brother," Kendra retorted. "This is what you would do to my people. *Our* people."

Trooogul growled, causing the tiny hairs on the back of her neck to prickle. Then he let go of her chin and with a slash of one great claw smashed a hole in the prison cart.

"Hey, yer gonna have to pay fer that!" Pugglemud cried— which was only met by another growl.

"Removezum magic," the Unger ordered.

"Are ya sure?" Pugglemud asked in surprise. "They're pretty sneaky, these Eenies, don't ya know, and with those magic collars, they can't do noth—"

"NOWZUM!" Trooogul roared.

"Someone sure got up on the wrong side of his rock, that's fer sure," Pugglemud muttered.

Kendra felt a peculiar instrument touch her neck—then, with a snip, the collar was gone. At that instant the magic inside of her flared to life, and she was so bombarded by feelings that she tumbled through the hole in the cart and lay writhing on the dusty ground. It was like opening the window shade after spending an eternity in the darkness; her mind was momentarily blinded as she struggled to absorb the multitude of zeens that surrounded her.

"Kendra!" Oki cried, coming to her side. "Are you okay?"

Trooogul was hovering over them. Amidst the haze in her mind, Kendra could just make out his zeen: he appeared to her like a claw of jagged lightning. Trooogul put Kendra and Oki into some sort of smaller cage built with bars of rough, twisted metal. Lurk went into a separate cage, next to them.

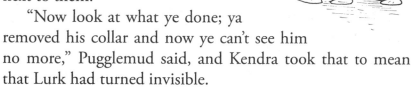

"Now look at what ye done; ya removed his collar and now ye can't see him no more," Pugglemud said, and Kendra took that to mean that Lurk had turned invisible.

"No matterzum," Trooogul said. "Trooogul havezum what importantzum."

"The Shard!" Lurk gasped. "The Unger took the Shard!"

"No!" Kendra yelled, her mind still throbbing amidst a storm of sensations. "Trooogul! Don't do this!"

But the Unger ignored her.

"My part's done," Pugglemud said. "Where's me gold?"

Trooogul snarled in reply. Then he gave a shout, and two other Unger guards appeared. "Takezum dwarfzum to Shuuunga," Trooogul commanded.

"Wait a nose-pickin' minute!" Pugglemud cried.

"They're dragging him away!" Oki squeaked.

"What kind o' treatment is this!?" Pugglemud wailed. "I'm Irko Vex! Why don't ya show some respect . . ."

As the dwarf's hollers faded into the night, Trooogul snatched up the two Een cages and trundled into the ring of tall stones. He hung the cages on two separate pillars, side by side, so that they were facing the center of the circle.

"Oh, Kendra!" Oki whimpered. "Right in front of is a stage. And on it is a . . . it's a . . ."

But Kendra knew what it was. She could feel its powerful magic. The cauldron of Greeve. She had seen it before, when she had been lost behind the Door to Unger. Back then, it had been in pieces, but she knew that wasn't the case now. The Ungers had painstakingly pieced it together, fragment by fragment, and now it was only missing one tiny piece—the Shard that was now in Trooogul's possession.

"They can finish repairing it!" Kendra panicked. "They can do it *tonight*."

At this moment, dozens of Ungers began spilling into the circle. Oki described them as being painted with bizarre tattoos and wearing long ceremonial robes. Some were carrying torches, while others held long staffs. (*Unger wizards!* Kendra thought.) And then there were those who had come with long, tusk-shaped drums.

"It's like they're going to perform a ritual of some sort," Kendra said.

"And we're going to have a front row seat!" Oki gulped.

CHAPTER 28

A Dance of Monsters

A thunderous chorus of drumming now erupted from the Ungers who had amassed around the cauldron. The ceremony had begun. Lurk began to cough and retch.

He's so afraid he's made himself sick, Kendra thought pitifully, but then Oki told her, "Trooogul just doused him with a clawful of some sort of powder!"

"To make him stay visible?"

"If so, it didn't work," Oki replied.

Strange, Kendra thought. *Is the powder just to prepare Lurk for the ritual?* Then she sensed Trooogul lumbering away. "Where is he going?" she asked frantically. "He still has the Shard!"

"Maybe he doesn't want the cauldron to be completed," Oki said hopefully. "Maybe he *is* on our side."

Kendra didn't answer, for now there was something about the rapturous beat of the Unger drums that was mesmerizing her. Many of the Ungers began to dance before the cauldron, flailing their crooked limbs and chanting in their strange, guttural language. Kendra could feel their energy; it was tribal and terrifying—yet somehow beautiful, too. The thump of the drums gripped her by the stomach, touching something wild and primitive inside of her. In spite of herself, Kendra began to sway to the rhythm.

How much time passed, she had no idea. It might have been minutes, or even hours. Then the tone of the drums abruptly changed—the Ungers began playing the long steady beats of the thunddrum.

"This is it!" Lurk wailed from his cage. "I'm doomed!"

And so this is the point of the ceremony, Kendra thought, snapping out of her daze. *They've caught their thief, and now they mean to destroy him.*

"Kendra, do something!" Lurk moaned, thrashing wildly in his cage. "I need to get out of—what!?"

"What is it?" Kendra cried.

"My cage . . . I just kicked open the door!" Lurk screeched in delight. "That imbecilic Unger didn't close it properly."

Even though he was invisible, Kendra could see Lurk by his zeen as he wriggled out of his cage and dropped lightly to the ground. But he did not leave.

"What are you doing?" Kendra cried over the rising crescendo of the drums. "Run for it!"

"No!" he cried. "I'll free you first."

His zeen was blazing bright and golden now, and Kendra felt her heart leap. *You do care,* she thought. *There's no denying it.*

Then, suddenly, the Ungers began to shout, "Killzum! Killzum! Killzum!"

"You have to go—now!" Kendra shouted at Lurk.

"But—"

"There's no time," Kendra cried. "You have to escape! Flee! Go to Een—you'll be safe from the Ungers behind the magic curtain!"

For a moment, Lurk said nothing. Kendra could see his zeen spinning wildly, its golden core sparkling and hissing as he wrestled with his decision.

"If you want to help me, go to Een," Kendra implored.

"I will," Lurk said at last. "But just so you know, I . . . I . . ."

"I know," Kendra said. "I know."

Then he slipped away and Kendra felt a twinge in her heart.

"Holy rhubarb," Oki murmured. "How angry are they going to be when they find out he's escaped? What if they take it out on us?"

Kendra had no reply, and now she could sense her brother whisking across the ground towards them.

"He's not wearing his armor anymore," Oki said. "Just a long cloak. Why?"

"So he won't make any noise," Kendra surmised. "But why all the secrecy?"

"Oh!" Oki cried. "He's looking at Lurk's cage. He's knows he's escaped!"

But Kendra could sense no surprise in Trooogul, no anger either.

"Something strange is going on," she whispered to Oki.

The next thing she knew, Trooogul had opened their cage and tucked them inside a large pocket inside his cloak.

"Where are you taking us?" Kendra demanded.

He gave no reply, but in short order stopped and uttered a strange word. There was the sound of rock shifting and Kendra realized that the Unger had spoken a password to open some sort of doorway.

"I think we're entering a cave," Kendra told Oki. "It feels . . . dark."

The beating of the Unger drums now became dull and muted. A moment later, Trooogul opened his cloak and emptied Kendra and Oki onto a rough, uneven floor.

Reaching out with her magic, Kendra surveyed her surroundings and knew at once they were inside Shuuunga's lair. Oki confirmed that it had all the trademarks of a sorceress's den, being cluttered with urns, rolls of parchment, and the skulls of strange, unidentifiable creatures. A fire was crackling nearby, filling the space with warmth. It was almost cozy.

Then Kendra discerned a strange zeen in one corner of the cave. It gave her the feeling of a bubble: simple, round, and clear, as if it had no character or personality. But what surprised Kendra the most was when the owner of the zeen spoke. Even though his words only came out as gibberish, Kendra recognized the voice as Pugglemud's.

"What . . . what's wrong with you?" Kendra gasped.

"Tee hee! Too hoo! Wee hee!" the dwarf jabbered. It was like listening to a small child.

Shuuunga suddenly entered from a side chamber. Kendra was struck by what she felt from the witch—or, better said, what she couldn't feel. Her zeen was flat, or false, as if it was somehow disguised. And that's when Kendra realized how powerful the witch was. Shuuunga was guarding herself against Kendra's magic. Whatever lay within the witch's heart, it was cloaked in mystery.

It made Kendra shiver. Now she could hear the great witch pace back and forth, like a wild animal deciding what to do with its prey. At long last, a quiet, mournful sigh escaped Shuuunga's lips. "Your eyes," she murmured. "I did not know this had befallen you. If . . . well, there is no point in ifs, is there? I learned that long ago."

Kendra started—Shuuunga's voice still had the rasp of an Unger, but here, in private quarters, she spoke like an Een! Her pronunciation was as perfect as her own.

Kendra could tell Shuuunga was staring at her. Not knowing what else to say, Kendra asked, "What did you do to Pugglemud?"

"I gave him his reward," Shuuunga replied. "A draught that turns the mind to innocence. He is like a babe now, and will never hurt you again."

"You didn't kill him?" Kendra wondered.

"Am I a monster?" the witch demanded. "Is that what you think of me?"

Yes, Kendra thought, but she dared not say it out loud.

"Perhaps I am," Shuuunga conceded. "For some would say that the dwarf's fate is worse than death." She paused again, and Kendra could hear her running one of her finger-nails along a piece of Eenwood; Kendra's own wand. "I have retrieved it for you," the witch said eventually. "It has grown long! Very long. Yes . . . Een magic grows strong within you; and so quickly! Who could have foreseen this? Not the old wizard. Not the sorceress. No one."

Who is she talking about? Kendra puzzled. *Uncle Griffin-skitch and Winter Woodsong?*

"So here, in one hand, we have the Eenwood," Shuuunga said. "And in the other . . . *this.*"

"The Shard!" Oki shrieked, and Kendra could now picture the witch holding out the dark stone by its long cord and watching it sway with her serpentine eyes.

"The Shard, too, is Een magic," Shuuunga declared. "After all, it was created by an Een."

"A terrible Een," Kendra said. "And now that you have the Shard, why don't you just repair the cauldron and get it over with?"

"You are as impatient as your brother," Shuuunga chided. "The cauldron *will* be repaired, all in good time. It must be done at exactly the right moment, and in exactly the right place, if my plan is to succeed."

"By *plan*, you mean the destruction of our people?" Kendra huffed.

"The Ungers are our people, too," Shuuunga countered. "All of them. Not just me. Not just your brother. *All of them.* Can't you see that?"

"In fact, *Mother*, I do not see at all," Kendra snapped.

Another muffled sound came from Shuuunga . . . one Kendra couldn't quite understand. Was the witch distraught?

But when Shuuunga next spoke, her tone was calm and even. "You are more right than you know. You have a gift, Kendra, the gift to look upon the world not with your eyes, but with your feelings, to see it for what it really is. The problem is that you have not yet harnessed the potential of your gift. Your mind remains closed to possibility. And if your mind is shut, then so is your heart." She paused, sighing. "It's just as I've feared; you've become too much like your father."

"What's that supposed to mean?" Kendra cried. "At least he's on the right side. You want to take the cauldron to Een! To destroy us! You'll resurrect the curse and transform as many as you can into your kind." She paused, seething. "But you won't find Een," Kendra continued. "It's invisible to your Unger eyes. It will be safe and—"

"That hidden flower will soon be discovered," Shuuunga said curtly.

"What do you mean?" Oki cried.

"The thief," Shuuunga explained, a hint of satisfaction creeping into her voice. "Even as we speak, he leads me right to Een."

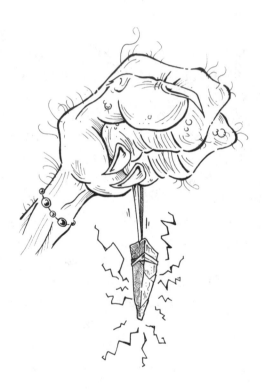

CHAPTER 29

Shuuunga Reveals Her Ploy

Sometimes the sting of realization is more sharp and painful than being kicked in the stomach. As the witch's words sunk in, Kendra suddenly felt woozy, like she was going to pass out or throw up.

Shuuunga and Trooogul planned all along for Lurk to escape, Kendra thought. *They purposely left the door to his cage ajar. And I told him to head straight for Een. Which is exactly what they wanted!*

"I've been such a fool," she gasped.

"It doesn't matter," Oki said. "None of this matters. Lurk is invisible. No one will be able to follow him."

"I can," Shuuunga declared.

"The powder," Kendra realized. "That's what it's for! You dusted him with it so that he would leave a trail . . . right to the magic curtain."

215

"Yes," Shuuunga confirmed. "The thief leaves a sign of his passing through the sky, one only monster eyes can see. It points like an arrow, straight to Een."

"The sky?" Kendra asked.

"I arranged for that crippled boy to find a skarm caught in a hunter's snare, just outside the camp," Shuuunga explained. "The thief has a way with those flying worms! He has already freed the creature and now wings towards Een, so quickly he can't be caught. My armies shall soon march in his wake."

"And you will use Oroook's spell to lower the curtain," Kendra guessed.

"Exactly," Shuuunga said. "Everything happens now according to my careful design. Everything comes to fruition! There will be no stopping us, Kendra. No matter what you do."

"Father was right!" Kendra exploded, the tears now running hot down her cheeks. "There is nothing left of my mother in you. Nothing!"

Another slow and sorrowful sigh slipped from Shuuunga's lips. "If that is what you believe, then so be it. It is the price I must pay. I would not have it be this way, Kendra. But it will be worth it by the end."

"I won't love you," Kendra said. "Even when I'm an Unger, I'll despise you."

"And who says you will be an Unger?" Shuuunga bristled.

Kendra could hear Trooogul fidgeting nearby. Even though he remained silent, he seemed at the point of bursting.

"What is it?" Kendra asked him. "Tell me!"

"No matter how much he wishes, he can say nothing of our plot," Shuuunga revealed. "I cast him with a spell, a magical muzzle, if you will. By pressing him, you only cause him torture."

"Tellzum Little Starzum!" Trooogul implored Shuuunga. "Little Starzum shouldzum join Shuuunga and Trooogul! Togetherzum—"

"NO!" Shuuunga bellowed, her voice so loud and furious that Kendra even heard Trooogul stumble backwards in fright. "I told you before. Kendra stays out of it. Her very presence here jeopardizes our plans. You must go now, Kendra. You and the mouse will return to your uncle, and wait, far away from Een."

"Wait for what?"

"For what happens next," Shuuunga answered. "It's the part I would spare you."

"So you care enough about me, then, to save me?"

"Care about you?" the witch croaked. "Kendra, I . . ." She seemed to be fumbling for words. At last she said, "This isn't helping. The more we talk, the more we endanger everything we've worked so hard to achieve. I wish you could understand that, Kendra. And you will. Soon enough. But for now . . . it's like I've said already. You refuse to see the possibilities. You are young, after all. Arazeen is not yet yours."

"Arazeen!?" Kendra cried. "You're on the war path and you dare to bring up Arazeen? Arazeen means peace."

"In here," Shuuunga growled, thrusting one of her bony fingers into Kendra's chest. "When you have found Arazeen, then you are at peace with yourself. With your path."

"Is that the case with you, *Mother?*" Kendra sneered. "Are you at peace with your path?"

A growl rumbled warningly in Shuuunga's throat, and Kendra shivered. "Judge me, if you must," the witch said eventually. "Despise me, even. Just like your father has trained you to do. But make sure you gaze upon yourself, too. You see the world by its energy, Kendra, by its zeens. But there is one zeen, I think, that you do not see at all."

"Yours?" Kendra guessed.

"Hmph," the witch grunted, shuffling close. "The one I mean is *yours*. And if you cannot see yourself, you can see nothing."

"I don't know what you're talking about," Kendra said.

"Tell me, Kendra," the witch rasped. "What is *your* zeen?"

"What? What do you mean?"

"Your aura," Shuuunga persisted. "Your symbol, if you must think of it that way."

"I don't know!" Kendra said in frustration. "How am I supposed to know that?"

Shuuunga sighed. "And this is why you are so dangerous, so unpredictable," she said. "Which is why you must go."

Kendra's mind began to spin. "What do you mean?" she asked. "I'm not the dangerous one! You are! What do you mean, *my* zeen?"

But Shuuunga ignored her questions. "Take them away," she instructed Trooogul. "Far from here. Make haste! We have an army to mobilize."

"Yeezum," Trooogul said with an obedient grunt. He lifted Kendra and Oki back into his cloak pocket, then carried them out of the den.

Kendra clutched at a braid, hoping it would somehow calm her thoughts. It had never even occurred to contemplate her own zeen. But of course she had one! Everyone did. Kendra had always cast her magic outwards, but now she tried sending it inwards. And what did she see?

Nothing. Only darkness.

"I'm so confused," she told Oki.

Then, suddenly, they were back in the thick of the Unger camp, and Kendra's mind quickly returned to their present situation—she couldn't help it; the throng of monsters had erupted into a beastly frenzy.

"They discovered Lurk's escape!" Oki guessed from their place inside Trooogul's pocket.

The hostility in the air was palpable. The drums had gone silent, their rhythm replaced by hoots and hollers, growls and grunts.

"EEK!" Oki squealed. "If they find us . . ."

Kendra cupped her hand over his mouth, trying to silence him. She knew what her friend was thinking, and he was right. The Ungers wanted their thief, but if they couldn't have Lurk, they might satisfy their bloodlust by ripping them to shreds.

"Stay calm; we must stay calm," Kendra whispered. The words were meant for herself as much as for Oki.

At long last, the riotous sounds began to fade and Kendra knew they had passed the perimeter of the vast camp. They weren't quite out of danger, for a few Ungers were still roaming about and searching for their escaped quarry. Kendra could hear them ripping stones from the ground and uprooting trees. Still, Trooogul trundled onward, into the night. Kendra was glad; she wanted to be as far away from the camp as possible.

An hour passed. Then another. Finally, they stopped, and Trooogul dumped them gently onto the ground.

"Youzum gozum to Een," he said. It was more of a statement than a question.

"What's it to you?" Kendra demanded.

"Shuuunga say stayzum awayzum. Be safezum."

"Listen!" Kendra said, desperately clutching at the Unger's cloak. "Join us. You don't have to be on her side. I know there's something good in you yet."

"Nozum!" Trooogul roared. "Youza! No understandzum. This is wayzum, Little Starzum!"

Kendra could tell he was looking around furtively; his zeen was twitching nervously, as if he was worried someone might overhear. Then he thrust one of his claws into another pocket in his cloak and pulled out Kendra's wand, which Shuuunga must have given to him at the last moment. He placed it in Kendra's hands.

Kendra's palms tingled as she touched the Eenwood. Now she could feel even more clearly than before; it was like lighting an extra candle in a darkened room. She heard her uncle's voice come through the wand. *Kendra,* he called. *We are here.*

Kendra turned her attention to the sky and cast out her feelings. Sure enough, she could sense the *Little Bang* headed towards them.

"Eeneez no catchzum thiefzum," Trooogul told Kendra. "Not evenzum with magic shipzum."

"We can try," Kendra retorted.

"Thiefzum quicker," Trooogul insisted. "Eenee no tryzum! Followzum Shuuunga's planzum."

"And if I don't?" Kendra demanded.

"Itzum wayzum," Trooogul grunted. "Itzum *only* wayzum." Kendra could feel him staring at her. "Little Starzum," he finally said, in what passed for a whisper. "Youza always dozum what mustzum."

"So?" Kendra snapped. "What of it?"

"And so mustzum Shuuunga."

"What is that supposed to mean?" Kendra asked.

But Trooogul didn't answer. Instead he simply turned and sped off into the night, back towards the vast and mighty army that was preparing to destroy Een.

CHAPTER 30

Winter Woodsong's Secret Weapon

It doesn't matter if you are human, Een, or Unger—everyone knows what it's like to quarrel with family members. Sometimes you end up so angry with them that you think you might never forgive them. Kendra, however, just didn't think it. She was certain of it.

"They plan to destroy Een!" Kendra shouted as she and Oki climbed aboard the *Little Bang.* "And they have the means to do it."

"We must hurry home," Uncle Griffinskitch said after Kendra had explained everything. "We may not be able to catch Lurk, but we can certainly fly to Een ahead of the Ungers."

And so they made all haste towards that magical land tucked between the cracks of Here and There. All through this journey Kendra was agitated. Shuuunga's words gnawed at her: *What is your zeen?* Perhaps it wasn't the question that bothered her so much, but the fact that she didn't have the answer. For, no matter how hard Kendra looked inward, she could find no hint of her own zeen. If she had one, it was hidden to her.

It took them two days to reach Een's enchanted border. Uncle Griffinskitch, who had been given the secret to the magic curtain by Winter Woodsong before last leaving Een, guided them through. Whatever sense of despair Kendra had been feeling was now instantly magnified, and it took her a moment to realize that it was coming from the land itself. It was like gazing upon a painting that had once been a masterpiece, but now had been vandalized, so that nothing remained but a marred and shredded canvas.

Burdock, Kendra fumed. *He's done this.*

Then, just as they were zooming over the Hills of Wight, a bolt of fire flew from the ground and caused the ship to lurch. Another bolt came and this one punctured the ship's balloon, sending them towards the ground.

"Hold tight!" Ratchet cried. Kendra heard him scramble to maneuver the ship's wings and steady their descent.

Luckily, their fall was broken by a large clump of ferns. No one was hurt, but Kendra could sense a group of Eens approaching. "It's Burdock's Red Robes," she told the crew. "They're the ones who shot us down; they've come to arrest us."

"How many of them are there?" Jinx asked.

"Six, at least," Kendra calculated. "Plus the Een Guard. Wait a minute . . ." She could now sense two more zeens, but the strange thing was that they seemed to come from beneath her. One felt like a flutter, while the other gave Kendra the sensation of smelling a rose—but touching its thorns at the same time. A moment later, a nearby rock lifted up and there appeared Mercy Moonwing and Timmons Thunderclaws.

"The Knights of Winter, at your service!" Mercy greeted, hovering just above Kendra. "I suppose no one told you that the only safe way to travel Een these days is by tunnel. Lucky thing Winter sensed your arrival; she sent us to fetch you."

"Oh, I suppose we'll have to go underground now," Oki fretted.

"Don't worry," Mercy consoled the mouse. "These passages are perfectly safe. I know them like the back of my wings."

"Er . . . you can't technically see the back of your wings," Oki pointed out.

"Never mind!" Timmons growled. "Grab what you must from your ship; we need to hurry."

They were soon all safely in the tunnel and Timmons secured the hidden door behind them.

"Come on," Mercy called as she flitted down the tunnel. "Winter Woodsong awaits."

It was a long trek, which was not helped by the fact that Mercy twittered the entire way—though in truth the hummingbird spoke so quickly that Kendra couldn't follow half of what she said. Eventually, they arrived at the headquarters of Winter's secret underground base and there was much rejoicing as they reunited with the old sorceress and the other members of her resistance. Even Opi and Oji, Oki's little sisters, were there. They eagerly smothered their big brother with kisses.

"Okay, that's enough now," Oki said after a few moments. "I'll end up with *smoochamosis!* Where's the rest of our sisters? And our parents?"

"I'm afraid they are all slaves," Winter Woodsong said gravely.

The ancient Een projected a beautiful zeen. It was like gazing close up at a snowflake that was pure and complicated—and ever so delicate, as if the slightest heat might melt it. But Kendra knew better. Winter was as strong as steel.

"Come," the sorceress said to Kendra and her companions. "We have much to discuss."

They soon found themselves huddled in one of the larger caverns in the underground complex. For the first hour or so, Uncle Griffinskitch related all that had befallen them, often asking Kendra or the other members of the crew to help explain things along the way.

"So," Winter mused, once all was said. "The time has come, at last. The Ungers have the cauldron and march towards

Een, following the trail left by Leerlin Lurk. How long before this army arrives?"

"Their numbers are substantial and, as such, I suspect they will move ponderously," Professor Bumblebean replied. "I estimate we have approximately two weeks before they arrive."

"That leaves little time to prepare," Winter said. "Given our current predicament, especially. After all, how can we sweep our front steps when we have not yet cleaned the inside of our house?"

"We ought not to waste any time sweeping," Ratchet said. "Besides—no offense, Elder Woodsong—there's not much sense taking a broom to *this* place."

"Er . . . Ratchet?" Oki said. "I think what Elder Woodsong means is that we need to take care of Burdock before we can prepare for the Ungers."

"Indeed," Winter declared. "The land is in shambles, divided against itself. Burdock, as self-proclaimed emperor, has been able to convince the people that the Een animals are against them, that they wish to take over the land for themselves. In this way he has been able to declare all Een animals slaves. Most toil in the Dragon Jaw Salt Mines or rot in the dungeons; except, of course, those who have escaped to the underground."

"All magic has been outlawed," Timmons added. "It can only be performed by Burdock and the selected few in his so-called Red Robes. They know when someone uses it illegally; this you experienced firsthand when you crossed the curtain."

"Have we no other friends?" Kendra asked. "What's happened to the former members of the Council of Elders?"

"They are dead, or in Burdock's prisons," Winter replied solemnly. "The only aid we shall receive has already arrived. The time to act is now."

"What is your plan?" Uncle Griffinskitch asked.

"If we are to defeat Burdock, we must have the people on our side," Winter explained. "Tomorrow, as is his custom, Burdock will assemble the Eens in the town square and hold court. He shall have an unexpected trial, I'm afraid! For, at last, I shall make my presence known. The Eens will discover that I did not perish as Burdock has told them all these months. They will finally know his lies. And, most importantly, I will warn them of the impending attack from the outside world."

"And if they don't believe you?" Timmons growled.

"They will," Winter said. "For you see, I have a secret weapon."

"And what is that?" Jinx asked.

"Why, it is young Kendra!" Winter responded.

Kendra started. "Me!? What are you talking about?"

"I may not be enough to inspire the Eens," Winter said. "For who am I but a reminder of the past? We need to show the Eens the future. And that is you, Kendra."

Kendra found herself fiddling uncomfortably with a braid as she remembered the conversation she had overheard between Uncle Griffinskitch and her father.

Bound for something . . . triumphant.

Isn't that what her uncle had said? Kendra wasn't even sure what that meant anymore. Shuuunga had said that Kendra couldn't see herself; and she'd been right about it.

Dangerous, Kendra thought. *Unpredictable. That's what the witch called me.*

"Think about it in this way," Winter said, disrupting Kendra's train of thought. "You are from Een; so you are one of the people. But you have also lived in the outside world. You are not an animal; yet, you are best friends with them. You are magical, but not quite yet a sorceress. You are blind, except you can 'see.' Why, you are many things at once. In fact, you make the perfect inspiration, Kendra. Or, put another way, a leader."

Kendra gave her braid an extra hard tug. Why was everyone trying to turn her into something she didn't want to be? First, it had been her father and the Arazeen putting her on a pedestal as a princess. And, now, here was Winter Woodsong calling her a leader.

And all I really want is to be a wizard's apprentice, Kendra thought.

But it didn't seem to matter what she wanted anymore. Before she could even speak up, the knights rose to their feet and began to shout, "Here's to Winter Woodsong and her secret weapon!"

"Spread word through every tunnel," Timmons boomed. "Tomorrow we rise . . . this year, winter comes early to the Land of Een!"

CHAPTER 31

The Elusive Emperor

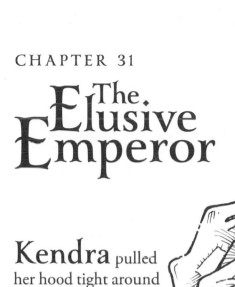

Kendra pulled her hood tight around her face and followed Winter Woodsong through a lonely tunnel. Both of them were disguised in simple brown robes that would help them blend into the crowd in Faun's End.

"Remember," Winter said, "no one must recognize you until the exact right moment."

"How will I know when that is?"

"You will know."

"And what about the others?"

"Everyone is positioned at the two tunnels that secretly open into the square. They will leap out upon my signal."

"But—"

"Now here is a girl who has faced dragon, Unger, and every other sort of obstacle," Winter chided, turning to stop

Kendra. "Surely nothing so frightening awaits you in the town square?"

"You expect me to speak like a leader," Kendra said. "I'm just a twelve-year-old girl."

"Hardly like any I have ever met," Winter said. "Tell me, child, what is bothering you?"

"Everyone has a zeen, don't they?" Kendra asked. "When I look at you, Elder Woodsong, I get the feeling of a snow-flake."

"A snowflake?" Winter chuckled. "That hardly seems inspired. I would have fancied a dandelion blossom."

Kendra sighed. That was Winter for you; always finding the tease during a serious conversation. "You know your own zeen, I know you do," Kendra pressed. "But what is mine? What do *you* see in me, Elder Woodsong?"

"Why, I see *you*, Kendra," Winter replied.

"That's not an answer!" Kendra growled in frustration.

"It's the best answer I have for someone who knows better than to ask such ridiculous questions!" Winter boomeranged. "As if it matters what I see in you! It only matters what *you* see in yourself."

"I don't want to be a leader or a princess or . . . or . . ."

"Well, then," Winter said firmly. "I suppose you should have never left Een to begin with. Just stayed at home playing with magic in your uncle's garden. But you *did* leave Een, Kendra. And you are so much more than you ever were. So come; we have work to complete."

Winter turned and Kendra knew that was the end of the conversation. They hastened to the end of the tunnel and popped out into the cellar of Luka Long-Ear's tailor shop, which was now abandoned and coated in dust. Then Winter led them into one of the backstreets and they navigated their way to the town square, where hundreds of Eens had already assembled for Burdock's weekly address.

Winter nudged her way to the front of the crowd, and Kendra followed, trying to make sense of the scene. There were the citizens of Een, who seemed mostly on edge. There were the Red Robes and the armed members of the Een Guard who were arranged around Burdock's throne in the center of the square. And then there was Burdock himself. Sitting on his throne, the paunchy emperor projected a sickening feeling that made Kendra think of a prickly fruit that was black with disease and slowly rotting away from the inside. The sensation was so strong that it made Kendra wrinkle her nose in disgust.

Then one of the Red Robes announced, "The court of Burdock Brown, Royal and Supreme Emperor of Een, is now in session."

The crowd responded with a perfunctory applause, and Burdock began to speak. "I have received some grave news," the tyrant proclaimed. "Old enemies have returned to bedevil our peaceful realm."

He paused to let the words sink in; the crowd buzzed in surprise and fear.

"Yes!" Burdock continued. "It is Gregor Griffinskitch and his traitorous niece. As we all know, they consort with Ungers, Krakes, and the other creatures of the outside world, the very creatures that would snatch us the moment we set foot beyond the magic curtain. I sealed the curtain to protect you! But do these renegades care? No! They flaunt my rules with impunity! We must protect what is precious to us: the Land of Een and its magical border."

"Alas, I'm afraid the curtain will protect us no longer," Winter Woodsong declared, now hobbling out of the crowd to stand in the empty space before Burdock's throne.

"What is this!?" Burdock snarled. "Who dares—"

"I am Winter Woodsong, the Eldest of all Eens!" came her reply, and Kendra could tell by the gasps from the crowd that the sorceress had thrown down her hood so that all could see her ancient face. At this very moment, the Knights of Winter sprang from the secret tunnels and charged into the square, weapons raised.

Kendra felt Burdock's zeen flicker with fury as he roared, "Arrest them! Arrest them now!"

Kendra could hear the soldiers in the Een Guard hesitantly raise their weapons; their zeens were beating fast and anxious.

"It's an illusion," Burdock berated the throng of spectators. "Winter Woodsong is dead!"

"Hear my voice!" Winter called.

Kendra sensed the old woman wave her staff, and then felt something soft land on her face; Winter had caused a flurry of snowflakes to flutter down from the sky.

"Behold my magic!" the sorceress cried. "Do I not seem real to you?"

More astonished gasps came from the crowd.

"All this time, I have been working with our allies," Winter continued. "The animals."

"They are not our allies!" Burdock screeched. "They are—"

"ENOUGH!" Winter cried, and Kendra started—for she had never heard such a timbre in the old woman's voice. "Burdock has ignored the outside world. I am here to tell you that danger is coming. If we are to survive we must unite with the animals."

"She lies!" Burdock accused with a stamp of his staff. "There is no danger from the outside world."

And now Kendra felt something twinge inside of her. She couldn't help thinking of her father, hiding atop his mountain. Her passion flaring, Kendra stepped forward, to stand alongside Winter, and cast down her own hood. There was a loud unified exclamation from the crowd; Kendra knew everyone was looking at her empty eyes.

"Winter Woodsong speaks the truth!" she shouted. "I am Kendra Kandlestar, and I have been in the heart of the enemy camp! The Ungers come with the ancient cauldron of Greeve to curse all of Een. They will destroy us in one fell swoop. Do not doubt the power of this dark weapon. I know its destructive magic all too well; for it has stolen my eyes."

"So . . . so you cannot see?" someone asked from the crowd. "You're blind?"

"I see now only with my magic," Kendra replied. "And what my magic sees is a contemptible scoundrel who cares for no one but himself. Burdock! Look what he's done to the Elder Stone! Turned it into a castle! Look what he's done to the animals! Turned them into slaves. And he dares to call *them* your enemy? They are here before you, prepared to defend you! They shall stand against the monsters

of the outside world. Now here is the question! Will you stand with them?"

"NEVER!" Burdock thundered.

He sent a claw of lightning sparking from his wand, but Kendra had been expecting it. Without turning, she simply raised her wand and cast an invisible shield in front of her. Burdock's lightning crackled over its surface, dissipating into nothingness.

"She did that without looking!" someone in the crowd cried, which was followed by: "She's barely more than an Eenling!" And: "Look at how long her wand is!"

One of the Red Robes now took a careful step out of the crowd. At first the zeen of the girl beneath the scarlet robe was dull and muted, but then Kendra could feel it begin to blaze, like a diamond in the light. "I stand with Winter Woodsong," the girl declared, tearing off her hood. "I stand with Kendra Kandlestar!"

This seemed to spark the crowd; many began to cheer. Then several Red Robes and members of the Een Guard began crossing over to stand with Winter's knights.

"TRAITORS!" Burdock exploded. "KILL THEM!" he screamed at his remaining forces. "KILL THEM ALL!"

But not a soul stirred. Burdock's forces were now clearly outnumbered and, for a long tense moment, the two sides just stared at each other.

"Humph," Uncle Griffinskitch finally growled. He thumped his staff against the ground, and this was enough to cause the remainder of Burdock's side to drop their weapons and wands.

"Wait a minute!" Oki suddenly cried. "Where's Burdock?"

"What do you mean?" Kendra asked. "He's right there! On his throne."

"No, he's not!" Jinx exclaimed.

Kendra suddenly realized that Burdock had somehow hidden himself from sight—a trick that had no effect on her. She could still feel the wizard's thorny presence, though, a moment later, she could feel that presence try to slip away.

"He's just invisible!" Kendra shouted. "And he's escaping!"

She sped off after the wizard's prickly zeen. Burdock turned and fired a bolt of lightning from his staff. Kendra was too flustered to react, and the bolt struck her right in the ankle, causing her to collapse into the dirt. She tried to pull herself up, but her whole leg was numb and she ended up falling again, this time face first. By the time she sorted herself out, Burdock was long gone.

"Are you okay?" Uncle Griffinskitch asked, hurrying over to inspect her leg.

"I'm fine," Kendra answered in frustration. "But Burdock's escaped."

"I have a feeling we haven't seen the last of him," Winter said calmly. "But for now, we have accomplished our goal, and that was to remove Burdock from power. His justice will come soon enough."

"He must have procured a shadow cloak," Uncle Griffinskitch surmised. "That is how he disappeared."

"But there's only one such cloak," Kendra said, suddenly worried. "If Burdock has it, that means he stole it from Lurk."

"Or the boy gave it to him," Uncle Griffinskitch suggested. "After all, he sided with Burdock in the past."

"Lurk would never give up his cloak—ever," Kendra insisted. "Where is he, then? Do you think Burdock hurt him?"

"And what do you care for that foul boy?" Uncle Griffinskitch growled.

"I . . . I'm not so sure he's foul," Kendra stammered. "Not anymore."

"It seems to me you have come to care for that boy," Winter ventured.

Kendra could feel her cheeks flushing red as she quickly pulled away to pluck at a braid. The old sorceress was right, as she almost always was.

CHAPTER 32

A Council of War

It's no quick task to clean one's house. You can take out the garbage, open the windows, and let in the fresh air, but nothing's truly clean until you sweep out all those dusty corners. Cleaning up the Land of Een was no different. It was true that Burdock had been deposed, but there was still a lot of work to do. The first order of business was to free all those imprisoned in the dungeons of the Elder Stone. Then messengers were dispatched across the countryside to spread news of Winter's return and to declare that all Een animals were now officially free. The Dragon Jaw Mines were closed and the former slaves began making their way back to their homes, including Oki's family. Within a week, the natural order of things had been more or less restored to Een—but for how long was as good as anyone's guess.

"One fight is over," Winter said. "But a war is coming."

And so the old sorceress called for an important confer-ence to be held inside the Elder Stone. Such meetings had once been reserved for the seven elders who officially sat on the council, but Burdock had long ago dissolved the council and there was no time to properly vote for a new one. Instead, Winter named an emergency council consisting of the most trusted wizards and knights—including Kendra and her com-panions.

"I can't say I care much for Burdock's taste in decorating," Winter announced as everyone gathered in the council cham-bers. "I much prefer the Elder Stone without all the makeup."

Even though Kendra could not see the adornments that the old sorceress was referring to, she could sense how the Elder Stone had changed under Burdock's rule. Once a sparse and solemn place, the Elder Stone was festooned with lavish carpets, garish tapestries, and bejeweled statues—many of which, as Kendra was told, depicted Burdock himself in arro-gant poses.

"It is a pity, and something we will have to rectify," Winter remarked. "But for now, we have more pressing issues to con-sider. Even though we have freed Een from Burdock's tyranny, an even greater threat now awaits us: The Ungers. They march towards Een, and we suspect that the other monster tribes will follow."

"Before we formalize any strategy we must accumulate as much information as possible about our belligerent foes," Professor Bumblebean said. "What are their numbers? And where exactly will they attack?"

"That depends on where Lurk made his entry into the Land of Een," Uncle Griffinskitch pondered, scratching his whiskery beard. "Remember, the Ungers are following his magical trail to our border."

"I will lead some scouts into the outside world," Jinx volunteered. "Then we can see firsthand where the monster armies are amassing."

"Your bravery is to be commended," Winter said. "But we have more magical means at our disposal."

"Indeed," said Enid Evermoon the sorceress, who had been one of those recently freed from Burdock's dungeons. "I propose that we call forth the magic orb. It is certainly precious magic, but if ever there was a dire time, it is now."

Everyone agreed with this course of action, and so Winter hobbled towards the small pool that stood in the very center of the chamber. Raising her withered hands above her head, the old sorceress began to hum from deep within her throat.

It was hard to imagine such a rich and vibrant sound coming from one so tiny and frail; it was so sonorous that it reminded Kendra of the Unger's ceremonial dance. Then, as Winter's voice grew louder, the pool began to bubble, like a cauldron over a fire—and a glimmering crystal ball shot into the air, riding on a jet of water. Kendra had seen the orb once before—and now it sparkled in her mind exactly as she remembered it: round and numinous, and crackling with light.

"Who awakens me on this dark eve?" the orb inquired, spinning calmly in the air. "Another has been trying to pry and thieve. But I rise only for one whose heart is pure. That is the secret of Een magic; this much is sure."

Burdock! Kendra thought. *He must have tried to awaken the orb.*

"We need your guidance, O Gracious One," Winter told the orb. "The monster tribes have gathered their armies and are poised to destroy the Land of Een. We teeter on the edge of ruin."

The orb spun slowly, considering. Then it said, "The pathway to victory is not easily seen. Make the wrong choice and it will be the end of Een. The monsters march on their determined course, their numbers united in a single force."

"They no longer war against each other?" Winter asked, concern rising in her voice.

"Coerced and cajoled by the brazen one—they do not rest until her purpose done," the orb replied, whirling in the air.

"Shuuunga!" Kendra cried out. "That's who the orb means!"

"Yes, I know, child—shush," Winter chastised. Then she asked the orb, "Where will they attack?"

"From the north the beasts do approach; the border at Clovinstand, they try to broach," the orb answered. "In three evenings they will be in sight, and descend upon Een with all their might."

"How can we defeat them?" Kendra blurted.

"Kendra!" Uncle Griffinskitch scolded. "It is not your place to—"

A snap of electricity crackled over the surface of the orb, so loud that the old wizard went silent. Kendra could sense the orb whirring in her direction; it felt like it was glaring at her.

"It is hard to know the path ahead; what will lead to hope or unfathomable dread," the orb proclaimed in its unvaried tone. "Darkness is coming; it takes deadly aim. It will only be vanquished by magic's flame. Now I have said all I know; return to my slumber, I do go."

Then, with a quiet whoosh, the enchanted sphere retreated to its pool. For a moment everyone just stared at the water in awe.

"Yeesh," Ratchet said eventually. "I think you offended it, Kendra."

"It talks in riddles," Kendra fumed. "Call it back, Elder Woodsong! Why can't it just tell us what to do?"

"It does not work that way," Winter explained patiently. "The orb merely senses what might happen. You should know enough about Een magic by now to not ask such questions."

Kendra sighed. "If only we could find Lurk. He's from the future; he knows how all of this turns out."

"Humph," Uncle Griffinskitch muttered. "I, for one, will not put the fate of Een in his hands. That boy knows how to look after one thing—himself. Leave him to hide in the shadows, with Burdock."

"What if he isn't hiding?" Kendra said. "What if Burdock captured him? Or worse?"

"I understand you are concerned for the boy," Winter said gently. "But we have no time to deal with ifs. We must make our plans now, with the knowledge at hand."

"The orb said the monster army will strike at Clovinstand in three nights," Uncle Griffinskitch said. "That means we should send every able-bodied Een to protect the northern border."

"That is not our only choice," spoke Hektor Hootall, a rather shy and timid wizard who had been quiet up till now. "Perhaps we should consider an alternative. Evacuation."

"Abandon Een?" Kendra cried. "Never!"

An argument now erupted in the council chamber. Many Eens, such as Hektor, were in favor of hiding or fleeing. Others thought the "flame" the orb had mentioned might be some enchanted weapon that could be used against the monsters—but what this was, nobody had any idea. In the end, they put it to an official vote and it was agreed that they would stand and fight.

"How will we muster an army that could face such a monstrous force?" Hektor asked.

"We are not without friends," Kendra said. "I can call my friend, the peryton, for help. I survived the Rumble Pit with him; he would surely stand with us."

"Bid him then," Winter said. "If we are to have any chance of defeating the Unger witch, we will need all the help we can get."

CHAPTER 33

The Battle Begins

Kendra stood atop the ancient tower of Clovinstand, the night breeze teasing her two braids. The tower, and the town for which it was named, lingered at the edge of a gloomy forest known as Fledgling Wood. The trees cast an imposing energy, but it was the landscape in front of Kendra that had her attention. Stretching before her was a long plain. Then came the magic curtain, invisible but strong, Een's most precious defense. The plain continued on the other side of the curtain, vast and empty—though Kendra knew it would not be that way for long. Somewhere out there, Shuuunga's army was amassing. Ungers, Krakes, Orrids, Izzards, and Goojuns—the enormous armies of each tribe, all assembled as one. Kendra could feel their zeens, thousands of them, piping hot and ready to wreak havoc.

Below her, at the base of the tower, was another set of zeens. These ones were agitated and flickering: the army of Een. How small and insignificant they seemed! Eens had journeyed from every corner of the land to fight, but Kendra couldn't help wondering if they would be of any use when the battle started. What did her people know of war? Most of the time, the rain clouds were enough to chase them away.

Then again, I don't know if I will be much help either, Kendra fretted.

Just stay on the tower and out of the fray, her uncle advised through her wand, as if he could sense her panic from his position on the ground below. *It will help you focus.*

Kendra wasn't so sure. She cast her feelings upwards into the sky. Three nights ago, after the meeting in the Elder Stone, she had sent out her magic call for the peryton, but so far there was no sign of the magnificent flying stag.

"I guess this is it," Kendra murmured as Oki and Jinx came to stand beside her at the edge of the tower. "Tonight, help or no help, the battle begins."

Then, as if in agreement, a low, long sound reverberated across the plains. It was followed by another, then another.

"The drums of Unger," Kendra gasped.

And now she could hear the grisly army begin to march. There were so many of them that the very ground began to quake. A murmur of trepidation rippled through the Eens below. Kendra knew most of them wanted to flee—and she didn't blame them.

"Th-that drumbeat," Oki stammered. "It's the thunddrum!"

"They play it for all of Een," Kendra said in a chilling realization. "No mercy! No quarter!"

"EEEEEK!" Oki cried.

Ratchet poked his head up from the stairwell below. "No time for *eekitis* now, my young apprentice. Time to help me and Professor B. warm up the cannons! We'll show them beasties a surprise or two!"

Just hearing the raccoon's voice made Kendra feel better. Ratchet had stocked the bottom part of the tower with all sorts of makeshift weapons that would fire his and Oki's infamous magic powders—*Snot Shot, Itch Twitch*, and even *Snore Galore*. But it was Ratchet's unabashed confidence that gave Kendra the biggest boost.

"If every Een was like Ratchet, we'd win for sure," she told Jinx as Oki scampered down below.

"He's got pluck," Jinx admitted. "I, for one, will think of Clovin Cloudfoot. He was the first captain of the Een Guard and the legends say that here, at this very tower, he stood against the Wizard Greeve and the first monster army. I too was once captain of the Een Guard; and so I will honor Cloudfoot by fighting with all my courage."

Only a few moments later, the drums stopped and Kendra realized that the enormous force had almost reached the curtain. Then she detected a zeen stride ahead to separate itself from the throng.

"Shuuunga!" Kendra uttered.

"She's stabbing her staff into the ground, right at the base of the curtain," Jinx told Kendra.

The Unger witch began to chant, so loudly and clearly that her rasping voice sailed across the wind. Then, all at once, Kendra heard a fizzling sound.

"She's tearing the curtain!" Jinx screamed.

The Eens began to chatter in fear. In the next moment there was a dramatic crackle—and Kendra knew the curtain was gone.

"She didn't just rip it!" Kendra exclaimed. "She pulled it down! The whole curtain!"

The only thing now standing between the Eens and the monstrous swarm was the meadow. Shuuunga lifted her head and emitted a terrifying, spine-chilling war whoop. Her warriors responded with a cry of their own—and charged. The pounding of their feet against the ground was deafening. To you or me, the stampeding monsters might have looked like an enormous flood of claws, tusks, horns and teeth, but they painted a different picture inside Kendra. The army felt like a roaring inferno, one that would scorch everything in its path.

Suddenly, a singular zeen danced out from the Een side to stand before this oncoming surge of fire. It was Winter Woodsong; Kendra could tell by that feeling of a snowflake, a snowflake that was so tiny and delicate that it seemed as if it must melt against the blazing heat of the monsters.

But Winter did not melt. Kendra could picture the whole scene as it unfolded below her. Winter

249

thrust her staff upwards and, in an impossibly loud voice, shouted, "FOR EEN!" And now a gale of freezing wind and snow unleashed from her magic Eenwood, sweeping upon the monsters with such potency that it sent many of them—even the gigantic Ungers—sprawling to the ground in a clatter of armor and dropped weapons.

When the old sorceress finally lowered her staff, it seemed to Kendra that the entire monster army had been flattened—at least temporarily. Kendra could sense Winter's snowflake flutter and fade, her magic taxed to near exhaustion. And yet Kendra knew why the ancient woman had taken such action. She had meant to inspire her army—and it had worked.

"FOR EEN!" Jinx yelled.

With these words, the entire Een force charged across the meadow, straight towards the monstrous rabble that seemed more than just a little befuddled. Kendra heard Shuuunga let loose another war cry of her own, snapping her warriors to attention. Weapons were quickly snatched up and the savage beasts continued their charge, head on towards the Eens.

The battle had begun.

As the two sides collided on the field in front of the tower, Kendra's ears were blitzed with grunts, growls, screams, and shouts. Weapons clanged and bolts of Een magic sizzled. Ratchet and Oki began firing their cannons, sending up clouds of smoke. Yes, Kendra could hear, smell, and feel the battle. She just couldn't see it—not with her eyes anyway. For the tiny Een girl, everything was just a bedazzling whirl of zeens.

"Are you okay?" Jinx asked, clutching her arm.

"Y-yes, I'm fine," Kendra lied.

"Good—stay here," Jinx warned. And then she launched herself from the top of the tower and torpedoed into the fray.

Kendra felt the grasshopper become engulfed by a tumultuous blur of zeens. She sensed Winter's snowflake flicker somewhere in the throng and then the whiskery shape of Uncle Griffinskitch, too. But she soon lost track of them.

Clear the clutter, came the sound of her uncle's voice through her wand. *Feel what you want to feel.*

But there's so much going on!

Humph! I hadn't noticed.

Kendra took a deep breath, suppressing her panic, and tried to tune her mind. *Feel what I want to feel,* she told herself.

Soon, the jumble of zeens before her began to make sense. She honed in on her friends, and the enemies surrounding them. An Unger was lunging at her uncle from behind. Kendra fired a crackle of lightning, nailing the beast just as he was about to land a crushing blow. The enormous creature stumbled backwards, only to be immediately struck by a cloud of sparkling dust that sent him crashing to the ground. There he lay, as if paralyzed. Then, of all things, he began to snore.

Not paralyzed, Kendra realized. *Asleep!* "Good shot!" she called down to her friends below.

And so the battle raged on. Kendra had been in these situations before; indeed, she had fought in the depths of the Rumble Pit and on the high walls of her father's city. But this time was different. It wasn't just the fact that she didn't have her eyes. Nor was it that this battle was so much larger in scale and scope.

It was the place. This was Een. This was *home.* And now Kendra came to realize this certain truth: even the tiniest, most timid creature has the fiercest desire to protect its own.

With her beloved land under siege, this desire had sprung to life inside of Kendra—and inside each and every other Een, too.

Who were the heroes amongst them? All of them. For here not only fought Kendra's uncle and the other great wizards, Winter Woodsong, Enid Evermoon, and Hektor Hootall, but the simplest of folk: the tailor Luka Long-Ears, the baker Gilburt Green, and the weaver Willow Windfingers. Sure enough, Timmons Thunderclaws, Mercy Moonwing, and the other Knights of Winter battled bravely—but so did those who had never before raised a weapon: Obyrt Openheart, Lissel Lightfoot, and many more. Here fought Kendra's closest friends: Oki, Ratchet, Jinx and Professor Bumblebean, but so too did those Eens that were complete and utter strangers to her. Even those who had been Red Robes, working for Burdock, fought. At this moment, they were all united by a single cause: to save Een.

Yet not even the stoutest of hearts can always vanquish the sheer power of muscle and limb. As valiantly as the Een army fought, they were slowly and surely being pushed backwards, across the field until they fought at the very foot of the tower. Then, suddenly, Timmons unleashed an agonizing wail from below: "NOOOOO!"

His cry was like a switch, for at that instant the entire Een army just turned and fled, leaving Kendra alone and helpless atop her tower—and completely surrounded by the monster swarm.

CHAPTER 34

Winter's Snowflake Rises

It was like being stranded on an island in the midst of a hurricane. On every side were the barbaric soldiers of Shuuunga's army, snarling, growling, and pounding at the tower walls. Many of the creatures, especially the flea-like Orrids, began scaling the steep slopes. Kendra desperately fired her wand, sending more than one tumbling down—but there were just too many.

Kendra! came the sound of Uncle Griffinskitch's voice through her wand. *There's an escape tunnel beneath the tower that leads into the forest. We'll rally there—the professor knows.*

An Unger throwing sword whistled past Kendra's shoulder, shredding her sleeve and drawing blood. It wasn't a serious injury, but the pain was so shocking that she stumbled backwards, right into the arms of Ratchet, who had come to fetch her.

"Time to skedaddle!" the raccoon cried.

Ratchet grabbed Kendra's wrist and led her down the spiraling stone steps. There were only windows in the top part of the tower—these were the slots where Ratchet had pointed his cannons—but the Orrids had now reached these from the outside and Kendra could hear them spilling through in swarms.

"Hurry!" Kendra screamed.

They reached the next level of the tower and Ratchet quickly latched a door behind them, leaving the Orrids to crash into it from the other side. They rattled the handle, shrieking in fury.

"That won't hold them long," Ratchet said.

They dashed down the remaining steps to the bottom of the tower, where Oki and the professor were anxiously waiting. They had already barred the entrance to the outside, but Shuuunga's warriors were thumping at the door with such wrath that Kendra knew it would only be a matter of moments before they tore it asunder.

"We must make haste," Professor Bumblebean urged.

He yanked open the hatch to the tunnel below and scrambled down the rickety ladder with Oki and Kendra right on

his heels. Then Kendra realized that Ratchet wasn't with them. She could hear him fiddling with the Snifferoo in front of the door, which (as she could also hear) was buckling and twisting on its hinges from the monstrous assault.

The Orrids had already broken through the door above; Kendra could sense them skittering down the steps towards them.

"Ratchet!" Kendra cried, popping her head back through the hatch. "What are you doing!?"

"Leaving a surprise!" he replied, as he scampered across the floor and squeezed past Kendra. "Can you use your magic to turn on the Snifferoo?"

"Which smell do you want?"

"All of them!"

Just then, the tower door burst apart in an explosion of splinters and mangled braces. A maelstrom of monsters thundered towards them. Kendra slammed the trapdoor shut, but not before sending a zap of magic to detonate the Snifferoo. The resulting boom was so cataclys-

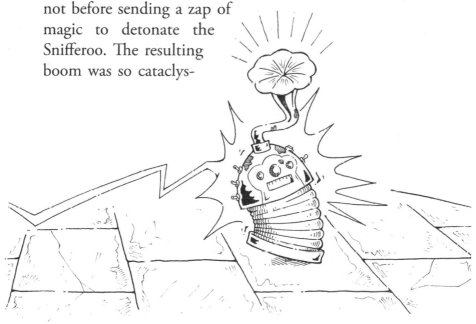

mic that the whole tower shook, down to its very foundations. Kendra tumbled from the ladder, taking her companions with her. They landed in a tangled heap on the tunnel floor.

For a moment they just lay there in silence. The riotous sounds from above had come to an abrupt stop.

"What just happened?" Kendra groaned.

"We added a magnifier to the Snifferoo," Oki explained, as he wriggled out from beneath Ratchet.

"What exactly does that mean?" Professor Bumblebean wondered.

Ratchet beamed triumphantly and said, "Biggest. Stink. Bomb. Ever."

A putrid waft now reached Kendra's nostrils. "Ugh," she gasped.

She could sense the dazed and woozy monsters above begin to pick themselves up. As they stomped around the debris, giant clumps of dirt began raining down on the Eens.

"Come on," Kendra said, leading the way down the tunnel. "Let's get out of here."

It didn't take them long to reach the end of the crude passage. Kendra could detect Eens ahead—the remnants of the army, hiding in Fledgling Wood. She thrust aside the bushes that disguised the tunnel exit, only to be struck directly in the chest by a needle-sharp point.

"Oh!" chirped a familiar voice. "It's *you!*"

"Mercy?" Kendra asked, staggering out of the tunnel to collapse in front of the fidgety hummingbird. "You have a sharp beak, you know!"

"I thought you were an Unger sneak attack," Mercy explained. "So sorry . . . er . . ."

"Kendra!"

"Oh, dear me!" Mercy hummed. "I can't remember anything."

"Maybe you have *forgetabetes*," Ratchet suggested as he, Oki, and Professor Bumblebean crawled out of the tunnel.

Kendra's mind slowly absorbed the state of the Eens around her. She couldn't see their injuries or wounds, but their zeens told the story well enough; they were faint, like stars at dawn. Jinx's was the brightest, though little did Kendra know that one of the grasshopper's antennae had been lopped clean in half, and that she had one arm in a sling. What hadn't been injured, however, was her tongue.

"Well, well, well," Jinx grunted. "Looks like we have *Professor Bumblescream* and the whole gang of misfits together again."

"Just like old times," Ratchet said. "How are we doing?"

"The usual," Jinx huffed.

"EEK!" Oki cried.

"What now?" Kendra asked.

"Er . . . nothing," Oki stammered. "It's just that . . . well, our usual is *terrible.*"

"Humph," Uncle Griffinskitch grunted, arriving on the scene. There was something in that humph that caused Kendra to tug at a braid.

"What is it?" she asked.

"Come," he said softly.

He took her by the hand and led her deeper into forest. The others followed, and they soon they came upon a small hollow. It was here where the majority of the Een army had congregated and at one end, leaning against a tree trunk and sobbing as if he was no more than an Eenling, was the mighty badger, Timmons Thunderclaws. He was cradling someone within his mighty arms, but the zeen was so pale and vague that Kendra could barely discern it.

Then, with a sudden chill, she realized why the Een army had retreated so suddenly. The zeen within Timmons's arms was a snowflake. Winter Woodsong had fallen.

Kendra rushed to the older sorceress and fumbled to find her hand. It was limp and cold.

"Ah, Kendra," Winter greeted, barely in a whisper.

"How could this happen?" Kendra demanded between her tears. "Why didn't you protect her?" she growled at her uncle.

"She was not even struck," the old wizard said, shuffling up from behind. "Her magic is simply exhausted."

"I don't believe you! It was Shuuunga, wasn't it?"

"No," Mercy said, fluttering down alongside Kendra. "The monsters seem to be only trying to capture or injure . . . in fact, it's like they're purposely trying *not* to kill us."

What do you mean?" Kendra asked intently. "That doesn't make . . ."

"Shuuunga wants as few casualties as possible," Uncle Griffinskitch explained. "The more of us left standing, the more of us will be transformed into monstrous forms once she resurrects the curse."

No mercy, no quarter, Kendra thought. "She has thought of everything!" she rued.

"The cauldron," Winter rasped. "You must find it."

Yes! Kendra thought. Amidst the chaos she had completely forgotten about it.

"Mercy . . . to the skies," Winter coughed, her words weak and broken. "Seek that vile weapon. Make . . . all speed. When you . . . when you have found it . . . tell . . . Kendra."

"Me!?" Kendra cried. "What about Uncle Griffinskitch? What about you, Elder Woodsong?"

"My season is over," Winter wheezed. "You, Kendra. You . . . will see the way."

"The way to what!?"

"Everything . . . is dark," the old woman said. "But *you* will see the way."

"What are you talking about?" Kendra asked, gripping Winter's hand.

"The darkness," Winter gasped. "It is your teacher. Not . . . your master."

After hearing these words, Kendra had the feeling of a snowflake blinking out of existence—but for just a moment. In the next instant, Kendra felt it more strongly than ever. It was as if it had suddenly burst free from sort of prison, for now it blazed in Kendra's mind with such radiance that she felt overwhelmed.

"She's alive!" Kendra cried.

"Kendra," Uncle Griffinskitch said gently. "What do you mean? She . . . she's gone."

But the snowflake seemed so vivid in Kendra's mind. She smiled at it, and somehow it seemed to smile back—then it whisked away, free and strong, beyond Kendra's imagination . . . and out of the living world.

CHAPTER 35

Help from Above

It is impossible to describe the sensation that Kendra felt. She was wracked with grief, yet somehow alive with possibility at the same time. She tugged at a braid and listened as Oki described a miraculous scene: Timmons placed Winter's body on the ground, only to have the roots of the surrounding trees emerge from the earth, embrace the old sorceress, and pull her into the soil.

"To cherish her evermore," Uncle Griffinskitch said, his voice hoarse with sadness.

And yet, the hard truth of battle is that it leaves no time to mourn, nor a moment to reflect. Even as the glow of Winter's zeen faded from Kendra's mind, an Unger's roar came from the edge of the woods, followed by the panicked shriek of an Een.

261

"Shuuunga's beasts are routing the forest," Uncle Griffin-skitch declared. "Our respite is over. Mercy, embark! Find the cauldron, as Winter Woodsong said."

"I will not let her down," the hummingbird declared, flitting away into the sky.

"What are we going to do?" Kendra asked.

"We are the Knights of Winter," Timmons proclaimed. "As long as I have life in these ancient bones, I shall fight!"

"And me alongside you," Jinx said.

"Aye," Uncle Griffinskitch said, stamping his staff against the forest floor. "Here is where we make our stand."

Now the old wizard became like a general, rallying the remaining Eens in the hollow. Kendra clenched her wand tightly, standing between Oki and her uncle. With her magical sight, she began to sense the approaching warriors. They were too many to count, but even more terrifying was the fact that they were coming from every direction.

We're surrounded! she told her uncle.

I know, came his reply. *There is no retreat for us this time.*

Then, suddenly, Kendra detected a peculiar zeen from high above. Was it Mercy? No, it was someone else; someone much bigger. It evoked in her mind the strangest of shapes, like a feather sprouting from a branch.

"The peryton!" Kendra exclaimed in sudden comprehension. "It's Prince!"

"Thank rhubarb!" Oki squealed.

"It's just not him—he's brought his entire herd!" Kendra said as she felt more zeens approach. "And—oh!"

"What is it?" Uncle Griffinskitch asked.

Kendra furled her brow. "It's like . . . it's like the perytons have *riders*."

"I thought perytons wouldn't allow that," Oki declared.

"It's true . . . but these perytons have riders all the same," Kendra insisted. "And they're . . . Eens! No, wait a minute. Some are . . . Krakes? Ungers?"

"My word!" Professor Bumblebean exclaimed. "That means they are Arazeens!"

He was right, Kendra realized. Did that mean her father had changed his mind? Was he with them? She cast out her mind to find the king's zeen—but at that moment the hollow sprang to life with battle. In came the monsters, swinging and slashing, only to be met instantly by the majestic perytons in a surge of antlers, hooves, and wings. The Arazeen leapt from the peryton backs to join the fray and, emboldened by these reinforcements, the Eens gave a cry of jubilation and began to fight with rediscovered vigor.

Everything was now a confused jumble. If you had been there, you would have thought it was the strangest assortments of soldiers, and not guessed whose side was whose. In one corner there was Een against Unger, in another Unger against peryton, and in yet another Goojun against Goojun. And it was all over in what seemed like an instant. The next thing Kendra knew, Shuuunga's warriors had retreated, leaving the Eens to greet their new allies.

"Oh, Prince!" Kendra exclaimed, running up to embrace the mighty peryton. "You came."

"Of course, Arinotta," the peryton replied, using his pet name for her. "You called me, after all. Ah! It is as I have heard: you have suffered the dark magic of the Shard."

"My eyes are gone," Kendra acknowledged. "But do not despair for me, old friend. I know your beauty still; it shines brightly as ever."

"Then you truly are a sorceress of Een," Prince said, nuzzling her cheek. "And I have brought you something, Arinotta. A gift."

He stepped aside, leaving Kendra to contemplate a zeen lingering hesitantly at the edge of the hollow. It cast a familiar feeling inside of Kendra, though one she couldn't quite put her finger on. Then it occurred to her.

"Father?" she called.

"Yes," he replied nervously. "I am here. Can you ever forgive me, child?"

Kendra replied by rushing forward and throwing herself into his arms. He squeezed her so close that she could feel the moisture of his tears.

"You came," Kendra said. "Whatever changed your mind?"

"It was you," he said gently. "You were right, Kendra. Arazeen was not . . . Arazeen at all. How could it be without you?"

Kendra realized why she hadn't been able to recognize his zeen. He had changed. Back in the City on the Storm, he had seemed like a frail and withering flower, but now it was like he was a bud, opening up from a winter's hibernation.

"There's so much to talk about, Kendra," her father said. "But we'll have to leave that for a quieter moment."

"Tell me one thing at least," Kendra said. "How did you come with the perytons?"

"I can explain," Prince replied. "When I heard your call, I asked my father, the great king of Mount Zephyr, for permission to lead the strongest of our herd to assist Een. With his blessing, we soared towards your beckoning. Along the way, we happened upon this strange collection of Eens and beasts, and so made landfall to investigate. Imagine my surprise to learn that the leader of this strange multitude was none other than the father of my old friend! We learned our purpose was one and the same; and so we carried them here."

"I thought perytons didn't allow riders," Kendra said.

"They do when their leader commands them to do so!" Prince snorted.

A few more perytons now entered the hollow, carrying the young and the old of the Arazeen.

"No one was left behind," Krimson explained to Kendra. "They were circling until it was safe to land."

"Kendra!" Charla called, bounding over. "I've made it to Een! Now you can show me all of the wonders you told me about."

"Maybe tomorrow, Little One," Kendra replied with a sad smile. "Today, we're a little busy."

Then, as if to prove this point, Mercy came swooping into the hollow. She was in a fluster—Kendra realized it didn't help the little bird to see Eens standing alongside monsters.

"They're on our side," Uncle Griffinskitch assured the hummingbird. "Now, quickly, Moonwing! Tell us your news."

"I found the cauldron!" Mercy sputtered, whirring excitedly in the air. "It's with a small band of monsters on the far side of Fudgling . . . I mean Fledgy . . . well, you know what I mean—*these* woods! They are carrying the cauldron straight towards Faun's End."

"Days of Een!" Uncle Griffinskitch exclaimed. "I see it all now. The entire battle was just meant to distract us. While we were busy defending Clovinstand, a secondary force was sent sneaking around the forest with the cauldron."

"It's Trooogul," Kendra realized, tugging at a braid. "I never sensed him in the battle, and now I know why. He's the one Shuuunga charged with sneaking the cauldron past us."

"What about the witch herself?" Krimson wondered. "She wasn't here in the forest."

"Humph," Uncle Griffinskitch grunted. "I suspect this attack was just a further diversion, allowing her to mobilize the rest of her army and march on Faun's End. She'll rejoin the cauldron there."

"Why wait to reach Faun's End?" Oki wondered. "Shuuunga could have just repaired the cauldron right at the border, the moment she lowered the magic curtain."

But Kendra knew what her mother was up to. Faun's End was not only the most populated place in the land, but the oldest too. Indeed, it was the symbol of everything that Kendra's people stood for. And that's why it would be in Faun's End where Shuuunga would resurrect the curse of Greeve and put an end, once and for all, to the Land of Een.

CHAPTER 36

A Duel of Wizards

Sometimes

life is like climbing a
tree. One moment
you're near the top,
enjoying the most
spectacular view—
then a branch snaps
beneath you and down
you tumble. And so it was
with Kendra. For just the
briefest flicker she had felt
that she was on top, everything
within reach. The perytons
had come to the rescue,
her father had joined her
side, and Shuuunga's army
had been repelled. And then
Mercy had delivered her news, and
Kendra was sent plunging back down to
earth.

"That's life," Uncle Griffinskitch said, as if he knew exactly
what she was thinking. "Sometimes you just pick yourself up
and begin climbing again."

"Indeed," Prince concurred, stamping one of his mighty hooves. "Come, perytons! Carry all who are fit to fight and let us speed to the Een capital!"

And so Kendra scrambled onto Prince's back, along with her uncle and father, and the mighty peryton galloped into the sky. The sun was rising (Kendra could feel the warmth on her face), but it did little to uplift her spirits. She could sense turmoil ahead and soon realized that it was just as her uncle had conjectured; while they had been busy fighting in the forest, Shuuunga had regrouped her remaining troops and laid siege to Faun's End. Much of the town was on fire, choking the sky with smoke and ash. As they neared, it became difficult to breathe. Prince fought bravely to stay aloft, but next came a wave of spears and arrows. One of the missiles struck the majestic stag in the wing and he began to plunge downwards in a dizzying spiral.

"Fur and feathers!" Prince cried. "Hang on!"

He struck the ground in more of a crash than a landing. Kendra, her father, and Uncle Griffinskitch were sent tumbling from the peryton's back, only to find themselves smack in the middle of the chaos that was now Faun's End. Flames crackled, monsters roared, and Eens screamed as they fled for their lives. Kendra leapt to her feet and sent a zap from her wand directly at an oncoming Izzard. Her magic, weakened by exhaustion, did nothing more than momentarily stun the snarling creature—but it was enough to let her dash past.

"Wait!" Krimson cried.

Kendra didn't heed his call. She could sense that the cauldron was somewhere ahead, and so charged alone into the smoky streets, leaving her father, uncle, and the rest of her companions to battle the swarming monsters—and hopefully

distract them. Navigating the
bedlam, Kendra finally
reached the middle of
the town square. Here,
on the very platform
where Burdock's throne
had once stood, was the
cauldron of Greeve. The
energy it emanated was
enough to bring Kendra to a
halt. The urn seemed to have a

life of its own, throbbing impatiently, as if anxious to receive
its final missing piece.

I can't let that happen, Kendra thought, pestering a braid.

Trooogul suddenly entered the square. He seemed fraught
with purpose and Kendra realized at once that it was because
of the Shard. Trooogul was clutching it in one of his enormous claws.

"Youzum!" the Unger growled. "No should comezum here!"

"Why?" Kendra lashed out. "Would you not have me witness your grand moment as you become the hero of all of
Unger?"

"He will be a hero indeed," crackled a voice from behind
Trooogul. "Not just for Unger. But for all of us."

Shuuunga swept forward to stand beside Trooogul. Her
breathing was broken and uneven, telling Kendra that the
witch's body had paid a terrible price in the battle at Clovinstand. And yet her zeen still flared with a wild and dangerous
energy that caused Kendra to shudder anew. And now
Shuuunga advanced towards the platform, just in front of the
cauldron, and began to chant. She slammed her long, tree-like

staff against the ground with such a resounding boom that it almost made Kendra lose her feet. For an instant the air crackled and snapped.

What is going on? Kendra thought desperately.

And then, somehow, she knew. Shuuunga had raised the magic curtain, once again sealing the Land of Een from the outside world. But this time the magic wasn't to keep the monsters out—it was to keep the Eens *in*. Every single creature now contained within that enchanted barrier, no matter how secret the nook or cranny they sought for hiding, would know the curse of the cauldron.

"Trooogul!" Shuuunga bellowed in her Unger voice. "Itzum time. Placezum Shard!"

He had already scrambled onto the stage, but before he could plunge the Shard into the cauldron's waiting gap, Kendra fired a zap with her wand, hitting her Unger brother with such force that he was sent tumbling backwards.

"Kendra! What have you done!?" Shuuunga screeched.

The witch lurched around the platform, Kendra right on her heels, where Trooogul lay sprawled on the ground. He had only been stunned, but the Shard had rolled out of his claw; Kendra sensed it brooding in the dust. She thought of snatching it—but now a new zeen appeared in the square and it caused Kendra to freeze.

Burdock. He was wearing the shadow cloak, but that didn't matter to Kendra. She could see him plain enough by the black and thorny feeling that he projected. And now he scooped up the Shard and cackled as the stone's magic began to surge through his decrepit body.

"What are you doing, Burdock?" Kendra cried. "You can't use the Shard! It will destroy you! Trust me; it nearly destroyed me once."

"Then it shall now have the chance to finish the job!" he screamed, discharging a gush of black fire.

Instinctively, Kendra shuddered—but the attack never reached her. It took a moment for her to realize that Shuuunga had launched herself into the path of the dark magic. Kendra could hear Burdock's lightning blaze across her mother's body, like a predator feasting on its prey. Shrieking in pain, the Unger witch collapsed to the ground in a smoldering heap.

"What is this!?" Burdock snarled. "An Unger saves an Een?"

Of course, he did not know who Shuuunga really was—but at that moment Kendra did, more than ever. Her mother had saved her.

"Nozum!" Trooogul sobbed. He had recovered from Kendra's earlier blow and now she could sense him stumble forward to cradle Shuuunga's body in his arms.

"How touching," Burdock mocked. "Who knew Ungers were capable of such affection?"

"I did," Kendra murmured.

"You!?" Burdock spat, turning his attention towards her. "You know NOTHING!"

Kendra directed her empty eyes at Burdock, but her ears were listening to Trooogul tug Shuuunga's shattered body away. *Save her, Trooogul,* Kendra thought. *Save our mother.*

Their escape went unnoticed by Burdock; or perhaps he simply didn't care. "You stupid, braided brat," he croaked. "You think you are so clever! You don't even understand what is going on here!"

"What do you mean?" Kendra asked.

"Imbecile!" Burdock boomed. "Repairing the cauldron won't resurrect the curse! *It will reverse it!*"

He might as well have dropped a boulder on top of Kendra. "Wh-what?" she sputtered. "H-how can that be? What are you talking about?"

"Why, your little sweetheart told me," Burdock chuckled. "Lurk! What a pitiful little toad. I caught him sneaking back into Een, and he lasted but a few hours in my torture chamber before spilling the entire story. He knows if the cauldron is repaired that it will result in your greatest triumph. For the longest time, he was trying to stop you—but it seems you have wormed your way into what's left of his feeble heart, Kandlestar. Oh, how he cried out in devotion for you!"

"Where is he?" Kendra demanded.

"Right where he belongs—rotting away in my dungeons!" Burdock chortled.

"But Winter Woodsong freed everyone," Kendra said. "He wasn't there."

"Perhaps that old biddy isn't so powerful as you think," Burdock spat. "But it hardly matters now. She can't help you, anymore, Kandlestar. Oh, how I've waited for this moment . . . to destroy you."

"Humph. You will have to wait a little longer."

Uncle Griffinskitch's hunched and crippled body was incapable of a strut, but Kendra would have never known it by the old wizard's zeen. From the point of view of her magical sight, he emerged from the confusing haze of battle like a giant. And now she used this same magic to watch the two wizards duel.

Hidden by the shadow cloak, Burdock fired dark lightning, but Uncle Griffinskitch repelled it with a skillful twirl of his long staff, sending the magic back to engulf Burdock in a spectrum of white light. For a moment, Burdock seemed ensnared in this enchanted net—Kendra could feel his zeen wriggling—but then, swinging the Shard as if it were a blade, the detestable wizard sliced his way to freedom and began scuttling across the square.

Kendra, help me, Uncle Griffinskitch urged through her wand. *I can't see h—*

Before he could finish, Burdock battered him from behind with a bolt of lightning that sent him spinning across the square as if he were nothing more than a puff of dandelion.

"Uncle Griffinskitch!" Kendra screamed.

She raced towards him, but Burdock struck again, this time sending forth an enormous ball of black fire that walloped the ground in front of her like a cannonball.

Kendra was thrown back amidst a shower of gravel and debris, her ears ringing.

Burdock seemed larger than life now, his zeen burning an image in Kendra's mind that looked like a giant, thorny weed towering over the town square. It was as if he had opened his heart to the Shard's poison—and it had granted him power beyond reckoning. He began blasting indiscriminately at anything that moved; Een or monster, it did not seem to matter. Buildings and trees exploded all about as he chortled in unabashed delight.

"HEED ME!" Burdock screamed, his voice seeming somehow amplified, as if it was coming from a thousand Burdocks instead of one. "NOW, ALL THE WORLD SHALL FEEL THE TERROR OF MY MIGHT!"

Kendra's mind was a whirl of confusion. She could sense no trace of her uncle. In desperation, she called for him through her wand. Then something fluttered down and landed against her cheek. She went to brush it away, only to realize it was a wisp of long white beard—all that was left of Uncle Griffinskitch.

CHAPTER 37

A Spark of Magic

Weeping,
Kendra fled the carnage,
stumbling through the
wreckage of Faun's End without direction. Her uncle was
gone, and she had no idea
what had become of the
rest of her companions. As
far as she knew, they had all
been claimed by the battle.
Eventually, Kendra collided into a wall
and realized that she had reached the
library. It had always been one of her favorite
places in Een, but the once-magnificent structure
had been so ravaged by the Shard's virulent power
that it was now nothing more than a mutilated
shell. Kendra clambered through one of the
giant, gaping holes that pitted the walls. She
could immediately sense the disarray. The smell of
charred and burning trees filled the air, as did the sound of
burning pages fluttering to the ground.

Then Kendra heard a stifled sob and she realized that she
wasn't the only one to seek refuge amidst the broken boughs

and fallen trees. She cast out her weary mind and found the zeen of her brother. She pressed ahead, into the refuse, and discovered the mighty Unger leaning against a stump. And now Kendra noticed a second zeen, this one faint and flickering. It was her mother, lying next to Trooogul. Kendra hurried forward and grasped at the witch's leathery claws.

"Is it true?" Kendra sobbed. "About the cauldron? Why didn't you tell me?"

"Too dangerous," Shuuunga croaked, struggling to speak. "I deceived them . . . all monsters. If even one Unger had discovered the plan . . . they would . . . have killed us . . . just as they killed Oroook . . . all would be lost."

"But surely there are monsters left in the outside world," Kendra said.

"Nozum," Trooogul told her. "Allzum here. Motherzums. Ungerlings. All!"

"I convinced all to come . . . to feast on Een in its final moments," Shuuunga explained. "But . . . it was all a ruse. Only Trooogul knew the truth."

"You should have told me!" Kendra moaned. "I could have helped!"

"No!" Shuuunga gasped. "We could not risk it . . . could not be seen working with Een. Everything depended on . . . deception. But now you must finish. Fix . . . cauldron!"

"It's too late!" Kendra cried.

"NO!" Shuuunga sputtered. "Kendra, you can see Burdock in his cloak. It's . . . your gift. Be the eyes, Kendra . . . Kiro, the might. Go together, my children . . . together . . ."

Kendra could sense Trooogul struggling to decide what to do. Then, at last, he touched Kendra on the shoulder and said, "Comezum, Little Starzum."

Kendra lingered next to her mother, thinking of Winter Woodsong's last moments. "D-don't go anywhere," she said, trembling.

Shuuunga was too weak to muster any more words. She simply squeezed Kendra's hand in a gesture of promise, and that was enough for the Een girl. She rose to her feet and scrambled after Trooogul, out of the shattered remains of the library, and into the tumultuous mayhem of the town square. For a minute, they just stood there, side by side, trying to absorb the scene of devastation before them.

Eens, monsters, and perytons dashed in every direction, amidst burning, collapsing buildings and the crackle of black lightning. These poor souls could not see their attacker, for Burdock was still hidden by the shadow cloak. They could not see his wicked sneer, or the fire that blazed in his eyes, or the giant red blisters that bubbled up on the skin of his hand, where he clenched the Shard. Kendra could not see these things either—but she didn't need to. For she could see one thing clearly enough, and that was Burdock's soul. It was cold, unforgiving, and black—as black as the magic that had consumed it.

"He's standing on the platform, just left of the cauldron," Kendra told her brother.

"Showzum Trooogul!"

Summoning every last bit of magic she could, Kendra sent a blast of lightning at Burdock. It caught him by surprise, sizzling over his form in a perfect outline and at that moment Trooogul charged. His claws might have touched the ground once, twice—then, with a blood-curdling roar that raised the tiny hairs on Kendra's neck, the Unger launched himself at Burdock.

He never reached him. Burdock burst free of Kendra's magic and unleashed a crippling flash of lightning that sent Trooogul crashing to the ground in a mangled heap.

"STUPID GIRL!" Burdock boomed.

He lashed out with a vicious claw of lightning, catching Kendra like an insect inside a fist—and began to squeeze. Kendra felt all the air flee her lungs; the pain was

unbearable, and she dropped her wand. After what seemed like an eternity, Burdock flung her to the ground, and she gasped helplessly as the dark wizard swept forward to loom over her.

"You fail," he proclaimed.

"But the curse," Kendra wheezed, clutching at the dirt. "Don't you want to reverse it?"

"Why would I want to vanquish the shadows of the outside world?" Burdock snarled. "Why, the Eens might step into the light! Much harder to control that way. Much harder for me to rule. Then again, why should I care about this pathetic land now? I have the Shard. I can rule the *entire world*." He paused, and Kendra could feel him flaring with pride. "And the best part is you squirming before me, Kandlestar. Not only did you fail to save Een—you *destroyed* it!"

"No!" Kendra cried. "You're the destroyer!"

"Oh, really?" Burdock snickered. "Me? Why, if not for you, Kendra, the Unger would have done his work. Een could have been saved! But now, because of you, it will be wiped from history. FOREVER!"

"No!" Kendra sobbed. "I tried to . . ."

"Think of it!" Burdock bellowed, relishing in her despair. "It's all because of you . . . because of YOU!"

The gravity of his words sunk in, like weights pulling at her feet and dragging her to the bottom of the deepest, darkest ocean. He was right, Kendra realized. Her father, her mother, her brother—they had all wanted her to just stay away from Een. If only she had listened! But she had chosen to interfere, and . . .

"Everything is ruined," Burdock said smugly, finishing her thought.

He fired the Shard once more, and Kendra writhed on the ground in excruciating pain. It was like losing her eyes all over again—but now the dark magic savaged every part of her body, from the tips of her toes to the roots of her teeth. Soon the anguish was so great that it was as if she was no longer in her body. The chaos of the battled faded away. She could no longer hear Burdock's cackling, or smell the smoke of the burning town. She was simply swirling away into complete and utter darkness.

But the darkness is your teacher, came a voice. *Not your master.*

The words echoed in her mind. *But why now?* Kendra wondered. What use were they in her final moments? She had failed! And so Kendra simply surrendered and let herself drift away into the empty blackness.

And that's when she saw it. Amidst the dark plain, it appeared tiny and insignificant, nothing more than a pinprick of light. And yet, it flashed ever so intently and Kendra suddenly realized what it was.

It was herself.

A spark.

It was the one thing she had always possessed. Her spark had urged her to rescue Trooogul while searching for the Box of Whispers. It had given her the courage to face the maze behind the Door to Unger. It had willed her to survive the terrors of the Rumble Pit. It had inspired her time and time again, throughout her entire life.

And now it would *save* her life.

For this is the magic of a spark: it appears the brightest in the night, when things are the blackest. Kendra had seen it, and now it blazed to life in her like an inferno. It was as if every part of her body was suddenly alive; she could taste color, breathe sound, and see *everything*. At last, she knew who and what she was.

She rose to her feet. Picking up her staff, she gushed magic, pure and bright, a power more true than she could have ever known possible. Light streamed from her Eenwood in every direction. Cussing in surprise, Burdock blasted at Kendra with the Shard—only to have the claws of black lightning now wither and fade in the spectrum of her brilliance.

"Curse you—and all of Een!" Burdock roared. He unleashed the full power of the Shard, striking with every speck of hatred that could be mined from his malevolent heart. It was as if he had opened the door to wickedness—a door that could not be closed. For now the dark enchantment of the Shard simply devoured him. There was a thunderous boom, and then Kendra knew he was no more. She could see it in her mind—a pile of ash, gray and sullen, with the Shard lying on top.

Kendra realized that her arms had been lifted in the air. Now she lowered them, feeling her staff of Eenwood strike the earth.

"Kendra?" She recognized Oki's voice as he scampered towards her. But there was something else that she could sense: hundreds of monstrous eyes staring from the edges of the square. They had watched in confusion as she had battled the strange invisible force that was Burdock, but now they were seething with fury.

"Oki," Kendra said calmly. "You must take the Shard. Place it in the cauldron. It will end the curse."

"Why not you?" he squeaked.

"I mustn't touch it. It will feast on me. But you are pure of heart, Oki. You can do it."

The little mouse gathered up the Shard, just as the monsters began to charge. They could not know what Kendra and

Oki intended, but the only thing that seemed to matter to them now was that all things Een should be destroyed.

"Kendra! Do something!" Oki shrieked. "Eek! Don't think of rhubarb!"

Kendra lifted her staff against the ground and radiated magic. Suddenly, giant green stalks erupted from the ground, creating an enormous, leafy wall that thrust back the horde of attacking beasts.

"Rhubarb!?" Oki cried.

"You put it in my mind," Kendra said. "Always thinking about rhubarb."

"To be fair," Oki said, as he scrambled onto the platform, "I was trying *not* to think of rhubarb."

The roars of monsters could still be heard beyond the leafy barrier. The strange plants had momentarily surprised them, but now the vicious beasts were tearing through the leafy fronds, their rage intensified.

"Hurry!" Kendra told Oki.

She turned to face the monstrous throng as it burst through the rhubarb. She flashed her magic, but even so, she could feel their claws ripping at her robe, scratching her face, pulling her hair. But one part of her could sense Oki as he thrust the Shard into the waiting hole in the cauldron. And then . . .

CHAPTER 38

The Land Between the Cracks of Here and There

It was like an explosion of light. Energy burst forth from the now-repaired cauldron, embracing everything in its path as it swept through the town square, across Faun's End, and over the entire land. Kendra's skin tingled, her ears buzzed, and her hair crackled with electricity. Indeed, her whole body felt more alive than she could have ever imagined possible, as if her heart was a bell and someone had suddenly discovered the secret to making it ring.

Then, in a flash, the light was gone. Kendra would have rubbed her eyes if she had them to see, for she felt like she was awakening from a dream—or perhaps a nightmare. The claws that had been clutching at her fell away, and what had been growls and roars melted into gasps. She was still surrounded by zeens, but these had changed too; it was hard to put her finger on it, but it seemed to Kendra that they were somehow more true.

"Eens," Oki gasped, scurrying up alongside her. "They're all Eens!"

He was right. Not an Unger, Orrid, Izzard, Goojun, or Krake was left in the square. All had been transformed, leaving behind a crowd of bewildered Eens. Only a moment ago they had been at war—but now it seemed as if none could remember why. Kendra and Oki just stood there, gaping.

"Little Star?" someone called from the crowd.

"Kiro?" Kendra replied. His zeen had previously invoked in her the feeling of a lightning bolt, but now it was different, filling her with a new feeling. It was warm and radiant, like a beam of light.

Of course, Kendra thought. *He is Trooogul no more. He's changed, and so has his zeen.*

"It worked, Kendra!" Kiro cried. "I . . . I can't believe it."

"Neither can I," came the voice of her father. He rushed forward to enfold Kendra and her brother in his arms. "I'm so very proud of you," he said.

"Wait!" Kendra cried. "Mother! She's here somewhere too."

"We left her in the library," Kiro said. "Come on."

Together, the three Kandlestars hurried towards the smoldering remains of the library. They only made it halfway up the steps when Kendra detected a zeen at the top. It made Kendra think of a tree with a wild, meandering trunk, bursting with blossoms, and she knew at once it was the very essence of her mother. Kendra raced up the rest of the stairs, into her mother's waiting embrace.

"Everyone has turned, then," Kayla said eventually. It was more of a statement than a question, one she followed with a sigh.

"Isn't that what you thought would happen?" Kendra asked. "Aren't you happy?"

"I have to admit, I wasn't sure *what* would happen," Kayla replied. "Would all monsters be transformed back into Eens? Or just some? Was it even my right to try and change them? But . . . after all, we were Eens originally, weren't we? It was dark magic that cursed us." She paused. "But it wasn't all darkness. Being an Unger unlocked something inside of us, I think. A type of wild beauty, a type of freedom. It's a part of ourselves we can't forget."

"We won't," Kendra's father said as he and Kiro arrived at the top of the steps. "You did it, Kayla. You were right all along. I should have listened to you."

"What are you talking about?" Kendra asked.

"She tried to tell me," Krimson told Kendra. "That night in Arazeen, when she came to see me, she told me we had to rebuild the cauldron. But I wouldn't listen to her. I was convinced she was on the side of the Ungers. I thought she was trying to betray us."

"You had every right to be suspicious," Kayla admitted. "But it angered me so much . . ."

"They turned against each other after that," Kiro told Kendra. "They are stubborn, both of them."

"But . . . but," Kendra stammered. "Everything turned out, didn't it? I mean, that was before. Surely, now you two can . . ."

"We can work it out," Kayla assured Kendra, placing her hands on her shoulders. "We just need some time."

"Not too much time, I hope," came a voice from the bottom of the steps. "Humph!"

It was the type of humph that made Kendra's heart leap in her chest. Could it be? But the whiskery feeling she suddenly sensed left no doubt in her mind; Kendra leapt down the stairs and launched herself so vigorously at Uncle Griffinskitch that she knocked him flat to the ground.

"Now, isn't this the mouse's job, to bowl me over?" the old wizard growled lightheartedly.

The square was now filled with many joyful and surprising reunions as Eens discovered friends and family amidst the transformed monsters. Tuttleferd was dancing with a pair of little moles that Kendra later learned were his grandchildren. Professor Bumblebean was fumbling for words as he was reunited with an elderly Een who turned out to be his real mother (there are those of you who might remember that Professor Bumblebean had been adopted as a baby). Oki and Ratchet were being introduced to a mouse that turned out to be Oki's cousin, Elsbeth, who had been missing since before Oki was born. But no one seemed more excited than Jinx; she was chirping excitedly over an old grasshopper that Kendra realized was her long-lost Uncle Jasper.

And yet, amidst this jubilation, something nagged at Kendra.

"What is it?" her mother asked.

"Lurk," she replied. "Seems everyone has been found except for him. Burdock said he was hidden away in the dungeons. But . . ."

"Come," Kayla said, taking Kendra's hand. "We'll seek him together."

So, into the dungeons they went. Together, they called upon their magic to probe for Lurk's zeen. Sure enough, they detected a faint trace of it in the utmost depths of the Elder Stone. Kendra and her mother followed the glow and at last realized that it was coming from behind a wall of solid rock—a dungeon cell that Burdock had enchanted with his magic to keep it hidden. With a spell from her staff, Kendra cracked open the wall and Lurk tumbled into her arms. He was half-starved and shivering with fever, but he was alive.

"Don't worry," Kendra told him. "We'll make you better."

For once, he had no retort.

As you can imagine, there was much to do in the Land of Een afterwards. There were wounded to heal, and some to bury and mourn. Much of Faun's End needed to be repaired or rebuilt. Slowly, the land began to recover. The weeks passed.

One morning, late in summer, Kendra awoke to the sound of chirping outside her window. She had been having a dream about adventuring in the outside world, facing dragons and giants; it was almost disappointing to find herself back in the safe familiarity of her bedroom, inside Uncle Griffinskitch's yew tree house.

There was more chirping from outside, and Kendra detected Mercy Moonwing fluttering amongst the branches near her window.

"Happy birthday!" the little hummingbird sang. "You're thirteen today!"

Kendra smiled, fetched her wand, and scampered downstairs where her father was bustling about the kitchen.

"Where's everyone?" Kendra asked as she pulled a chair to the old oaken table.

"Your mother and uncle had an early council meeting at the Elder Stone," her father replied. "Gregor is Eldest of the Elders now—no time for dillydallying. As for Kiro, Jinx collected him before dawn to run drills outside the magic curtain. I guess she's training him."

"Training him for what?" Kendra asked.

But Kendra's father simply replied by saying, "Don't worry—everyone will be here for your party."

"Party?" Kendra asked, tugging at a braid. She had never really had a proper party to celebrate her birthday.

Humph—that's my fault, came the sound of Uncle Griffinskitch's voice through her wand. *But never you mind. Today we shall make up for lost time.*

It seemed the entire Land of Een showed up to celebrate Kendra's birthday that evening. Oki and Ratchet brought her a hiccupping music box, which was one of the featured items at the new toy shop they had recently opened in Faun's End. Professor Bumblebean gave her a talking book. ("The first one plucked from the book trees in the new Een library," he said.) Jinx read her a poem that she had written herself, while Charla sang a song. (Mercy helped with the tune, though she forgot the last half of it.) Many guests came from afar, including the peryton prince and Effryn Hagglehorn, who made a grand entrance riding atop Skeezle.

The yew tree house was decorated with lumabloom vines planted by Kendra's father, who also whipped up many wonderful desserts, including Eenberry tarts, fudgery pie, bumblepops, and glum pudding (which tastes better than it sounds). A band of musicians played throughout the event with their womboes, fizzdiddles, and flumpets, with Kendra's mother performing a solo on her narfoo. Uncle Griffinskitch capped off the evening with a display of fireworks that danced in Kendra's mind.

It was during this spectacle that Kendra noticed Lurk lingering at the edge of the garden, beyond the crowd of guests.

Old habits are hard to break, Kendra thought, wishing he would come join the party.

She knew Lurk was still shy of his looks—though she also knew that many of his injuries had been healed. Having let the wizards of Een finally work upon him, his skin had gained new color, his pockmarks had faded, and he had even grown hair. Most importantly, he had been relieved of the crippling pain that had plagued him for so long.

Lurk slipped away, and Kendra decided to follow after him.

Don't disappear yet, came Uncle Griffinskitch's voice through her wand. *There's something we need to discuss.*

What is it? she asked impatiently. She could hear him fiddling with something, like a piece of parchment or a scroll.

The future, Kendra, Uncle Griffinskitch replied. *Yours . . . and all of Een's.*

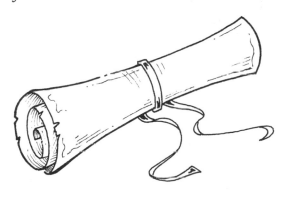

An hour later, Kendra caught up with Lurk at the banks of the River Wink, where he sat dangling his feet in the gentle current.

"I know you're there, Kendra," he said as she lingered in the shadows. "You shouldn't be missing your own party."

"It's mostly over," she replied, coming to sit alongside him. She dipped her own feet into the cool water.

"I wanted to bring you a gift," Lurk said. "I mean . . . I made one, but it seemed so . . . inadequate. Compared to what I really wished I could give you."

"What's that?" Kendra asked.

"Your eyes," Lurk murmured.

Kendra took a deep breath. "I think I've come to realize that losing them was my gift."

"That's . . . ridiculous," Lurk snorted. *"You're blind."*

"No," Kendra said. "I just don't have my eyes. But I can see—like Uncle Griffinskitch says, the way a wizard needs to, the way that was needed to make it all work out. And now what I see is what I've gained. My family. Een. And . . . well, I don't know how to describe it. Happiness. Tonight it feels like I'm floating in the clouds, like I'm in some sort of paradise."

Lurk grunted. "Sounds like your father's kingdom in the sky."

"That place turned out to be an illusion," Kendra said. "It was wonderful . . . but not right. Do you know what I mean? But what I know now, what I feel . . . it's . . ."

"Arazeen," Lurk ventured.

Kendra smiled. "Perhaps."

For a while they didn't speak, but just sat listening to the river. Eventually, Lurk said, "The Council of Elders called me to the Elder Stone today. They asked me to join the new exploration crew."

"Really?" Kendra said. "Well, you have a way with creatures. And there are lots of those in the outside world to deal with."

"I haven't made up my mind yet," Lurk said quickly.

"It would be a shame if you didn't come," Kendra told him. "We could use you."

"We?" Lurk asked in surprise. *"You're* joining?"

"Not exactly," Kendra declared. She took out the scroll her uncle had given to her and passed it to Lurk. "Uncle Griffinskitch just told me—a birthday gift for me, I suppose—he asked me to *lead* the group."

Lurk exhaled. "That's . . . that's . . . what did you say?"

"Well, someone has to keep Jinx in line," Kendra replied. "Not to mention my brother. And *you*."

Lurk chuckled. "More adventures then?"

"I hope so," Kendra said. "I wouldn't have it any other way."

OFFICIAL
PROCLAMATION

As agreed by Gregor Griffinskitch,
Eldest of the Elders, and the Council of Elders,
the following Eens have been chosen to explore the
outside world, with the aim of establishing and improving
relations with the creatures, races, and societies
beyond the magic curtain.

Kendra Kandlestar, Wizardess
Juniper Jinx, Captain of Arms
Professor Broon Bumblebean, Cartographer
Mercy Moonwing, Scout
Kiro Kandlestar, Explorer
Paipo Plumpuddle, Explorer
Joymus Jinglehoot, Explorer
Leerlin Lurk, Creature Communicator

Tools and supplies provided by
R.O. Toys & Gadgets of Faun's End

Signed by the Elders
Gregor Griffinskitch, Eldest
Enid Evermoon
Timmons Thunderclaws
Jasper Jinx
Hektor Hootall
Kayla Kandlestar
Luka Long-Ears

THE
CHRONICLES
OF
KENDRA
KANDLESTAR

Book 1: The Box of Whispers
Book 2: The Door to Unger
Book 3: The Shard from Greeve
Book 4: The Crack in Kazah
Book 5: The Search for Arazeen

Visit
www.kendrakandlestar.com
for activities, teacher guides, news, and to
send an Een-mail to Lee Edward Födi

Author's Note

Bill Moyers: In all of these journeys of mythology, there's a place everyone wishes to find. What is it? The Buddhists talk of Nirvana. Jesus talks of peace. There's a place of rest and repose. What is it?

Joseph Campbell: Nirvana is a psychological state of mind. It's not a place like "Heaven." It's not something that's not here. It *is* here, in the middle of the turmoil . . . the whirlpool of life conditions. Nirvana is what? It's the condition that comes when you are not compelled by desire, or by fear. Or by social commitments. When you hold your center, and act out of there.

An excerpt from *The Power of Myth*

It seems each time I send Kendra on a journey, I take one of my own, a journey inevitably filled with many challenges, obstacles, and questions. For the writing of this book, there was plenty of self-doubt. Was I making Kendra's final journey too mystical? Too elusive?

Then, one day, I was revisiting *The Power of Myth*, a series of famous conversations between the mythologist Joseph Campbell and journalist Bill Moyers. When I heard the section that appears at the top of this page, I found myself scrambling to transcribe it. These few sentences by Mr. Campbell reinvigorated me, helping me to complete Kendra's journey—and, of course, my own. Somehow, it just feels right to include these words here.

Acknowledgements

I've never gotten into the habit of writing acknowledgements. I suppose I'm always worried that I will leave someone out, or not quite mention everyone in the right order, or in the right way. But better to try and fail than not try at all. So, here it goes . . .

First, I thank my beautiful wife, Marcie, who stood by me through the many ups and downs of bringing Kendra's adventure to life, and who was always eager to play any part I needed (and sometimes that part was dressing up as an Een at my book events!).

Second, I want to thank Paige, whom I only met because of Kendra. Little did "Paipo" know that being an über-fan would mean that she would end up being coerced into reading the multiple versions of my manuscripts!

Next, I thank Charlotte, my goddaughter, who now, at long last, is released from the duty of having to dress up as Kendra for various book launches and events. (I need to also thank Charlotte's mom, Danie, who brought to life that pesky Kendra hairdo on so many occasions.)

Of course, I want to thank Simply Read Books and, in particular, my editor, Kallie George, who helped push the story further and held it (and me) to a higher standard.

Thank you, as well, to my mentors, Dōv and Ren, whose support has been unwavering. Then there are my families—mine (Mom, Dad, Brian, Nola, Crystal, Mike, and Isabella), Marcie's, and the one I adopted along the way, otherwise known as the Scooby Gang: James McCann, kc dyer, Sarah and Rob Bagshaw—plus all the rest of you who have supported my career.

The Blevis clan—Mark, Andrea, Lucy, and Bayla—thank you for all of your pre-reading and promotion of little Kendra. You must have Een blood in your ancestry! The same goes for the Winters clan: Kari-Lynn, Jonah, Liam, and McKenna.

I'm also extremely thankful for the friendship and support of Joon Park and everyone at CWC, the creative writing company that seemed to take birth at just about the same time as Kendra, all those years ago. Our journeys seem entwined.

Lastly, I want to thank the readers. You sustained me during the writing process with your many Een-mails, your fan art, and photos of you in full Een costume. You are martyrs for having waited so long for this final installment. I hope, in the end, it was worth the wait.

Readers Respond to Kendra Kandlestar

Lee Edward Födi shares some of his favorite letters

Dear Mr. Födi,
I love your books. I have read all your books at least five times. My favorite book is the first book. It's the best because everyone goes on a huge adventure and meets Pugglemud. My favorite scene is when Oki screams. My favorite character is Professor Bumblebean because he loves books and I do too.

~ Sydney, age 10

Amazing book! I can't wait for the next one! I hope you continue making another series after the last one.

~ Kaniel, age 11

I loved all four of your books! They were so full of suspense and mystery. My favorite book was *Kendra Kandlestar and the Crack of Kazah*. Great job!

~ John, age 9

I loved all your books and I could not stop reading them. They were truly inspiring and had a lot of suspense. I read them so often that one day my mother hid the one that I was reading from me because I had to finish my homework. I can't wait until the last book in the series comes out!

~ Samantha, age 8

I am a huge fan I love your books! I went to a book store and bought your books. My favorite character is Kendra because she is brave and goes to adventures.

~ Melynda, age 10

When I was nine or so my brother lent me a book *Corranda's Crown*. The next day I was already finished it twice. Now, at the age of twelve, I read all of the Kendra Kandlestar books so far. Then one day I realized that both those books were by the same person! I was amazed! I truly love all your books, keep the awesome work up.

~ Megan, age 12

I love these books! I cannot wait for the next one! My mom and I read them every night and we are on book four already! My favorite characters are Kendra because she tests things just like me and I love Jinx because she's unstoppable like me. My favorite part is in *The Box of Whispers* when Kendra opens the box and sets the whispers free. My mom loves the peryton and the part when Kendra realizes she is responsible for ruining the beautiful prince. She even cried when reading that part to me.

~ Isabella, age 9

I finished *The Crack in Kazah* yesterday. It was one of the best books I have ever read in my life.

~ Jonathan, age 10

I LOVE your Kendra Kandlestar series. My favorite character is Kendra.

~ Priya, age 10

This is one of the most fun books I ever read. This book is fun and adventurous. Kendra is a fun character. If you like magical creatures, fun, and adventures, than this is the book for you.

~ Fiona, age 10

Dear Mr. Födi,
My name is Simone and I'm seven years old. I really like the Kendra Kandlestar books so much that I even dressed up like Kendra for Halloween, but I also like Oki and Jinx. My mom did my hair so I guess it might have been hard, it took her a long time. My favorite book is *Kendra Kandlestar and the Crack in Kazah*, because she meets her mom. I'm looking forward to the next book of Kendra Kandlestar. When is your next book going to be out? Are you going to make a movie with Kendra? I hope so.

~ Simone, age 7

This book is amazing! In *Kendra Kandlestar and the Crack in Kazah*, you get whisked away on an adventure not to where, but to when. This was a real page-turner.

~ Alison, age 11

Thanks for being such a great inspiring author! I love your books and could never put them down. Now I am waiting for your next book to come out! My favorite book is *Kendra Kandlestar and the Crack in Kazah* and my favorite character is Oki because he is always scared and funny. My sister and I suggested your first book for the school district's Battle of the Books competition and it was selected for Grade 5.

~ Luke, age 10

I LOVE YOUR BOOKS! My favorite book is *Door to Unger.*
My favorite chapters are *Into a Maze of Monsters, Who Kendra
Finds in the Labyrinth, The First Elder of Een, A Brave Sacrifice*
and *A Whisper Given.*

~ Navin, age 9

My favorite book is the first one. My favorite character is
Uncle Griffinskitch. Can you make a book that makes Kendra
get kidnapped by humans but Gregor, Jinx, Bumblebean, and
Oki save her but you can add more details? My Een name is
Jelinda Emberstar!

~ Jelani, age 10

I love your books! I like the first one the best because that's
when it all started. My favorite character is Kendra because I
like her hair.

~ Esther, age 10

Hi, Mr. Wiz! I just adore your books. They are the best! Please
make 20 more books. No, make that 100. No make that
99999999999. Thanks!

~ Erika, age 11

Hurry up with the fifth book already! I love your books! So
what are you waiting for?! Hurry!

~ Zoi, age 10

I have been waiting for the new *Kendra Kandlestar.* I really
want it I can't wait! Mr. Wiz, if you are reading this, please
send me an e-mail when it comes out!

~ Airan, age 9

I really enjoyed the first four *Kendra Kandlestar* books. So far, my favorite *Kendra Kandlestar* book is *The Crack in Kazah* because I think it would be pretty cool to have the Kazah Stone. My favorite character is Kendra. I hope you write a new series once you finish this one. I had fun creating my own Een name when my mom and I checked the website.

~ Lily, age 11

I'm a huge fan of these books. My favorite book in the book series is *Kendra Kandlestar and the Door to Unger*. My favorite character is Kendra Kandlestar. I created my Een name. It's Boboon Upbeak.

~ Cayla, age 10

I just finished reading the third *Kendra Kandlestar* book and it is awesome! I can't wait to read your next book! I hope that Trooogul gets turned back into Kiro again!

~ Natalie, age 10

I just want to let you know that I love all of your books, especially *The Crack in Kazah*. Could you please write some more. I was wondering if you could make movies based on the books also.

~ Andrew, age 9

I really liked your book *Kendra Kandlestar and the Door to Unger*! Can't wait to read more of your books! P.S. I would probably rate this book 7 out of 10 if I had to rate it. My favorite character is Jinx, because she is strong, kind, and sneaky (because she is small).

~ Fred, age 10

I'm looking forward to book 5. I'm hoping Trooogul comes back in his Een form. He is my favorite character because he was so selfless in his sacrifice for Kendra. My favorite book is *Book 2: The Door to Unger.*

~ Virginia, age 11

I love your books! They are great. I like the part of *The Box of Whispers,* where they fought the dragon. It was not an easy task for me! Best for your fifth book.

~ Megan, age 8

Dear Mr. Födi,
I've read the first three books in the Kendra Kandlestar series and they were AMAZING! My favorite characters from *The Box of Whispers* are Kendra, Oki, Jinx, Rumor, and Uncle Griffinskitch. From *The Door to Unger:* Kendra (of course), Oki, Effryn Hagglehorn, and Trooogul. From *The Shard from Greeve:* Prince, Oki, Jinx, and Uncle Griffinskitch. I love your books and drawings! P.S. My fave book is *The Box of Whispers.*

~ Victoria, age 12

I just finished *The Shard from Greeve.* It was awesome. What was Prince's real name? Prince is my favorite character. Can't wait to read the next book!

~ Abby, age 9

I really want to read your next book. Your books are amazing! I love the way you put so much detail and really tell what Kendra is thinking.

~ Grace, age 10

I like Kendra Kandlestar because she is adventurous, and she teaches us to be not afraid and she also has the courage to stand up for herself. I like Uncle Griffinskitch because in the book he tells us the right thing to do and even though he is grumpy in the book I believe he is only like that to protect Kendra. I like Honest Oki because he is honest, and at the end of the book even though he is scared he tried his best just to help Kendra. He is also a great friend to Kendra; he helps Kendra with a lot of things. I like professor Bumblebean because he is smart and I wish I was smart as him too. I like Jinx because she is strong and she is not afraid to try.

~ Mariel, age 11

My Een name is Genel Jinglebloom. I have only read your first book, *The Box of Whispers* and your fourth book, *The Crack in Kazah*. I love them. I do not have a favourite book, but my favourite character is Kendra as she is very adventurous and brave. Eengards,

~ Genie (a bookEen named Genel Jinglebloom), age 10

I love *Kendra Kandlestar!* I think my favorite characters are Oki, Trooogul, and Kendra. As long as you keep writing, I'll keep reading.

~ Megumi, age 8

Want to send your own Een-mail to Lee Edward Födi?
eenmail@kendrakandlestar.com

Or visit:
www.kendrakandlestar.com

Lee Edward Födi likes to think of himself as a daydreaming specialist. Constantly daydreaming used to get him into a great deal of trouble, but now he finds it keeps him out of it. When not daydreaming himself, he teaches it—mostly to kids, who, it seems to him, are already pretty good at it; it's just that they haven't yet learned how to put it to good use. He enjoys mythology, history, and the mysteries of the universe. He loves to visit exotic places where he can lose himself (literally) in tombs, mazes, castles, and crypts—not to mention tiny places tucked between the cracks of Here and There. He lives in Vancouver, Canada, with his wife and unhelpful cat.

Find out more at www.leefodi.com and www.kendrakandlestar.com.